CHRISTOPHER BUSH
THE CASE OF THE SAPPHIRE BROOCH

CHRISTOPHER BUSH was born Charlie Christmas Bush in Norfolk in 1885. His father was a farm labourer and his mother a milliner. In the early years of his childhood he lived with his aunt and uncle in London before returning to Norfolk aged seven, later winning a scholarship to Thetford Grammar School.

As an adult, Bush worked as a schoolmaster for 27 years, pausing only to fight in World War One, until retiring aged 46 in 1931 to be a full-time novelist. His first novel featuring the eccentric Ludovic Travers was published in 1926, and was followed by 62 additional Travers mysteries. These are all to be republished by Dean Street Press.

Christopher Bush fought again in World War Two, and was elected a member of the prestigious Detection Club.

He died in 1973.

CHRISTOPHER BUSH

THE CASE OF THE SAPPHIRE BROOCH

With an introduction
by Curtis Evans

DEAN STREET PRESS

Published by Dean Street Press 2022

Copyright © 1960 Christopher Bush

Introduction copyright © 2022 Curtis Evans

All Rights Reserved

The right of Christopher Bush to be identified as the Author of the Work has been asserted by his estate in accordance with the Copyright, Designs and Patents Act 1988.

First published in 1960 by MacDonald & Co.

Cover by DSP

ISBN 978 1 915014 64 1

www.deanstreetpress.co.uk

For

DOROTHY GARDINER

With Love

INTRODUCTION

Rosalind. If it be true that good wine needs no bush [i.e., advertising], 'tis true that a good play needs no epilogue. Yet to good wine, they do use good bushes, and good plays prove the better by the help of good epilogues.

–Shakespeare, Epilogue, As You Like It

The decade of the 1960s saw the sun finally begin to set on that storied generation which between the First and Second World Wars gave us detective fiction's Golden Age. Taking account of both deaths and retirements, by the late Sixties only a bare half-dozen pre-World War Two members of the Detection Club were still plying their deliciously deceptive craft: Agatha Christie, Anthony Gilbert (Lucy Beatrice Malleson), Gladys Mitchell, John Dickson Carr, Nicholas Blake and Christopher Bush, the subject of this introduction. Bush himself would pass away, at the age of eighty-seven, in 1973, having published, at the age of eighty-two, his sixty-third Ludovic Travers detective novel, *The Case of the Prodigal Daughter*, in the United Kingdom in the spring of 1968.

In the United States Bush's final detective novel did not appear until late November 1969, about four months after the horrific Manson murders in the tarnished Golden State of California. Implicating the triple terrors of sex, drugs and rock and roll (not to mention almost inconceivably bestial violence), the Manson slayings could not have strayed farther from the whimsically escapist "death as a game" aesthetic of Golden Age of detective fiction. Increasingly in the decade capable of producing psychedelic psychopaths like Charles Manson and his "family," the few remaining survivors of the Golden Age of detective fiction increasingly deemed themselves men and women far out of time. In his detective fiction John Dickson Carr, an incurable romantic, prudently beat a retreat from the present into the pleasanter pages of the past, setting his tales in bygone historical eras where he felt vastly more at home. With varying success Agatha Christie made a brave effort to stay abreast of the times (*Third Girl,*

Endless Night), but ultimately her strivings to understand what was going on around her collapsed into the utter incoherence of *Passenger to Frankfurt* and *Postern of Fate*, by general consensus the worst mystery novels that Dame Agatha ever put down on paper.

In his detective fiction Christopher Bush, who was not quite two years older than Christie, managed rather better than the Queen of Crime to keep up with all the unsettling goings-on around him, while never forswearing the Golden Age article of faith that the primary purpose of a crime writer is pleasingly to puzzle his/her readers. And, in contrast with Christie and Carr, Bush knew when it was time to lay down his pen (or turn off his dictation machine, as the case may be), thereby allowing him to make his exit from the stage on a comparatively high note. Indeed, Christopher Bush's concluding baker's dozen of detective novels, which he published between 1957 and 1968 (and which have now been reprinted, after more than a half-century, by Dean Street Press), makes a generally fine epilogue, or coda, to the author's impressive corpus of crime fiction, which first began to see the light of day way back in the jubilant Jazz Age. These are, readers will find, "good bushes" (to punningly borrow from Shakespeare), providing them with ample intelligent detective entertainment as Bush's longtime series sleuth Ludovic Travers, in the luminous twilight of his career, makes his final forays into ingenious criminal investigation.

*

In the last thirteen Ludovic Travers mystery novels, Travers' *entrée* to his cases continues to come through his ownership of the Broad Street Detective Agency. Besides Travers we also regularly encounter his elegant wife, Bernice (although sometimes his independent-minded spouse is away on excursions of her own), his proverbially loyal secretary, Bertha Munney, his top Broad Street op, Hallows (another one named French, presumably inspired by Bush's late Detection Club colleague Freeman Wills Crofts, pops up occasionally), John Hill of the United Assurance Agency, who brings Travers many of his cases, and Scotland Yard's Inspector Jewle and Sergeant Matthews, who after the first of these final novels, *The Case of the Treble Twist* (in the U.S. *Triple Twist*), are promoted, respectively, to Superintendent and Inspector. (The Yard's ex-Superintendent George Wharton, now firmly retired from any form of investigative work whatsoever, is mentioned just once by Ludo, when, in *The Case of the Dead Man Gone*, he passingly imparts that he and Wharton recently had lunch together.)

For all practical purposes Travers, who during the Golden Age was a classic gentleman amateur snooper like Philo Vance and Lord Peter Wimsey, now functions fully as a professional private eye—although one, to be sure, who is rather posher than the rest. While some reviewers referred to Travers as England's Philip Marlowe, in fact he little resembles the general run of love and leave 'em/hate and beat 'em brand of brutish American P.I.'s, favoring a nice cup of coffee (a post-war change from tea), a good pipe and the occasional spot of sherry to the frequent snatches of liquor and cigarettes favored by most of his American brethren and remaining faithful to his spouse despite encountering a succession of sexy women, not all of them, shall we say, virtuously inclined.

This was a formula which throughout the period maintained a devoted audience on both sides of the Atlantic consisting, one surmises, of readers (including crime writers Anthony Berkeley, Nicholas Blake and the late Alan Hunter, creator of Inspector George Gently) who preferred their detectives something less than hard-boiled. Travers himself sneers at the hugely popular (and psychotically violent) postwar American private eye Mike Hammer, commenting of an American couple in *The Case of the Treble Twist*: "She was a woman of considerable culture; his ran about as far as Mickey Spillane" [a withering reference to Mike Hammer's creator]. Yet despite his manifest disdain for Mike Hammer, an ugly American if ever there were one, Christopher Bush and his wife Florence in the spring of 1957 had traveled to New York aboard the RMS *Queen Elizabeth*, and references by him to both the United States and Canada became more frequent in the books which followed this trip.

Certainly *The Case of the Treble Twist* (1957) features tough customers and an exceptionally cruel murder, yet it is also one of Bush's most ingeniously contrived cases from the Fifties, full of charm, treacherous deception and, yes, plenty of twists, including one that is a real sockaroo (to borrow, as Bush occasionally did, from American idiom). Similarly clever is *The Case of the Running Man* (1958), which draws, as several earlier Bush books had, on the author's profound love and knowledge of antiques. By this time Bush and his wife, their coffers having burgeoned from the proceeds of his successful mysteries, resided in the quaint medieval market town of Lavenham, Suffolk at the Great House, a splendidly decorated fourteenth-century structure with an elegant Georgian-era façade which he and Florence purchased in 1953 and resided in until their deaths. The dashing author, whom in 1967 *Chicago Tribune* mystery reviewer Alice Crombie swooningly dubbed "one of the handsomest mystery writers on either side of the Channel or Atlantic," also drove a Jaguar, beloved by James Bond films of late, well into his eighties.

The Case of the Running Man includes that Golden Age detective fiction staple, a family tree, but more originally the novel features as a major character a black American man, Sam, the devoted chauffeur of the wealthy murder victim. Sam, who reminds Ludovic Travers of Rochester, "Jack Benny's factotum of television and radio," is an interesting and sincerely treated individual, although as Anthony Boucher amusingly pronounced at the time in the *New York Times Book Review*, he speaks "a dialect never heard by mortal ear"—an odd compounding of "American Negro" and London cockney.

The Case of the Careless Thief (1959) takes Ludo to Sandbeach, "the Blackpool of the South Coast," as the American jacket blurb puts it, with "a dozen hotels, a race track, a dog track, a music hall and two enormous dance halls." Anthony Boucher deemed this hard-hitting, tricky tale, which draws to strong effect on contemporary events in England, "one of Ludovic Travers' best cases." Likewise hard-hitting are *The Case of the Sapphire Brooch* (1960) and *The Case of the Extra Grave* (1961), complex tales of murderous mésalliances with memorably grim conclusions. The plot of

The Case of the Dead Man Gone (1961) topically involves refugee relief groups, while *The Case of the Heavenly Twin* (1963) opens with a case of a creative criminal couple forging American Express Travelers Checks, concerning which Americans of a certain age will recall actor Karl Malden sternly enjoining, in a long-running television advertising campaign: "Don't leave home without them." In contrast with many of his crime writing contemporaries (judging from the tone of their work), Bush actually learned to watch and enjoy television, although in *The Case of The Three-Ring Puzzle*, a tale of violently escalating intrigue, Travers dryly references Scottish philosopher Thomas Carlyle's famous observation that England's population consisted of "mostly fools" when he comments: "I guess he wasn't too far out at that. But rather remarkable an estimate perhaps, considering that in his day there were no television commercials."

Of Bush's final five Ludovic Travers detective novels, published between 1964 and 1968, when the Western World, in the eyes of many, was going from whimsically mod to utterly mad, the best are, in my estimation, the cases of *The Jumbo Sandwich* (1965), *The Good Employer* (1966) and *The Prodigal Daughter* (1968). In *Sandwich* a crisp case of a defrauded (and jilted) gentry lady friend of Ludo's metamorphoses into a smorgasbord of, as the American book jacket puts it, "blackmail, black magic, a black sheep, and murder." It all culminates in a confrontation on a lonely Riviera beach in France, setting of some of Ludovic Travers' earliest cases, between Ludo and a desperate killer, in which Bernice plays an unexpectedly active part. Ludo again travels to France in the highly classic *Employer*, which draws most engagingly on the sleuth's (and the author's) dabbling in the world of art and is dedicated to his distinguished Lavenham artist friends, the couple Reginald and Rosalie Brill, who resided next door to Bush and his wife at the fourteenth-century Little Hall, then an art student hostel for which the Brills served as guardians. In *The Guardian* Francis Iles (aka Golden Age crime writer Anthony Berkeley) pronounced that *Employer* represented Bush "at his most ingenious."

Finally, in *Daughter* Travers finds himself tasked with recovering the absconded teenage offspring of domineering Dora Marport, sober-sided head of the organization Home and Family, which is righteously devoted to "the fostering, so to speak, of family life as the stoutest bulwark against the encroachment of ever-more numerous hostile forces: sex and violence in literature, films and on television; pornography generally, and the erosion of responsibility and the capability for sacrifice by the welfare state." Can Travers, a Great War veteran who made his debut in detective fiction in 1926, bridge the generation gap in late-Sixties London? Ludo may prefer Bach to the Beatles, but in this, the last of his recorded cases, he proves more "with it" than one might have expected. All in all, *Daughter* makes a rewarding finish to one of the longest-running and most noteworthy sleuth series in British detective fiction.

Curtis Evans

1

STRANGE BURGLARY

NEITHER Norris nor myself has any set hours at the Broad Street Detective Agency. As a kind of managing-director, he's more in the office than out, whereas I'm more out than in. But naturally there's a lot of changing around. We have a contract or two in the provinces and I take over the office when he's paying periodical calls. On that particular evening of late January he was away. My wife was away, too, so there was no need to worry about getting back to the flat, and that's why I was putting in some time over accounts.

Bertha Munney, our secretary-receptionist, had brought me in a pot of tea and a cake before she left at her usual five o'clock. The first night man had reported for duty and taken over in Bertha's room, and we two had the place to ourselves. And it wasn't a bad place to be in on that January night. Outside, the weather was filthy, with snow and slush and patches of fog. Not one of those impenetrable fogs which you can taste and smell, but patchy, as I said: clearish one moment and then, a few yards on, a visibility of only a few yards. It had been like that all the day, with now and again a bleak sun trying to get through and finding the job too tough.

It was well after six o'clock when I knocked off work. I wasn't in any particular hurry to get away, so I stoked my pipe and picked up one of the evening papers. Spread across the front page was the account, with pictures, of yet another hold-up: almost a replica of one that had taken place a few weeks before.

A bank delivery van had been on its rounds. It had left a branch bank in South Westminster and was making for Victoria Street, and to avoid traffic had cut down Butter Lane, intending, as usual, to come out not far from Victoria Station. It's a one-way street, and as it nosed through the mist at about ten o'clock, it was stopped by a smallish saloon car in front. At the same time another van drew in behind it and two masked men at once attacked the bank employees, while a third man, who'd come from the saloon car, held up the driver at the point of a gun. The whole thing was over in a couple of minutes. The employees were blinded with pepper, the cash was transferred to the saloon car, and that was that. The total amount taken was about fourteen thousand pounds.

The police had little to go on. Both the attackers were tall men, one burly and the other on the slim side. Their van, a stolen one, had been abandoned. The number of the saloon car had been taken, and later that car had also been abandoned on the Embankment, not far from the turn into Wedmore Street, and it too had been stolen. Its driver—the one with the gun—had been described as slim and shortish, wearing a heavy brown overcoat and a brown beret and, of course, a mask. He hadn't spoken a word—just made the gun speak for him. Altogether it was a slick job that must have taken quite a lot of casing. It had also been timed to a nicety, with the weather an enormous help. Visibility in Butter Lane had been about twenty yards. A few yards on it had been much clearer and on the Embankment it had been a good hundred yards.

But that, I couldn't help thinking, didn't make the whole affair less stupid. Week after week there were these holdups: mail vans, bank delivery vans, vans carrying wages. The proportion of attacks might be almost infinitesimally small, but that didn't make their owners less negligent. The responsibility was theirs, not that of the police. That's what I was thinking, a bit complacently perhaps, when the buzzer went.

"A call for you, sir. A Mr. Farrell."

"Farrell?" I thought. "Who's Farrell? I know the name. Can't place him, though."

The call was put through, and as soon as I heard the voice I knew its owner. A youngish, gaunt and rather unkempt Welshman who'd reminded me when I'd first clapped eyes on him of a certain John the Baptist in the National Gallery.

"How are you, Mr. Farrell?" I said. "It's quite a time now since I saw you."

"It is that," he said, and went on with never a pause. "I want you to help me. I look like being caught up in the very devil of a mess. Can you get over here? The same address—135 Mayes Road, Pimlico. I'll be waiting for you."

"Just let me get my breath," I told him. "What's it all about? Give me an idea."

"Not over the phone. I just can't explain it. You'll have to come."

"Very well," I said. "In an hour's time? I can't do it in less."

"Make it less if you can. I'll be here. It's about three minutes from the Tube station."

"And your telephone number? Just in case anything should go wrong?"

He gave it to me. I rang off and got up at once. I put on my hat and coat and then asked for Bill Fraser's number—City Detection, Limited. He has a flat above his premises and he happened to be in. He said he'd be delighted to see me. Maybe he was thinking I was going to put some job or other in his way. There's quite a lot of stuff that we prefer not to handle, that we pass on to Bill Fraser. Occasionally, too, he passes something on to us.

It's only a short bus ride that didn't take me out of my way. The light was on in Bill's office and that's where he was. A few of the usual remarks and I came to the point.

"I'd rather like a little information from you. Nothing particularly secret, but you remember us passing on to you about three years ago a man called Farrell? Paul Farrell. Something to do with a missing wife."

He frowned. He went to one of the cabinets and after a minute came back with a file. He ran a quick eye through it.

"That's right," he said. "Just over three years ago. His wife ran out on him suddenly and we were supposed to find her." He looked up. "You knew him, didn't you?"

"Years ago. I think I told you at the time. He used to have a little photographic shop just off Cheapside and we used to put work in his way. The usual stuff: enlargements, reproductions and so on. Did wonderful work, even in those days. Always had his eye on further up the ladder, though. When we sent him to you he was getting pretty well up, too. Now he's quite a big shot in his way. Doing documentaries and shorts as a free-lance. Won a prize at Cannes for a documentary. And he does quite a lot of stuff for television."

"I seem to remember," Bill said. "But why the enquiries now?"

I told him in strict confidence what had happened. He agreed it had a queer sound to it.

"Still has the same address, though—if that means anything. It sort of makes him the same man, even if he *has* got on. But what do you want from me?"

"Just, briefly, what did you actually do for him? Any impressions you formed and so on."

It was a very slim file and it didn't take him long to skim through it.

"Well," he said, "he was living at that Pimlico address with his wife. Only been married to her about three weeks and then she walked out on him. When he got home, she'd vanished with all her things. We found out she'd rung a local taxi service and had gone with a couple of bags to Charing Cross Station. She'd got there about seven o'clock. We made a preliminary report and suggested an enquiry as to whether she'd taken a train or moved on in another taxi. He didn't want either. Just clamped down on the whole thing. Paid up and that was that."

"What was the wife like?"

He passed me a photograph: a glossy about five by three. A fine-looking woman, even if the face was a bit drawn. Her blonde hair hung round her shoulders and gave her the look of a half-starved show girl.

"A smart-looking piece," he said as I gave him the photograph back. "Which reminds me. She'd been in show business in her time so I suggested we might enquire at the agencies. He clamped down on that, too. There's a note here by one of our operatives, by the way. He thought Farrell a most unsatisfactory client. Holding far too much information back. That's why we weren't sorry to lose him. That's nothing against you, by the way. Very good of you to have sent him along."

I glanced at my watch. Twenty-five minutes of the hour had gone.

"Nothing else you want?" he asked me as I got up.

"Thanks, Bill, no," I told him. "Time I got along to see what the hullabaloo's all about. If there's anything you ought to know, I'll pass it on."

I was slightly early when I left the Tube station and in less than no time I was in Mayes Road. Number 135 was at the far end so I still had quite a little way to walk. There was a swirling kind of mist but nothing much to worry about, but the night itself was bitterly cold: the kind of cold that has a raw dampness that gets clean into one's bones.

Mayes Road was an approach to the busier shopping centre of Morley Street. It had a few old dwelling houses and a warehouse or two and then the first shop appeared. Then there were more of them: a grocery, a newsagent's, the inevitable junk shop, and all with the drabness of the older suburbs. Number 135 looked like a shop, too, an empty one, but wasn't. Its window was plain glass of what looked in that light a yellowish tinge, and by the door was a brass plate. I shone my torch on it. The street lamp was too far away to give much else but shadow.

C.W. HIPMAN, M.B.
R.G.P. CAVER, M.B., F.R.C.P.

Under it was a kind of white plaque with wording in black.

SURGERY 9.15 a.m. to 10.0 a.m. 5.15 p.m. to 6.0 p.m.
(Sundays and Wednesday evening excepted)

The sudden thought came that Farrell must have given me a wrong address, but when I looked back I saw another door just short of that of the surgery, and on it was the number I wanted. Almost as soon as I opened it a light went on at the head of a flight of stairs just beyond me. A door to the landing opened and a man appeared.

"Farrell, here. That you, Mr. Travers?"

"Yes," I said. "Shall I come up?"

He drew back at the open door to let me pass and I stepped straight into a cosy-looking if desperately untidy living-room that ran parallel to the road and the whole length of the surgery beneath. An electric fire was going full pelt, but the room was only comfortably warm. Books had overflowed everywhere from the lines of shelves; some on the floor and some on chairs. A couple of ashtrays were heaped with cigarette stubs. The worn, brown carpet looked as if it had been there since Victoria's time. A blue haze of cigarette smoke hung heavily about. But there wasn't any particular dust. An untidy room but friendly somehow, and lived-in.

"I can't stand formality," he told me, waving a hand at the room. "That woman of mine has a mania for balancing: you know, something on the right has to have something on the left. Not that I'm here all that much nowadays. Suppose it's more of a place to sleep in than anything else. Let me take your overcoat."

"You've not changed a lot yourself," I told him. "I'd have recognised you quite easily if I'd met you."

He was still in the thirties and still looking ten years older. The six foot of him was as lean, or even gaunt, and his shock of black hair just as unruly. A review of a film of his had referred to him as a tone poet, and if that meant anything, it was that he dealt with light and shade as a poet does with words. And as I saw him in that artificial light he had something of a poet with every now and again that faraway look in the eye. There was a restlessness, too, and an impatient disregard. With a hand he swept some books from a chair to the floor to make room for my overcoat. He took an old waterproof from the corner of a worn settee, looked round for a place to drop it, and once more chose the floor.

"Sit here," he told me. "And let me get you a drink. Never drink a lot these days but I always keep it—just in case."

"Thanks, no," I said, and felt the hard springs of the settee as I sat down. "I'm a pretty modest drinker myself."

He passed me an almost empty packet of cigarettes and then lighted another for himself and, before, as you might say, I was ready for him, he began to talk. At one moment he'd be standing bang in front of me and then he'd move a restless yard or two and as suddenly come back as if to confront me. Everything about him was such sheer restlessness and nerves that all at once I found myself smiling at a sudden thought. His wife had left him after three weeks. It was a wonder she'd stayed that long. If ever a man was a confirmed bachelor, it was Farrell.

"You must have been suspicious about me not explaining things over the phone," he began, "but I think you'll agree I was right after what you're going to hear. And what I want you to see."

His story was far too garbled for you to hear it direct. There was quite a lot that had little, directly, to do with the affair, and he constantly kept harking back, but what it all amounted to was this. He had a partner and they had an office just off Fleet Street. In the morning he'd done some filming—mist effects—and then he had gone to the office. After lunch he'd had an hour at Television House and finally he'd got back to the flat at about half-past four. He'd brewed himself some tea and it was about five o'clock when the telephone went. The man who spoke was an American.

He gave his name as Fred Steinberg, Jr., of Atlanta, Georgia, and said he was staying for a day or two at the Somerton Hotel, just off St. James's, before flying home. He was most interested in Mr. Farrell's work and had an immediate and, he hoped, gratifying proposition to put up to him. Time was important, so could Mr. Farrell see him at once at the hotel. They could talk business before dinner and, if necessary, during it. He gave the name of the television circuit which he largely owned and added that details could be gone into when Farrell arrived.

In a quarter of an hour Farrell was on his way. He'd tried without success to contact his partner, but that was of no great importance. He could be brought into things later, before any decisions were arrived at. It was about ten minutes to six when he asked at the desk for Steinberg's room number. *There was nobody of that name at the hotel.* Nobody had made a reservation under that name. There was nobody in the hotel who came from Atlanta, Georgia.

"Extraordinary!" I said. "What was the idea? A practical joke?"

"I was simply knocked all of a heap," he said, "but that's what I thought it might be when I got round to thinking at all. But what was the point? And who'd do it? Nobody that I knew of."

"What else did you do then?"

"What was there to do? I just grabbed a taxi and came back here and I was feeling pretty damn mad, I can tell you. What I came back for was because I had to do some reading on a place in north Finland. A possible film. Very much in the air at present. At any rate, I got back here and almost as soon as I got inside the place I knew someone'd been in while I was out."

At the far end of the room was a somewhat battered mahogany bureau, on the top of which the telephone stood. He went over to it and pointed out a drawer that hadn't been properly shut. A corner of paper was protruding from it. All the drawers, he said, had had their contents pawed over. I had to take his word for it.

"But that's nothing," he told me. "Just have a look in here."

He went through the nearer of the two doors and we were in what had to be his bedroom. It was a fair-sized room and not too untidy. Oddments of clothing were draped over a chair, and others strewed the floor, but the bed was neatly made. He pointed out the wardrobe door. It was ajar. Two of the drawers of the burr walnut chest were partly open. It was a mystery to me how he could tell that anything had been disturbed, but maybe he had a photographic eye that could detect a new untidiness among the mass of the old. Again I took his word that everything had been pawed over.

"I remember how I left things after I'd changed in here before going to that hotel," he said. "But let's go to the bathroom."

It was quite large but hopelessly old-fashioned. The ancient bath stood high on claw feet, the walls had begun to peel from damp and heat, and the linoleum flooring was badly cracked. There was a hot-press in the far wall with the door wide open, and on the floor by the off-white basin was quite a deal of water. As his arm went out and halted me just inside the door, it was that water I noticed first. My mind must have registered the fact that there was something strange about it, and when I looked at it again, a second or two later, I saw that it had a pinkish tinge. I asked him what it was.

"Water," he said. "And some blood in it. Can't be anything but blood. And look at this."

He edged nearer to the basin, keeping to the dry linoleum. When I looked over his shoulder I could see some faint, dried smears of red by the basin top.

"There's something else," he said. "The towel's gone. I had a clean-up before I left and I left it hanging on that rail. And look here."

He straddled the wet patch and landed up by the small hot-press. Both the bottom and the single shelf were heaped with linen and blankets. It was the bottom layer that had been turned over. Whether anything had been taken or not he didn't know, but on two of the white towels were faint pinkish marks where they'd been handled.

There was a dampness on the floor that had come from wet boots, and when I looked back towards the door, the light showed more faint marks that petered out just short. We straddled again and hugged the side of the bath to the door and the outside passage. There were two more doors. The one that faced us led to a spare room, its contents piled all ways and partly covered with dust sheets.

"Used to be my mother's room," he told me. "She owned a little bit of property round here. Didn't bring in a lot but about enough to keep her. It was the only one I kept after she died. I get a rent for the surgery and I'm used to it. Handy for town, too."

"Nothing touched here?"

There wasn't, and we went through the other door to the kitchen: an old-fashioned room with a gas-stove and a huge porcelain sink with the corners brown stained. There was a plate-rack over it, and at each side was a standing cupboard that had recently been repainted white. Just beyond was a kind of pantry annexe with a ventilation grating and a frosted glass window. There was little but oddments of china on the shelves, and the clear white enamel of a medium-sized refrigerator looked out of place like one white tooth against the yellow remnants in an old man's gums.

"Used to be my dark room," he told me. "A couple of years ago, when we took those premises in town, I had the window put in. Mrs. Back—my woman—said she had to have a pantry. God knows why."

"Well," he said, as we came back through the living-room door, "what do you make of it? Think I did right to ask you to come?"

I hardly knew what to say. I had the feeling that I was only on the fringes of something. There was a kind of simplicity about it all, and yet something was telling me it couldn't be so simple as it seemed. But I had to start somewhere: to assume, as a beginning, that Farrell himself had nothing to conceal and that all he'd told me was implicitly true.

"Looks as if you were more than justified," I said. "But might I have a look at the lock? No possibility of any other entry?"

"Never a hope," he said. "You can't get to the back at all—not from the street."

I shone the torch on the lock and had a good look through my glass. The faint scratches were just those of ordinary use.

"A cylinder lock. Couldn't be an easier one to manipulate. Don't think I'm spreading myself, but if I had the little gadget on me I could open it in a couple of shakes. But what about keys? Your Mrs. Back has one?"

"Always has had," he told me. "But she's been with us since long before my mother died. Absolutely reliable. But what made you think of her? I mean, why should she come here tonight? She has her two mornings, Tuesday and Friday."

"Then that's that," I said. "But let's look at what happened. Someone got in through that door and after making a search of the place, happened to cut himself pretty badly. Any other way to account for the blood? If it *is* blood?"

"What else *could* it be?" He made a quick gesture of exasperation. "Ever since I rang you I've been worrying my wits out. Why did he come here, whoever he was? There's nothing valuable in the place. An old camera or two that wouldn't pawn for more than a pound or so."

"He wouldn't know that."

"But dammit! does it look like a place worth bothering about? And how'd he come to injure himself? What'd he cut himself on?

And where is it?" He snorted. "The whole thing's sheer lunacy. There's neither rhyme nor reason nor any other damn thing."

"Maybe you're right," I said. "It couldn't have been that woman of yours, because if she'd cut herself she'd have cleared up the mess. And you can't think of another person?"

There was no missing the hesitation. It took him two or three seconds to say there was no one at all.

"Well," I said, and let out a breath, "the problem is what to do about it all. Or what you want me to do. Or ought the whole thing to be reported to the police?"

"My God, no! It's too fantastic. And nothing's been taken— except perhaps that towel."

I gave my horn-rims a polish, and when I replaced them he was watching me.

"Thought of something?"

"Yes," I said. "There must be more in this than meets the eye. That scheme to lure you away was too well planned. Someone knew a good deal about you. I know you've been in the papers and so on quite a lot, but this chap had worked out just the right line. You couldn't help falling for it. An American voice was it? Not a fake?"

"Absolutely genuine."

"Know any Americans?"

"Plenty. I've been over there twice and met all sorts. That voice was the genuine thing. You can take that as read. The voice of a man in the prime of life. Typical business voice. Brisk and assured and all that."

That didn't help. It wasn't even a confirmation of his story. And something kept telling me that he was keeping a whole lot back. What he had to conceal I didn't know, but there it was. Bill Fraser's man had said the same thing, and it was while I was frowning away at that, that something suddenly caught my eye—the shine of something like broken glass. Somehow I must instinctively have connected it with that bathroom blood, for I got up to see what it was. It lay by a small pile of books between two chairs in the direction of the door.

"This is interesting." I gave it to him. "A piece of jewellery."

He squinted at it. "That's right. Costume jewellery by the look of it." He gave me a look that was almost startled. "Never saw it before in my life. How'd it get here?"

"You had any women visitors?"

"There hasn't been a woman here since—well, not for years."

It was a sort of brooch or clip: the kind of thing women wear on a lapel. It was smallish: just an imitation sapphire in the centre, a surround of tiny imitation diamonds and the whole set in imitation gold. It looked superior to the usual run of costume jewellery.

"Does your Mrs. Back ever wear this kind of thing?"

"Never. A wedding ring, that's all. Well, all I've ever noticed."

I did a bit more thinking, then made up my mind. "Where's this Mrs. Back live?"

"She has a bed-sitter out Paddington way. Why?"

"Well, if you don't object, I think I'd like a word with her. There's just the off-chance she might know something about this clip."

He didn't like the idea. He didn't say so but I could see it on his face. Then he did some rummaging in the bureau and found the exact address—15 Farnham Road, Paddington. I put the clip in my wallet.

"Right," I said. "What about leaving things like this. I'll have a brief word with your Mrs. Back and then I'll do some more thinking. In the morning I'll come here again, whether I've had any fresh ideas or not. That suit you?"

Again I thought there was something he wanted to say and again he kept whatever it was to himself. We agreed on nine-thirty next morning, he to ring me meanwhile if anything cropped up.

"Don't disturb a thing here," I told him. "There's always the possibility that we'll be forced after all to go to the police."

And then I thought of something else. "That doctors' surgery under here. Did you think of asking if anyone had heard anything?"

He smiled wryly. "It's a Wednesday. No surgery Wednesday evenings."

I'd forgotten that, though I didn't tell him so. I said it was bad luck. We went down to the street together and said goodnight. A taxi passed me as I walked towards the Tube station and I wished I'd hailed it.

2
ONE DEAD MAN

I WAS just turning out of Mayes Road when I happened to look round and see another taxi approaching. This time I did hail it.

"Didn't think this would be a road for taxis," I told the driver. "Yours is the second in a couple of minutes."

"One of the busiest streets there is," he said. "Straight run through to the river. Misses the traffic. All us what're stationed at Victoria use Mayes Road. Where do you want to go, sir?"

The streets were fairly clear of traffic and we made good time. It's rarely a slow route across the Park in any case unless you get held up at the Arch. We hit a green light and after that the luck was average. I hadn't said I was in a hurry, but if I had we wouldn't have made it much faster. It was just before nine o'clock when that taxi picked me up and at twelve minutes past the driver was slowing down into Farnham Road and looking for numbers. He made a complete turn and drew up.

"Here you are, sir. Number fifteen."

I asked him how far we were from Paddington Station and he told me two minutes' walk. He even indicated the way. Had it been further I'd have asked him to wait. When he'd gone I had a look down Farnham Road: a road of terraced houses three storeys high. In daylight that road would be hideous. Now the light of the lamps and a rising moon softened it down. There was frost in the air and I slipped on the pavement as I turned towards the house.

The small iron gate hung open on crooked hinges and I went gingerly along the short concrete path. Light was coming through the Victorian fanlight above the door and I could hear the sound of a radio. If there was a bell-push I didn't see it. I used the knocker. Just as I was about to use it again the door opened. A tall, thin man barked out a "Yes?"

"Sorry to disturb you, but may I see Mrs. Back?"

He peered out at me. I think I was an unusual caller and I don't mean my six-foot three and horn-rims, but what must have been the general look of me: black homburg hat, black overcoat and all.

"Better come in," he told me. "It's perishin' cold out there."

He gave me another look as I stepped into the light of the passage. A flight of stairs was at the far end.

"What name, sir?"

"Travers," I said carefully. "Tell her I'm a friend of Mr. Farrell."

I could hear him saying it to himself as he went to the foot of the stairs. He called her name and a door opened on a landing.

"You'd better go up, sir, and tell her yourself."

She stood at the door of her room: a dumpy woman of well over sixty. She looked a motherly sort of soul. As soon as I mentioned Farrell's name she smiled and drew back to let me in.

"So you're a friend of Mr. Paul's, sir. Nothing wrong, I hope?"

"Nothing at all," I told her. "Just a message he wanted me to give you as I was coming this way."

"Sit down, sir. Don't mind the bed. I don't often have visitors and there isn't no sense in covering it up. I was just going to make myself a cup of tea."

There was an enquiring look, and it didn't take me a second to say I'd like one, too. She asked me how I liked it and I told her. There was a curtained recess in the corner beyond the end of the bed, and I could hear her pottering about in it while I looked round the room. There was an old-fashioned fireplace with a gas-fire full on. The mantelpiece above it was crowded with knick-knacks and little framed photographs. A horse-hair settee stood head-on to the bed, and there were a couple of matching easy chairs, one of which I had. A table with a wireless set was on my right. The floor was covered with coconut matting, with a flowered rug in front of the gas-stove. Cheap coloured prints hung on the walls and a couple of willow-pattern plates. The whole thing brought a whiff of nostalgia. There, in the heart of the suburbs, though different perhaps in many ways, was a room I knew long ago as a boy: a cottage room in a Suffolk village and an old nurse who used to give me milk and buns. A snug room, like this one, and a dumpy old woman with a motherly face. All that was missing was the kettle on the hob and a cat asleep on the rug.

It was a good cup of tea, strong and sweet, and she brought some biscuits with it, and it was only then that I knew how long it was since I'd had a meal. I suppose, too, that I must have an honest face. She didn't ask me about myself: just took me for granted as she began telling me about Paul Farrell. Her sister had worked for the father and mother, and when the sister suddenly died Mrs. Back—Elsie apparently—took over, and that was fifteen years ago. The father had had a furniture shop in the High Street, and after his death Paul and his mother moved to the flat in Mayes Road. Always a good boy to his mother, she said, and always the one who meant to get on.

"I suppose you knew his wife?"

"Her!" she said. "Did you know her, sir?"

"Never met her. I was away at the time."

"Well," she said, and her ample bosom heaved, "you could have knocked me down with a feather when I got a letter about him coming back—he'd been in France, you know—and saying as how he was bringing his wife. I had to read that letter twice before I believed it."

"He wasn't the marrying sort?"

"Not Mr. Paul, sir. Never heard even the mention of a girl's name. At any rate, I had to get the flat all spick and span and have both bedrooms ready. *Both* bedrooms, mind you! I told myself there was something fishy about that, soon as I read it. And then when I clapped eyes on her! A regular hussy for all her smarmy ways. And that blonde hair of hers hanging all over her shoulders, looking like—well, I won't bring my tongue to say it. And 'Paul, dear, this,' and 'Paul, dear, that,' and then as soon as he was out of the flat mornings, she'd be off, too. And then there was the morning when she brought a girl up, thinking I was gone. I was in the bathroom just doing a bit of tidying up and I heard her say, 'I think she's gone,' and I said to myself, 'No, my madam, I ain't gone,' and when I came out and she saw me she put on that superior voice of hers and they went into the bedroom."

"A friend of hers, was it?"

"A smart-looking woman, just about her age. Birds of a feather, if you ask me. And that was the day before she gave me the sack. He didn't want her to soil her pretty hands, so I used to come every morning then, except Saturdays, and this was a Tuesday, and I was just a-going when she says, 'Oh, Elsie, I've talked it over with my husband, and we shan't be wanting you any more. We're making other arrangements.' She brought out her purse to pay me but I told her I wasn't taking any notice from *her*. I said only Mr. Paul was going to give me notice, and then I flounced out." She smiled. "I was so upset that when I got out in the street I had a good cry."

"This is all news to me," I said. "And what happened then?"

She gave herself a little hug as if there was something coming that had to be enjoyed.

"I'll tell you," she said. "It was the very next day when she up and left him. Took every stitch. All the clothes she'd bought there with his money and everything. Later on he told me he'd employed one of them private detectives to find out where she'd gone, but that wasn't no use. She'd just used him for her own ends if you ask me. Good riddance to bad rubbish was what I thought, and that's what he thought when I told him what I suspected. Well, not suspected: what I knew. I've had two of my own—two boys; both in Canada they are now. Want me to go and live with them but I'm too old now to make a change. Not that they aren't good boys. No mother could wish for better."

"It's nice to hear you say so," I told her. "But what was it you found out?"

"Oh, yes," she said, and settled herself again. "She left, as it were, on the Wednesday, and on the Friday he come all the way here to see me and that's when I told him. ' Suppose you knew, Mr. Paul,' I said, 'that she was going to have a baby?' That's what I told him and, do you know, he went as white as a sheet. I told him about that sickness and her retching her insides out, and how she looked and the smarmy tales she told me about having a delicate stomach. Thought I was a fool. Couldn't take me in, though. I knew."

"How'd Paul take it?"

"Knocked him all of a heap, sir. Then he asked me to come back, and I said I would, but only two days a week. I have my pension and there's what my boys send me and I wouldn't do it at all if it wasn't for him."

"He thinks a lot of you, too."

She smiled. "Well, I've known him since he was a boy, and I was almost a mother to him, as you might say, till he got over his own mother, though she didn't suffer much, poor dear. Went off in her sleep."

I got slowly to my feet. "Well, it's getting late. Thank you for the tea, Mrs. Back. One of the best cups of tea I ever had."

"Glad to see you, sir, any time you're this way." She looked round the room. "It isn't much to ask anyone to, but it suits me. No place like home, as the saying is."

"True enough," I told her, and then gave a start of surprise. "I don't know. I've got a head like a turnip, as my old nurse used to say. I've forgotten the very thing I really came for."

I brought out that clip and gave it to her. "Paul found this lying on the floor behind some books when he came home tonight. He thought perhaps you might have dropped it."

She shook a reluctant head. "No, sir. 'Tain't mine. Never saw it before in my life." She smiled as she held it at arm's length. "Pretty, though, isn't it? Make a rare nice brooch. Go well with my black."

"Perhaps he'll give it to you," I said, as she handed it back. Then I frowned. "I've thought of something. This is strictly between ourselves, but you know how untidy he is. . . ." She clicked her tongue. "I ought to know, sir. He's one o' them that just can't stand tidiness. I'm always telling him. I've wore out my tongue telling him but it never was no good. It's just the way he is."

"Well then, Mrs. Back—still strictly between ourselves—could that clip have belonged to his wife? Could it have been dropped before she left?"

"Oh, no, sir!" She looked quite horrified. "Because he does more or less what he likes in the living-room don't mean I don't give it a going-over when he ain't there. I'd have spotted it at once."

"Did the wife have any jewellery?"

"Not that I knew of, sir. Only her wedding ring and some of that stuff you can buy at Woolworth's. Showy sort of stuff."

"What was her name, by the way?"

"Laura. Don't know what her maiden name was. He never used to call her anything, really." She clicked her tongue again. "Hardly like husband and wife, somehow. Still, they say it takes all sorts to make a world. Not that she was my sort, or his either. He never likes me to mention her now, but as I told him after she'd left him, it was the luckiest day of his life. Count your blessings, that's what I always say."

I shook her hand and thanked her and she warned me to go carefully down the stairs. I waved up to her before I closed the front door and then I made for Paddington Station. A waiting taxi took me home and it was half-past ten when I got back. I asked the night-porter to scrounge me something to eat and then I went up and made myself some coffee. The central heating was full on but I switched on the electric fire as well, and after I'd eaten the cold meat and bread and cheese George brought me, I stretched out my long legs before the fire and tried to think.

It was no good. The cold air had made me sleepy and too many things kept crowding in on my thoughts. As I was getting ready for bed there was only one thing that kept coming again and again to my mind: that now I knew why Farrell had called off Bill Fraser. He'd believed what Elsie Back had told him, and maybe for special reasons of his own. He knew also that he wasn't the father of his wife's child and that's why he didn't want her found. My guess was that the possibility of her returning was for weeks something of a nightmare. And I also thought I knew something else.

That night in his flat there had been things he had almost said but which he had kept back, and now I came to think things out, all were somehow connected with his wife. Even after three years and more a mere reminder was still something to fear and avoid. The sight of that clip had been a reminder: not that he knew it had ever been hers. If he had told me one truth, it was that he had never seen it before and that its presence in the flat was a mystery.

I kept thinking of that clip just before I fell asleep. It was the first thing I remembered in the morning when I woke: that, and the pinkish water by a wash-basin and the same pinkish marks where someone had turned over a pile of towels.

Norris should have returned overnight so I rang him at his private address. I told him a case had cropped up and I'd be busy on it for an hour or two and then I'd be back at the agency. After that I made myself some coffee and toast, then I brought in the two morning papers from outside the door and settled down in front of the fire. It was still only eight o'clock and I wasn't due at Farrell's place till half-past nine.

I glanced at a front page and didn't feel at all happy. Khrushchev was breathing out threats about Berlin and I couldn't help a premonitory shiver. Then my eye caught something else on the far right-hand.

DRIVER FINDS DEAD MAN IN TAXI
MYSTERY OF IDENTITY

That word *mystery* was enough to set me off and I began to read. There were only a couple of paragraphs which made it a late hand-out by Scotland Yard, with a minimum of editing.

The police are anxious to discover the identity of a man who was found dead yesterday evening in a London taxi. William Boydale, a taxi-driver, whose stand is at Victoria Station, was returning last night at about six-fifteen with an empty cab when he was hailed in Mayes Road—

I think my heart skipped a beat. For a moment or so I saw nothing, not even the blur of printed words. I sort of gave myself a shake, slowly polished my glasses, and began to read again.

. . . was hailed in Mayes Road, within a few hundred yards of Victoria Station, by a man. The man appeared to stumble as he came forward, and his speech seemed blurred as he asked to be driven to Charing Cross Station. On arrival the fare was apparently asleep in the cab corner, but was found to be dead.

At Charing Cross Hospital the man was found to be suffering from a shot wound in the stomach. No identity papers were found on him. He is described as about 45 years old, six feet tall, weight about fourteen stone, hair black and complexion sallow. No visible distinguishing marks. He was wearing a worn Merrimac waterproof, a dark worsted suit and snap-brim brown hat. It is understood that a photograph will be issued later. Meanwhile, the police will be glad of any information that may definitely establish the identification of the victim. A gang shooting is not ruled out.

I read it again. Everything was too apposite. That dead man must have been shot in Farrell's flat. It wasn't hard to visualise the whole thing—the shot and the quick getaway of the one who'd fired it. It couldn't have been an accident. Had it been that, then the one responsible would have stayed with the shot man and helped to get him at least to safety.

A shot in the stomach and the wounded man left alone. I could see him clutching his stomach with his hands and trying to staunch the blood: grabbing in the bathroom the first towel that came to hand and managing somehow to find a clean towel in the hot-press for a rough bandage. I could see him making a painful way down the stairs and out to the road, and leaning, perhaps, against a wall and praying for a taxi.

Maybe the shot had been fired in the actual bathroom. Maybe it would never be known where it had been fired. But what about the other man? *Or* woman? Did the dropping of that clip necessarily ensure that it had been a woman? Even the dead man might have dropped it. That's what I told myself—that one had to keep an open mind, and yet, deep down, I was somehow sure it had been a woman.

I took that clip out of my wallet and had a good look at it by the window in the hard, cold light of that frosty morning. It was the first time I'd really seen it. In Farrell's flat the light had been none too good, and when I had shown it to Mrs. Back I'd been more anxious about her identification than inspecting it again myself. Now it seemed to me to be just a bit dirty, so I mixed a little detergent and gave it a scrub with an old toothbrush. I dried it as best I could and had a look at it through the glass.

It wasn't a couple of seconds before I knew that that clip wasn't something picked up for a few pence at a chain store. I had no means of testing it but I was pretty sure that the metal wasn't a cheap yellow alloy but honest-to-God gold. Sapphires I knew nothing about, but the blue of this one had a lovely velvet lustre. The small diamonds, too, looked as if they might be real. I put the metal under the glass again. It had various letterings, but so filled with ancient dust or grime that I couldn't make them out.

I think I gave a little grunt. Why bother about valuing something about which I knew comparatively little when there were experts about? Why shouldn't I take it to Sumners of Bond Street. They knew me well enough there. And no sooner thought of than put into action. Just one thing that had to be done first.

I looked up Farrell's number in my notebook and rang. I could hear his bell ringing and ringing and just when I knew he couldn't be in, his voice—a sleepy one—was at the other end.

"Travers here, Farrell. Sorry to've disturbed you."

"I didn't turn in till late," he said. "What's the time?"

"About twenty to nine. I know I'm not due yet but I wanted to know if you'd seen the morning papers. I gather you haven't."

"Just this minute out of bed. Why the papers?"

"Listen," I said. "I'm in a hurry and I've got things to do before I get to your place, but read your papers. Get hold of two or three. Read what they say about a wounded man picked up yesterday evening in Mayes Road. And don't do anything about it till I see you."

I rang off at once. Ten minutes later I was on my way. I took the Underground at Leicester Square, and it was about ten minutes past nine when I walked into Sumners. I looked round and spotted a salesman who knew me. He gave me a smile.

"Good-morning, sir. A slightly better morning?"

We came to an agreement about the weather, and then I handed him that clip.

"Can you give me a quick valuation of that? Just a very approximate one. Naturally I'll pay any fee."

"Don't worry about that, sir."

He picked up a jeweller's eye-glass, switched on a swivel light and had a good look. I couldn't tell a thing from his expression.

"I'll get our Mr. Harris to have a look at it, sir, if you don't mind. Shouldn't keep you a minute."

He disappeared in the recess behind the main showroom and I took a look at a showcase of early silver. It couldn't have been more than three minutes before he was back. As he talked he was wrapping that clip, as I'd called it, in tissue paper.

"A late Victorian brooch, sir. Value about a hundred and fifty pounds. They're coming right back into fashion now. I think you'd appreciate it more, sir, after it was cleaned. If you cared to leave it, it'd only be a matter of a day or so."

"I'll mention it to Mrs. Travers," I told him. "She's away at the moment. Very good of you, and what do I owe you?" He waved a hand and smiled it away.

"Always glad, sir, to oblige a client."

Within a hundred yards of Sumners I picked up a taxi. I was five minutes late at Mayes Road and Farrell had his door open as soon as I set foot on the stairs. To say he was perturbed was a gross understatement. He was grabbing at my arm and babbling away as soon as I came within reach on the top landing. I just pushed him gently aside and went into the living-room.

"If that surgery's on downstairs, we'd better talk a bit quietly," I told him.

"They can't hear down there," he said. "But about this man. It's incredible. It just can't be anything to do with me."

"Take it easy," I told him. "Just light a cigarette and listen to me, because we haven't got a lot of time. Don't say a word and don't think I'm mad because I'm virtually whispering. Perhaps we'd better go through to your bedroom. And for God's sake make no noise."

He stared, but he followed me. The bed was unmade and I sat down on it.

"Listen," I said. "You know what I saw as my taxi came into Mayes Road? Plain-clothes men are systematically working this way, making enquiries. A few minutes and they'll be here, but we're not going to open the door. We're doing nothing till we've talked things over. The first thing you've got to do is sign an agreement with the Broad Street Detective Agency, dating it from last night. That'll put me in a position to act as a buffer on your behalf and to go on making private enquiries. You agree?"

He could only shrug his shoulders. He had a pen on him and we found a writing block in one of the drawers. I drew the agreement up in duplicate, signed his copy and he signed mine. It called for an advance of ten pounds and a further ten pounds a day, plus expenses, until mutual termination.

"Eyewash, largely," I told him. "Any financial matters we can settle up when the time comes. And now listen to this. To my mind there isn't a shadow of a doubt that that man in the taxi was shot here."

All the time I was talking I had to wave him down. It was like trying to force a bung into a bottle full of effervescence.

"For God's sake wait till I've finished," I told him. "If you have anything to say, you can say it then, but get this into your head. I'm prepared to believe that you personally had nothing whatever to do with it, but that man was shot here. Everything proves it: the missing towel, the blood, the timing—everything. In other words, when we're ready—I repeat, *when* we're ready—we've got to call in the police."

There was a sound outside and I held my breath. Steps were on the stairs and then on the landing. The bell rang. I gently moved the bedroom door to, so that there was only a crack of light. The bell rang again and we could hear low voices. It rang a third time and the voices grew fainter with the receding steps. I waited a good minute before I spoke.

"Just one last thing. The police have to be rung. If you don't do it, I must. All you have to do is tell everything you know or don't know, with my evidence in support. Anything you'd like to add to what you told me last night?"

The stuffing had been knocked clean out of him. I don't think he'd have resisted if I'd taken him by the arm and led him down-stairs. All he could do was give a helpless shake of the head.

"That's all then," I said. "Let's go quietly back in there. I've got to do some telephoning."

I didn't dial 999. I found another number in my notebook and I dialled that. When I heard the voice from the Yard, I asked to be put through at once to whatever officer was in charge of last night's man-in-the-taxi case. I gave my name and said I'd hold the line.

"Why exactly are you ringing, sir?"

"Because I have urgent and important evidence. Superintendent Jewle will vouch for me if you care to enquire."

"That's all right, sir. Some of us here know your name well enough."

That at least was something. I was even hoping that Jewle himself might be in charge of the case. Too much to expect, though. Jewle had gone right up the ladder since I'd worked with him. He'd be a Yard tycoon; all telephones and diagrams and little flags stuck in large maps.

"You're through, sir."

I cleared my throat.

"Hallo, Mr. Travers. What's this about you having something for us?"

"Good God!" I said blasphemously. "It's you, Matthews!"

"Me as ever was," he told me.

Always on the hunt for a witticism and generally missing the mark. I'd known him for years, even before he was Jewle's regular side-kick. I'd worked with him and joked with him. We'd even thumbed noses together at authority.

"To be serious," I told him. "I happen to have got mixed up in this case. I'm plumb in the middle of it. You can have all I know on just one condition—that you come personally and get it."

"Where're you speaking from, sir?"

"Never mind that. Do you agree? It'll be more than worth your time."

"Why not?" he said. "I'll be along at once. Where to?"

"Just one other little thing. You're not to send any of your myrmidons in beforehand. I and my client are talking to you and you alone."

"Why not?" he told me again, and that's when I gave him the address.

3
GIVEN IN EVIDENCE

"WE'RE in luck's way," I told Farrell. "You probably gathered that Inspector Matthews is an old friend. I don't say we're in need of it, but we'll get a square deal."

"You think he'll believe me?"

The smouldering cigarette was burning his fingers and he hastily stubbed it out.

"All you have to do is tell the absolute truth. What's called 'the truth, the whole truth and nothing but the truth'. So far I've believed you and so will he. I know, I know," I said, "You think it's all too fantastic. But don't you believe it. It's so fantastic that it just *has* to be true."

"Perhaps yes," he told me grudgingly. "But even the word police—"

"Stupidity," I said bluntly. "The police are as human as you and I—perhaps more so."

In all my experience he was unique. I suppose in a way he was a kind of visionary: poet and artist combined. And the matriarchal shackles still on him and the tighter—if you get what I mean—for not actually being there.

"We've got about half-an-hour, maybe less," I told him, "so let's go over last night again, up to the time you called me."

What he told me varied by hardly a word.

"Right. Let's hark back a bit. Tell me all about your wife."

He just gasped.

"B-b-but why?"

I let out a breath. I handed him that brooch. I told him what I'd found out and the nothing I'd learned about it from Mrs. Back.

"For heaven's sake pull yourself together! I know how these things work. It's my job. Inspector Matthews has to be shown this brooch. If we don't mention it he'll hear about it from Mrs. Back when he sees her, and, believe me, he *will* have to see her. Almost the first thing he'll ask you when he hears about it is if you're married."

He was trying to speak but somehow couldn't.

"Look," I said patiently, "the odds are enormous that this brooch was dropped here last night by a woman and the odds are just as great that it was she who shot the man. Have you seen your wife or heard from her or about her since she left you?"

He shook his head.

"Right," I said. "You tell me everything about her. The first time you met her—everything. Then I'll decide if there's anything you needn't tell the police. And make it quick because Matthews might be along here in a few minutes."

If the story of the previous night's happenings was fantastic, all I can say is that what I dragged out of him demanded the coining of a new adjective. Not that it wasn't credible. It was more than that: it just couldn't help but be true—once you knew Farrell himself. There was a man, attached to his mother's apron strings, who'd never even looked at a woman. To him, maybe there'd been nothing quixotic or generous in what he did and it wasn't perhaps so much a generosity as a sudden, overwhelming impulse that had made him do it. The whole thing had been a tremendous experience, sexually and emotionally, and how he'd come out of it without a nervous breakdown was something I'd never know. A kind of queer warmth suddenly flooded me when at last he'd finished.

"That's fine," I said, and it must have been lamely. "I shall do some talking with Inspector Matthews first, and then—"

I broke off. Steps were on the stairs and the bell rang.

To some people, the off-handedness of the next minute or two might have looked like indifference to duty, or even worse.

Matthews and I, for instance, greeted each other like the old friends we were. He introduced his sergeant—a tallish, sparely built young fellow in the late twenties. Both were introduced to Farrell. Sergeant Hassack thought he'd seen Farrell before and it turned out to be to do with a television short. We might all have been assembled there for a christening or something, with Farrell the nervous father.

"You're fatter," I told Matthews. "Must be doing pretty well for yourself."

But he hadn't altered much in the year or so since I'd last seen him: the same rather loose-limbed six foot of him, the same readiness to break into a grin, and the hair as black as ever.

"Can't grumble," he told me. "And now what's all this about information? Who's going to speak first?"

He and I were sharing the settee. Hassack had taken the chair on which my overcoat had laid the previous night. Farrell had cleared another chair for himself. I said I thought it would expedite things if I gave my story first. And it did.

"You confirm that, Mr. Farrell? Anything you want to add?"

Farrell confirmed, and he didn't. Matthews made a note or two and got to his feet. "Right. Let's see that bathroom."

We waited in the passage while he and Hassack went carefully round.

He closed the door when they came out. He asked if he could use the telephone. Farrell and I stayed where we were till he'd finished. He called us in. He'd want the run of the flat for a bit, he said, in about half an hour's time. Sergeant Hassack would stay on but he'd like both of us to see the dead man.

He sat down again and we sat too.

"Now, Mr. Farrell, let's hear your own version of last night. Tell it in your own way and don't worry about repeating Mr. Travers."

It was, in fact, practically a repetition. Matthews didn't show any impatience.

"And the whole thing's utterly inexplicable as far as you're concerned?"

"Absolutely."

I wanted to get Farrell off the hooks and ready for a far more trying story. That's why I produced that brooch. Matthews was told everything I'd discovered about it. He took down Mrs. Back's address and asked a few questions about her. And then—

it couldn't have been better timed from my point of view—came the vital question.

"Any women friends likely to come up here?"

Farrell said he had none.

"You married? Or been married?"

I cut quickly in. "That's a long story. Not a happy one from Mr. Farrell's point of view. I've only just learned it myself. If I might suggest it I think he should tell you something about his career and why he's living here and so on."

"That'd be fine," Matthews said. "Just how did you get into your line of business, Mr. Farrell?"

Farrell's account was a modest one. When he mentioned coming to the flat and life with his mother, I hoped it was registering. From what I learned afterwards, it did.

And so at last to that tale of his marriage. He started haltingly, but once the first nervousness was over, the words came in a spate. It was as if a dam had burst.

It all began in Marseilles. Farrell had been making quite a lot of film in the dock area. It was in December and there were some wonderful effects with winter sun. Then on almost his last evening he dropped in at a little café for a drink. A girl came in while he was sipping his *pernod* and took the stool next to him. Afterwards she owned up that she'd seen him before and had guessed he was British and had followed him there. It was she who got into conversation.

"You're British, aren't you?"

He said he was. Then, shyly one imagines, he asked if he might buy her a drink.

"You'll have to," she told him. "I haven't any money."

She took her drink to a table and he followed her. Ninety-nine men out of a hundred would have taken her story with more than a grain of salt, but he swallowed it, hook, line and sinker. A week before she had gone to Nice from England, after some correspondence, to take up a job with a dancing troupe. She hadn't liked either the place or the two men whom she met and, to cut a long story short, she was beginning to be scared of the whole thing and especially of the *madame* of the pseudo-hotel where they had found her a room.

Then when one of the men began putting a certain proposition up to her, she knew the kind of racket into which she'd been lured and the same night she managed to get away with virtually only the things she stood in, and very little money. She took a train to Marseilles and managed to get a room at a cheap hotel. She'd been there three days, hoping for something to turn up that would get her back to England, and now she couldn't go back to the hotel. Her last francs had been spent that morning on a brioche and coffee.

Well, there was her story and Farrell fell for it. She'd also given him the idea that she was in danger from the men, even in Marseilles, because of a possible exposure of their racket, and the upshot was that Farrell found her a room at his own hotel, and advanced her some money to buy clothes. The next night she came sobbing with gratitude to his room. He didn't say so, but I think that was where she spent the night. The next day they went to Paris and there, later, he married her. That's one reason why I think she spent that night with him. After that he'd have felt himself bound in some peculiar honour to marry her.

She claimed she'd had to leave her passport behind in Nice, but she married under the name of Laura Mann. She had no relatives at all, she said, except a step-brother whom she hadn't seen for years, and she claimed he was a doctor. At any rate, they came back to England and the flat in Mayes Road, and, almost as soon as they arrived, she was announcing that she was going to get a job. That made him furious. I don't know if you'd call it a mother complex, but he'd imagined things would be from then on as they were in his mother's time. And something else came up at the same time: the fact that she insisted from the first on having her own bedroom.

One gathered that from the day of their arrival at the flat, it was a pretty queer relationship.

And so to a certain Tuesday night, just three weeks after the marriage. He arrived home at about six o'clock to find a wholly changed Laura. Not only was she extraordinarily affectionate, but she announced that she'd changed her mind about getting a job. From then on the flat was going to be as it was in his mother's time. She said they must drink to it, and they did. After that, all he remembered was suddenly being sleepy, and then he passed out. He didn't actually wake till five the next morning. Laura had gone and with her everything she owned, including more clothes that she'd bought in England. Every penny he'd had on him had gone, too, and later he discovered she'd drawn out from his bank the full fifty pounds which had been arranged she was entitled to draw as the maximum necessary to run the flat if he were away for some time.

"Can I cut in here?" I said, and told Matthews about Farrell's application to me to find her and what Bill Fraser had found out.

"Better get the whole thing off your chest now," I told Farrell. "Tell Inspector Matthews what Mrs. Back found out."

And so Matthews heard that final sordid ending. He shook his head.

"Well, sir, you'll pardon me saying so, but she certainly played you for a sucker. And you've never seen her or heard anything of her since?"

Farrell had finished with talking. He just shook his head.

"She took her key with her?"

Farrell didn't actually know. He thought she had. Then he thought that she must have.

"Right," Matthews said, and got to his feet. "We'll have to get a complete statement from you later on, but meanwhile, if you get yourself ready, Sergeant Hassack will take you down to the car."

It didn't take Farrell a minute to get ready. Matthews motioned to me to stay behind. He wanted to know what I thought of that marriage story. I told him I thought it was implicitly true.

"Yes," he said. "Nobody but him could have been such a damn fool. What's the word for him? Quixotic. That's it. Quixotic."

"Or lack of social experience. And what they call a one-track mind. All his life he's wanted to do one thing. To put it simply, to make a record of things that appealed to him. And then, when he was just a bit out of his orbit, shall we say, he met the wrong woman."

"I think I get you," he said. "Later on this morning I'd like to expand that a bit. Also by then we might have a few more ideas."

*

I sat in front with the driver: Matthews and Farrell sat chatting at the back. I couldn't catch much they were saying but it was about Farrell's job, so Matthews, I guessed, was trying to get him at his ease. I'd never worked with Matthews when he was in charge of a case. As I've said, in my time he was Jewle's side-kick, and I was wondering whether or not he'd made up his mind on promotion to model himself on his old chief. So far I'd had no inkling. In the flat he'd been free and easy: just enough reserve, perhaps, to show who he was and what he stood for. If he'd tumbled quickly to the fact that Farrell was a bit out of his experience—an oddity who'd require special handling—then I thought he'd been dead right all the way.

There was only the faintest mist about that morning, though it was still bitingly cold. We were going the Embankment way and the trip didn't take more than ten minutes. I wasn't looking forward to that morgue. A morgue has always struck me as an annexe of Limbo: a no-man's-land between something and nothing; the very chilliness, and the sweetness of formaldehyde, as much a *memento mori* as the sickly scent of lilies. With me it's something that takes hours to shake off. And you see some queer sights in morgues; faces that can haunt you for days.

There was nothing like that about the face of the man we looked at that morning. I'd thought Farrell might be nervous about the whole thing but he wasn't. He stood there for perhaps half a minute and then shook his head.

"Never seen him before?"

"Never."

"I don't suppose you have, Mr. Travers?"

"No," I said. "He's a perfect stranger. Formidable looking, don't you think?"

He certainly looked a tough character to run up against. Pain or surprise had slightly twisted his mouth into something almost as ugly as a snarl. The nose was slightly askew as if it had been broken and badly reset. There was a deep dimple in the chin, visible even against the blue of the jowls. The neck was thick: the neck of an eighteen collar. Here and there was a tiny touch of grey in the jet black hair.

"Something of the Italian about him," Matthews said, "except that they don't often run to his size."

We moved away up the steps and through the door to the long passage. We halted at the foot of the main stairs and Matthews asked us to wait. It was five minutes before he was back.

"If you'll be so good as to accompany this officer, Mr. Farrell, he'll take you up to make your statement."

"The Old Man wants to have a look at him," he told me, and I guessed he meant Jewle. "We might as well go up to my room. Don't know about you, but I can do with a coffee."

I couldn't help smiling as I went into that room: it reminded me in some idiotic way of the handing down of a pair of trousers along the line of a family of boys. I'd known that room before it was Jewle's, and now Matthews was third in the line of ascent. There was the same Victorian stand on which to hang hat and overcoat, and I could have sworn that the coffee that came in was on the same tray. I definitely sat in the same chair.

Matthews took a rash gulp of the coffee and made a face. He gave it another stir to help it cool and lighted a cigarette. I was stoking my pipe.

"Now then, sir," he said. "You and I have got to have a little talk. By eight o'clock last night you knew everything that I know now, except perhaps about Farrell's wife, so why didn't you ring up the local police?"

"All sorts of reasons," I said. "Last night I could have justified them but to tell the honest truth, I don't think I can do so now. So if you want to read the Riot Act, carry on." He shook a sad head. "Not like you, you know, sir. Here's a man who was lured out of his house and proves to you there's been an entry, and then you see that blood in the bathroom, and what do you do? Go off and see his woman in case she came in on the wrong day and cut herself, and then you go home to bed. What on earth came over you?"

What I told him must have sounded pretty lame: that we didn't actually know it was blood: that Mrs. Back *might* have cut herself: that Farrell himself was an unusual character about whom I couldn't be sure, and the whole extraordinary thing a something on which I felt I had to sleep.

"If there'd been a body there or real, actual blood, that would have been different," I told him. "All the same you have to admit that I foresaw the police. I cautioned him not to touch a thing. When you look at it, the investigation was only postponed for twelve hours."

There was an incipient grin.

"You always could talk yourself out of anything. Twelve hours, he says, just like that. With those twelve hours we could have had the photo in the morning papers and by now we'd know who he was. Now the first hope is for this afternoon." You mightn't believe it but I was rather pleased about that wigging from Matthews. If it had happened a couple of years ago, I'd have had the shock of a man who'd been savaged by his goldfish. Matthews was settling down well. He had a job and he damn-well meant to do it.

"Well, I made a mistake," I said. "Saying one's sorry is always a bit footling, so just imagine it's said. And now what?"

"Well, maybe I can square it with the Old Man, to look up to you, you know, sir."

"I know," I said. "And now the idol's got feet of clay. If you'd been worth twopence as a detective you'd have found that out long ago."

He did grin then. And he took a real gulp of the coffee.

"Well, we'll take that as read," he told me. "So long as you don't do any more side-stepping. And that reminds me. Just what *do* you propose to do?"

"Do?" I said. "Farrell's my client. He's paying me money to look after his interests."

He gave me a sideways squint. "That couldn't mean, by any chance, that we're not capable of doing the same thing, buckshee?"

"Far from it," I told him blandly. "But two heads are always better than one. When I was a boy the harvest wasn't over when the farmer'd cleared the fields. The gleaners took over after that. So let's say I'm just a gleaner."

"My God, how you can talk!" he said. "But let me add a rider. A new law's been promulgated—"

"By whom?"

"By me. In future the gleaners bring in what they've gleaned and then, if we're in a generous mood, we do a hand-out."

"Just the way I like things," I told him. "I'll just go grubbing unobtrusively around and bring in what I find. Mind you, I've passed a new law, too, that I'm entitled at any time to demand a *quid pro quo*."

"Yes," he said. "You've caught me out on that one or two times in the past. Not that I'm not prepared to see how it works. So suppose you start handing over one or two things straight away. This client of yours, for instance—is he all he appears on the surface?"

"If you understand me, he's even more so."

He grunted. "I get you. But that tale about the American calling him up. It can't be proved. The fact that he went to that hotel and enquired is no proof. Let me tell you how some people might see things. He knows, we'll say, that his wife's coming to see him. She may have some hold on him for all we know, but he has a scheme of his own. He's going to get rid of her for good, only when she turns up it's with a man. the man in the morgue. There's a row and the man pulls a gun. There's a struggle and the man gets shot. He and the woman do what they can for him. The woman goes off and the man is feeling too queer to move. Farrell nips off to the hotel to establish a kind of alibi, and when he gets back he finds the man has done some rough bandaging on himself and gone. So he calls you."

"Ingenious," I said, "but it doesn't fit the known facts. That flat was searched—"

"I know. Farrell did that himself while he was waiting for you."

"Very well, take it as something that might have been done. But the whole thing still doesn't fit Farrell. I was listening to a wireless talk the other night and four speakers were giving evidence of a certain man's integrity. One speaker said that he once said to him, 'Have you ever told a lie?' to which he replied 'Yes'. And that, said the speaker, was probably the only lie he ever told in his life.

And that's the kind of man I believe Farrell to be. The man who told us that appalling story of himself and his wife wasn't one to conceal. In fact, you people can take what line you will. I'm going to work on the assumption that every word he's told us was true."

"Maybe you're right," he told me doggedly. "I still say it's got to be proved."

The buzzer went and he picked up the receiver. He didn't do any talking. A grunt or two and then, "Right, I'll be along."

But wherever he was going, he didn't make a move.

"I promised you a hand-out," he told me. "At the hospital they found a couple of towels on our friend's stomach. One staunching the wound and the other, a long bath-towel, holding it in place."

"According to your theory that was done by Farrell himself and the woman who dropped the brooch."

"Not a theory. Let's say a straw chucked up to see which way the wind blows. And one other thing. Two things. The dead man had also been hit on the head, almost certainly just after he was shot. And even though he might have been late in getting to a hospital, the wound itself wouldn't probably have killed him. He'd a wonky heart and the shock did it." He got to his feet.

"I ought to go back to that flat." He gave me the real old Matthews grin. "Suppose you don't want to come along?"

4

IDENTIFICATION

WE SWUNG out into the Embankment again and this time I was sitting with Matthews in the back. It wasn't till we were idling in the traffic stream in the straight stretch that I put a question.

"What was actually found on the dead man?"

"I could have shown you if I'd thought of it," he said. "But it wasn't what he had so much as what he didn't have. He didn't have keys and he didn't have a wallet. You can add, if you like, any correspondence or anything that might have identified him."

I own up at once to being the owner of an agile, hither-and-thither sort of brain. An old friend at the Yard once told me indignantly that if I were suddenly fired the question of how Balaam's ass came to talk, I'd produce a theory inside two seconds. Be that as it may, I did see a connection between those various hand-outs.

"Could this have happened?" I said. "A man and a woman consider it necessary to get inside Farrell's flat. Since the only woman even remotely connected with the case—as far as we've gone—is his wife, let's assume the woman was his wife."

"His wife might have kept her key, so it wasn't a break-in. It was a walk-in."

"A possibility and I'm not denying it. But you can't deny that a Yale lock isn't exactly Gibraltar. At any rate, Farrell is got out of the way and they get in. What they're looking for is found and as a result, the woman has no further use for the man and she shoots him. When he falls, she daren't risk the sound of another shot, so she hits him over the head. You don't happen to know with what?"

"One of the things we're going to see."

"Right. So that knocks him temporarily out and gives her the chance to take what they've come for, and his wallet. Since he must live somewhere, she took his keys so as to pay a visit. Something to conceal there or something else she wanted."

"It's feasible."

We crossed in front of the traffic at the green light and into Morley Street. A couple of minutes and we were in Mayes Road and pulling up outside the flat. The finger-print men and photographer had gone but Hassack was still there. Mrs. Back had been fetched while we were away and she'd just gone, too. Never a print in the place, Hassack said, but hers and Farrell's. The two who'd been there must have been wearing gloves.

"Sound like professionals to me," Matthews said. "When that wound was being dressed you'd have thought someone would have had to take off a glove. Nothing on that candlestick?"

It had been one of a pair of Victorian brass candlesticks in the living-room: heavy candlesticks about ten inches high. Hassack was sure it was what had been used to give the dead man that crack on the temple. It had gone to the Yard in any case.

I'd been looking at the chalk circle on the living-room carpet. It enclosed an almost invisible spot or two of dried blood. It was the colour of the carpet that had kept it from being spotted sooner. Hassack said he'd sent a snippet of the nap to the Yard to see if the blood group was that of the dead man.

Matthews glanced at his watch. It was half-past twelve. He said he was hungry and I said I could do with something, too. Hassack went off to Morley Street to get sandwiches. I accepted responsibility for using Farrell's tea for a brew.

I think I was frowning away at something else and Matthews wanted to know what was on my mind.

"The shooting took place here," I said. "Weren't we working on the assumption that he was shot in the bathroom?"

He shrugged his shoulders.

"Here or there—what difference does it make?"

It was curious but I couldn't answer him. Something had told me it made a deal of difference but now, when I faced up to the direct question, whatever it was that had struck me so suddenly had just as suddenly gone.

"If the shooting was an accident, this was the likely place," he went on. "What I'd like to know is what those two came here for. This isn't the sort of place a couple of crooks would have cased. The odds were a thousand to one there wasn't a thing in here worth taking, so why all that elaborate flummery about getting him out of the place?"

"Wait a minute! I've got an idea."

I didn't like his incipient grin.

"Better hear it before you turn it down," I told him. "It starts when Laura Farrell was living here and according to Mrs. Back, and unknown to her husband, she was pregnant. Now I ask you, knowing even the little we do about Laura, was she the one to let that baby be born?"

"Well—no."

"Right. So what might she do? For one thing she'd probably have a word with the doctor down below. I don't say anything illicit happened, but if my theory is right, something did: not necessarily an illegal operation but, say, a course of medicine that might have much the same effect. And if a record was kept, then that is what those two might have come for."

"But the doctor didn't keep his records up here? She knew that well enough."

"Wait a minute," I said. "We've been working on some pretty facile assumptions. The shakiest is that the one who shot the confederate was Laura Farrell. We don't even know it was a woman! Because a brooch was dropped is the very devil of a way from proof."

"And what then?"

"Well, then I arrive at only a hunch. Say Laura has died under suspicious circumstances. Those involved have to eliminate every bit of evidence. It might be what I said or it might be only her marriage certificate. If she hadn't it, they might assume that Farrell had it."

He didn't grin. He laughed. "That's the best I ever heard from you. You can't be serious."

I said it was a hunch, and a hunch was something you couldn't get to grips with till a chance piece of evidence gave a first bolstering up. But we didn't do any more arguing. Hassack came back with a mixed cold lunch and I'd brewed a pot of tea. But somewhere at the back of my mind that hunch persisted. So let me jump a long way ahead. What has been nagging at me was a kind of formula, none of whose terms at the moment appeared to fit. But they were there and they *ought* to have fitted: that's what kept nagging at me. All that was needed was just one missing term: some kind of rearrangement or even a sort of flux. And the simple, the almost obvious solution lay—if I'd only known it—in Farrell himself.

While Hassack and I washed up, Matthews did some telephoning. All he told us was that Farrell had gone straight from the Yard to his office off Fleet Street. And then came something apposite. The telephone rang and he took the call. He listened for a moment or two with a grunt or a "Yes, sir," and then he told Hassack to take something down. *Alder and Son, Mark's Passage, Camden Town. A Thomas Cantrill.*

Another moment and he was hanging up. And he was looking pretty pleased with himself.

"Talk about clockwork? That picture can't have been on the streets half-an-hour and we've got an identification. Let's get going."

Then he gave me a look. "What about you, sir. Where can we drop you?"

"Depends where you're going. Might be handier if I went with you. There's a cut through to Camden Town without having to go near my place."

"Also there're buses," he told me. "Still, we'll see. You can always stay in the car."

We drove through streets that were strange to me, at least till we crossed Lower Oxford Street. We went along Tottenham Court Road and then away to the left. We pulled up and asked for a direction and found ourselves a couple of hundred yards from Mark's Passage. It was a wide entrance to a kind of yard. The car stayed just beyond and Matthews and Hassack got out. I let them move off, then trailed behind like Mary's little lamb. The wide-ish entrance took a sharp, left-hand turn after some twenty yards, and in front of us was a kind of enormous garage. Two haulage trucks were drawn up in the open yard. At the end of the covered, open-fronted building was an office. Matthews made for it. A shortish man wearing a boiler suit came to meet him. They had a word or two and shook hands. I closed up to within a yard or two. Matthews made as if he'd no idea I was there.

"Where's Mr. Cantrill then?"

"Gone a few minutes ago, sir. Wanted for an identification."

"He hadn't any doubts?"

"No, sir: nor have I. It's Mr. Charles all right."

"Martin Charles, isn't it?"

"That's right, sir. He bought the business about a year ago from old Mr. Alder's son."

It was a haulage business. Plenty of work usually, that foreman said. Mr. Charles turned up most days but only for an hour or two. Mr. Cantrill was the manager. He'd been taken over, as it were, with the business. He'd been with Alder and Son all his life. No, Mr. Charles didn't interfere hardly at all. What was he like? Well, a biggish gentleman. Been in America most of his life.

"You got his address?"

The foreman knew it by heart. Flat 3b, Dresden Gardens, St. Pancras.

"He drives a car?"

"Yes, sir. A big Buick."

"Garages it here?"

"No, sir. I believe he leaves it outside his flat. Sometimes we give it a clean down here."

"I see. Think I might use your telephone?"

They went the few yards to the office. Hassack stayed on. I made my way back to the car. It was another ten minutes before the other two arrived. Matthews took the back seat with me.

"That manager made the identification all right," he told me, when the car moved off. "Martin Charles, that's who he is. Had that business just over a year. Probably bought it as a blind."

I could have said something but it didn't pay me to—that that elaborate theory that Matthews had reeled off earlier that morning had been knocked endways. Matthews was feeling his way with me. I wasn't official—just an old friend whom he felt bound to oblige. I didn't want to go over his head and yet it wasn't very comfortable to keep on insinuating one's self where one strictly had no right. What I did say was more in the nature of a gambit.

"Interesting about Charles being in America?"

"Yes," he said, and didn't spot the trap. "He must have been the one who got Farrell out of the flat. That hotel's been checked, by the way. Farrell did go there asking for Steinberg."

"Could be, then, that everything in his statement is true?"

"Maybe, but he's a hell of a long way from being out of the wood yet. He might have known Charles. A half-truth is always more tricky than a lie."

The same old routine, I thought, and Matthews true to the school in which he'd been brought up. An *idée fixe* as a basis.

No flexibility. Never trust a hunch. There's no such thing as a short cut. That it brought results was hardly the question. If

I'd been cabined and confined by all that slow-and-sure I'd have looked years ago for another job. Not that I said so.

It took about a quarter of an hour to work our way round to that St. Pancras area and it was three o'clock when we drew up outside Dresden Gardens. I don't know what I'd expected that block of flats to be like but it was pretty second rate. I wasn't too familiar with that part of town but it appeared to me as if it had been there a good few years. The whole building looked as if it could do with an exterior coat of paint. The reasonably large concrete parking space had plenty of cracks in it. Only one thing about it was interesting. Two cars were there: one a fairly new Buick. As we got out, Matthews told his driver to have a look at it.

"Probably locked, but you might get it started. We've got to get it down to the Yard. We'll check first if it's the right car."

"Mind if I tag along?"

"Why not?" he said. "But let me do all the talking."

We went through swing doors into a smallish foyer. An old-fashioned lift was on the left and stairs led up ahead of us. The office was on the right. No one was there. Matthews pressed the bell-push and he pressed a second time before anyone came. It was a middle-aged man in an oldish, blue serge suit. Matthews handed him his warrant. The man's eyes popped a bit when he looked at it.

"You're the manager?"

"No," he said. "The superintendent. We don't have a manager. Same thing though. No trouble, I hope?"

Matthews explained. A key was produced and we went up the stairs. There were only six of them. Charles's flat was the second door on the right. Penhouse—the superintendent had given his name—opened the door and peered round inside before drawing back. Matthews told him he needn't wait. We'd leave the key at the desk on our way out.

It was a small flat: lounge, bedroom, miniature kitchen and bathroom. The furniture and carpets had had plenty of use.

The large lounge window overlooked Atwell Street and took up most of the wall. There was a well-stocked cocktail cabinet and a 21-inch television set. A reproduction Queen Anne bureau was locked. Matthews pulled open the drawers. From what I could see, there was nothing in them but odds and ends. Then Hassack got to work on the locked flap and had it open in a couple of minutes. There were plenty of papers in the various pigeon-holes. Matthews drew up a chair and began going through them. He told Hassack to have a look through the other rooms. I went with him.

There was nothing out of the way. Charles had plenty of clothes and half-a-dozen pairs of shoes stood on the rack at the bottom of the bureau. As we went through the bathroom we could hear Matthews telephoning in the lounge. Nothing noteworthy in the bathroom but a couple of electric razors, one bought in America. It had the American prong type of plug, and new fitments showed that Charles had had special wiring put in. The kitchen had a small electric cooker, a tiny dresser for crockery with cupboard beneath, and a small refrigerator. Everything was clean. Probably room service.

We went back to the lounge. Matthews said the correspondence was pretty innocuous, most of it to do with that haulage business. The last bank statement showed a very big balance, and besides the cheque book there was a bank deposit book. Hassack was to stay there, he said, till a man came along.

Penhouse was at the desk when we went back. Matthews told him what we were doing about the flat.

"Any lady visitors did Mr. Charles have?"

Penhouse looked a bit hurt. "Sorry, Inspector, but I don't know. So long as our tenants behave as we expect them to, we never enquire into their private affairs."

"Now, now, now," Matthews told him. "Don't tell me you haven't got eyes. Ears, too, if it comes to that."

It was no use. Penhouse said they never tried to keep track of visitors. Anyone could walk in.

"You've never seen him with a lady?"

"No, sir."

"All right, let's be vulgar. His bed is a four-footer. Might hold two. If anyone was there all night and your chambermaid spotted it, would she report it?"

"Under no circumstances."

"That Buick outside is his?"

It was. And Penhouse had never seen Charles arriving in it with a lady. The flat had happened to be vacant a year ago and he'd taken it. The rent, with room service, was £275 a year.

"Right," Matthews told him. "We don't want to upset anything here, questioning people and so on, so we'll give you twenty-four hours to make your own enquiries. Anything you can find out about him from your staff or any of the other tenants we'll be grateful for. In return we'll shut down on any publicity. You think you can do that?"

Penhouse said he'd try. Matthews turned on the charm, said that'd be fine, and we went out. The driver was still examining the car. All doors locked and no keys. Matthews told him to force the door and get the car to the Yard. We got in our own car and moved off.

"Where to now?"

"The Yard," he said. "Better see the Old Man and report progress. You seen him lately?"

It was a pretty cunning question: an opening, if you like, through which I could wriggle. That was why, when we drew into the Yard, I went with him up to Jewle's room. As we came up to the door we could hear him telephoning so we sidled unobtrusively inside. Jewle caught sight of me, smiled and gestured with his free hand.

He's about the most undemonstrative man I've ever known but I was sure he was glad to see me. He didn't ask if I wanted tea but rang for it, and he and Matthews had a brief talk while we waited for it. I learned only one thing new: that he was having all Charles's papers brought in and having an expert to give them the once-over.

"So you're mixed up in all this," he said to me, when tea came in. "What's your honest opinion of Farrell?"

I told him. He seemed inclined to agree.

"Only wish we were sure," he said, and quoted a case he and I had been concerned with in which we'd been taken in by a man on whose integrity we'd have gambled our lives. "But just what does he want you to do? Aren't you rather taking his money—"

He smiled. "I was going to say under false pretences, but you know what I mean."

"That'll be up to him," I said. "All the same, I'm prepared to bet he'll want me to keep an eye on his interests. A sort of fatherly eye, if you get me."

"That's a new one on me," Matthews told me. "One thing about Mr. Travers," he told Jewle, "he never says the same thing twice."

"Which reminds me," I said. "I'm not one to keep things to myself, so you people ought to be glad I've got Farrell for a client. Anything I unearth I'll turn in. So what about doing the same for me? Just between ourselves."

Jewle gave Matthews a look. Something must have passed that I didn't see.

"Don't see why not," Jewle said. "Unofficially, of course. And unobtrusively. And that reminds *me*. We haven't had any kind of official statement from you yet, so what about making one now?"

A quarter of an hour later I was on my way out. I won't say I was feeling uproariously happy. The proof of the pudding would still be in the eating, and I wondered just how much those two would pass on to me. I was a bit more optimistic by the time I was out on the Embankment and thinking how friendly we'd all been in Jewle's room. Just like old times. And that was when I suddenly remembered Norris. It was hours since I'd rung him and said I'd be in before lunch.

I managed to hail a taxi and made it to Broad Street, and it was five o'clock when I left. Something in that particular time brought something else into my mind and I began looking for a taxi again. I didn't get one till I came to the traffic lights and it was half-past five when it dropped me in Mayes Road.

I opened the surgery door and found myself in a waiting-room. There was nothing palatial about it. Coconut matting covered the floor, a small electric stove was burning, and the usual table had its pile of ancient magazines. There were about a dozen chairs and only two were occupied. There was an elderly man who was breathing a bit asthmatically and a young mother holding a child wrapped in a shawl.

I'd just taken a chair when the inner door opened and a patient came out: a woman who smiled at the mother and left. A young-ish doctor looked out.

"Who's next?"

The mother went in. Before she came out a new patient arrived: a middle-aged woman who apparently knew the asthmatic. Five minutes and it was his turn to go in. I told the last-comer that if she was in any hurry she could go next. That sparked off a chat and she was telling me all about her second daughter when her turn came.

"You're sure you don't mind, ducks?"

I waved her on. She was in so long that she might have been having an operation. But no new patients arrived. In fact, it was just after six o'clock when I went in. The young doctor was entering something on a card. When he looked up he seemed a bit surprised. He'd given me a curious look when he'd seen me earlier in the waiting-room.

"I haven't seen you before, have I?"

"No, doctor. Unless you saw me this morning."

He stared. "You weren't here this morning?"

"Not actually in here," I said. "I was with the police. Enquiring into that burglary up above."

"A burglary?" he said. "I wondered what it was."

He stared. Then he smiled. "Oh, you want to ask me if I saw anything."

I took out the agency warrant card and let him see it. The quicker you make that gesture, the easier the trick works. It was ten to one he wouldn't hold out a hand.

"No," I said. "What the police are anxious to find is something very different. What's your name, by the way?"

"I'm Hipman. I'm in partnership with Dr. Caver."

"You always take this particular surgery?"

"Except when I'm on holiday."

"That's fine," I said. "Strictly between ourselves, we're anxious to get into touch with the wife of your landlord—Mrs. Farrell. They're separated. She left about three years ago."

"Before my time," he said. "I've only been here eighteen months."

"And your predecessor, if there was one. What's happened to him?"

"That was Forester. He's dead."

That was bad luck and I said so. "All the same, we have an idea that she consulted this Dr. Forester. And as a private patient. If so, would you have any records?"

"I think so."

It was the usual room with the usual smell, and the furnishings no different from a hundred others. He went to one of the filing cabinets. "What was the Christian name?"

"Laura. Laura Farrell."

A couple of minutes and he was saying there was nothing there. If there'd been a consultation, there should have been. Those records went back five years. So that was that. I offered him a cigarette and lighted one for myself and he saw me out at the front door. I moved on a few yards. When he'd gone back in I came back, too, to the side door. There was a wall switch a few feet on. I went up the stairs but knew somehow that Farrell wouldn't be in, and he wasn't. As I came out to the street, Hipman was leaving too.

"Hallo, sir. You still here?"

"Just been to see if your landlord was in. But tell me something. What did your Dr. Forester die of?"

"Good lord!" he said. "What on earth do you want to know that for?"

"Curiosity. Logical curiosity. I imagined he'd be someone youngish like yourself. A junior partner. Youngish doctors oughtn't to die."

"I see. Well then, strictly between ourselves, he got the drug habit."

"Unfrocked?"

"That's it. Hasn't applied for reinstatement. Simply dropped clean out." He tittered slightly. "Just a euphemism saying he was dead. That's between ourselves."

He turned back towards Morley Street. I went on, hoping for a taxi. I didn't get one till I was almost in Victoria Street.

5

CAFÉ MEXIQUE

THAT had been a queer, muddled sort of day, and in the morning I took things a bit easy. The papers were making a big thing of the Charles shooting. I wondered what they d have made of it if they'd known even half the story: about that piece of jewellery, for instance, and the inside dope on Farrell's marriage.

I'd had the sense at the Yard to get Farrell's address in town. He and his partner operated as Art Features, Ltd., at Warren House, in Sutton Court, just off Fleet Street. I rang him there soon after nine and found him in, and he sounded pleased that I was coming along. I went straight away. Warren House was a pretty old block of office buildings, and Art Features Limited had two rooms and a cubby-hole on the third floor. A secretary-receptionist had the cubby-hole. A larger room was partitioned off into small reception rooms for the partners, and the really large room was cutting-room, general workshop, dark-room and miniature cinema combined. When I got there, Kewton, the partner, had just nipped out for breakfast.

You'd never have thought that Farrell had had the experiences of the previous day. As soon as we were in his little room he handed me, rather diffidently, his cheque for ten pounds, and once I'd taken it he began telling me what luck he and Kewton had had to get the place.

"Hadn't we better talk business before your partner gets back?" I said.

"But he knows all about it."

"You're coming along," I told him. "Yesterday we had to winkle everything out of you."

"It's the police," he said. "You were right. It wasn't an ordeal at all."

Maybe you've missed a continuity in that, but that's the way he was. The way I heard it was that he'd found it so far from alarming when he'd been making his statement to Jewle, that he'd also told the whole thing to his partner.

"And you want me to carry on with the agreement? To look after your interests till all this business is cleared up?"

"Why, of course!" he said.

"Look," I told him. "You're making me feel as if I'm slipping my hand into your wallet and helping myself. You really want me to go on trying to clear up what happened on Wednesday night?"

That's how I had to pin him down, and just as he was telling me that he'd thought that was all understood, Brian Kewton, his partner, came in. I liked the look of Kewton: a chubby, good-natured-looking chap just a bit older than Farrell. You didn't have to be in his company for more than a minute to know he was his partner's antithesis. He was the good, hard common-sense of the business. I liked the way he grinned at Farrell and told him to get off for a minute while he had a chat with me. Farrell didn't seem to mind at all.

"What's your honest-to-God opinion of all this?" Kewton asked me. "Mind you," he went on quickly, "I ought to say Paul's story is true in every way. I've known him for the last ten years. There isn't an ounce of deception in him."

I brought him up to date.

"Well, I'm glad we've got you with us," he told me. "If the police go on keeping that wife story out of it, there's no publicity that'll harm us. And don't worry about any fees. He can afford whatever you charge." He gave me one of his grins. "That doesn't mean raising the ante. I'm the one who runs the accounts here."

"You're doing pretty well?"

He gave me one of those looks that he wouldn't give his inspector of taxes. "Enormous demand for the kind of stuff we're doing. And it looks like growing. Mind you, we're not out to push shoddy stuff through, not that Paul would ever handle it. Like to see anything while you're here?"

I said I hadn't much time but I'd be delighted. We went into the big room, and inside five minutes Farrell was running off a fifteen-minute documentary that was just about to be offered. It was in colour, the title *Bargains*, and it fascinated me. There wasn't a real soundtrack—no voices—but only accompanying sounds and faint wisps of music that were there and not there. The photography was exquisite and its range incredible. The whole thing was a series of bargain hunters, each brief episode fading unobtrusively into the next: shots of people at kerbside stalls, counters at a big store, children in a sweet shop, Teddy boys at the window of a tailor's shop, a woman selecting a cabbage and a finale of a street band with the collector holding out his box.

Fascinating wasn't the word. I just sat there, eyes glued, as one says, to the screen, watching the play of people's emotions. You'd have said there couldn't be suspense in a thing like that, but there was. Each was a little drama in which you were caught up, and when that film ended I'd have loved to see it all again. When Kewton switched on the lights, I clapped.

"Glad you liked it."

"Grand stuff," I told him. "Any of the actors professionals?"

"A very, very few. Mind you, we had to take an enormous length of film to select from."

"You were the photographer, Mr. Farrell?"

"Oh, no," he said. "Some of it was Brian's."

I thanked them: told Farrell I'd keep in touch, and then Kewton took my elbow and we went out to the lobby.

"Practically all that film was his," he told me. "He's a genius. When he gets an idea into his mind you can hardly get him to stop for a meal. But about this awful business. You honestly think things are going to be all right?"

I said there was no need to worry. He smiled. "He's like a babe in some things," he said. "Sometimes I've got literally to pull him down to earth. He's beginning to forget about it already."

As we shook hands I told him to keep it that way. Then as I walked on towards Broad Street it suddenly struck me that in a way I *was* taking money under false pretences. There seemed nothing that I could personally do except wait for a hand-out from Matthews or Jewle. To try to trace Laura Farrell seemed impossible. She'd vanished at Charing Cross Station, and over three years ago, and the trail would be deader than New Zealand mutton.

And then I thought of something. Charing Cross Station! Hadn't the dying Charles asked to be driven to Charing Cross Station? And why? He lived at Dresden Gardens and his business was in Camden Town. Why Charing Cross Station? Why not a hospital? Or his doctor, if he had one. The whole thing made no sense. And yet it *had* to make sense. Charles wasn't delirious. He knew where he wanted to go, and I could only wish to heaven I knew why. Matthews must be wondering the same thing and I made up my mind to ring him from the agency.

My own thoughts weren't too clear. Always at the back of them was that film I'd seen. It was a clear, frosty morning and everything I was seeing was through the eyes of that film. Its episodes would flash through my mind and I'd find myself looking at people's faces with a new interest and even making up little dramas of my own. I told myself I'd have to find out if that film was going to be released in London so that I could take my wife to see it.

I couldn't get hold of Matthews, but a little later I rang Tom Holberg, an old friend who runs the biggest theatrical agency in town. Tom was busy but I spoke to Ruth, his secretary. She asked me to ring back in a quarter of an hour. When I did ring she told me neither they nor a couple of other agencies had any record of a Laura Mann. I can't say I was surprised. I never ought to have considered seriously as evidence a single word that liar of a woman had told Farrell.

I'd only just hung up when the buzzer went again. This time it was Matthews on the line. "You busy?"

I said I wasn't.

"Know Medway Street, Soho?"

I said I did.

"Just had an anonymous tip," he said. "Tell you about it when I see you. Half an hour from now, suit you? At the corner of Wedlow Street."

He rang off. I finished what I was doing and went out to find a taxi. I only just made it to Wedlow Street in time. Matthews was looking in a tobacconist's window. In his well-cut dark overcoat and bowler hat he looked like a Lombard Street executive.

"A tip about Charles," he told me. "Some cove rang and suggested we should enquire about him at the Café Mexique. There it is: just along there. You know it?"

"Seen it, but haven't actually been in."

"Well," he said, "this tip gave us time to make some enquiries from Division. Let's stroll along past and I'll tell you about it."

The story began with an Enrico Cavallo who'd had a Mexican father and an American mother. He'd come to London before World War I and had worked as a chef before becoming naturalised and then buying the Poule d'Argent as it then was, and renaming it Café Mexique. The place had never given any trouble and it must have made money, for after the last war old Cavallo bought a bit of blitzed property at the back and so added a high-class dance room to the restaurant. Four years ago he'd died and a son, also Enrico, but known as Harry Cavallo, came back from the States and took over. He'd had his own ideas, and since there was an enormous demand for somewhere where the better-class younger generation could dine and dance at a not exorbitant price, he'd catered for the business. The place was well spoken of still, and Cavallo was doing pretty well.

I'd had a look at it as we'd passed and I had another as we came back. There was a double-windowed front with the door between and rods for a sun canopy above. All unpretentious.

"Right," Matthews said. "Let's go in."

We went straight into the main restaurant. Lunches were on, but it was fairly early and only about six of the score or so of tables were occupied. Stairs went up on the left at the back of the desk, and there was an open door to the cloakrooms. A youngish woman was at the pay desk: a foreign-looking woman: darkish skin, black hair in a pony tail and almond-shaped eyes. Swing service doors were half-way along, and at the far end curtains were drawn. Beyond them, I guessed, would be more tables and the dance floor. A tall waiter who'd been talking to a couple of men at one of the far tables said a last word to them and made for us. He was a good-looking man of about forty, dark-haired and with a Gallic kind of face. His English was perfect.

"The cloak room's this way, gentlemen. Lunch?"

"Just a word with you first."

He followed us through the men's cloak-room and the expression on his face seemed partly puzzled, partly amused. Matthews gave him his warrant card. The waiter looked surprised. He shrugged his shoulders and handed the card back.

"What is it, Inspector? You want lunch, or—?"

"You're the head waiter?"

"Yes, sir."

"Name?"

"Lemon, sir. George Lemon."

There wasn't anything obsequious about him. And he didn't seem too perturbed. In his time he'd probably handled far too many queer situations for that.

"Thank you, Mr. Lemon. And now will you tell Mr. Cavallo we're here."

"Mr. Cavallo, sir?" He shook his head. "I doubt if Mr. Cavallo could see you, sir. Mrs. Cavallo, perhaps. She's at the desk."

"And why not Cavallo himself?"

Lemon shrugged his shoulders. "It's ever since his accident, sir. He sees very few people."

"Sorry, but we've got to be among the few. You see him and tell him so. Say we shan't keep him more than a minute or two."

Another shrug of the shoulders and Lemon went up the stairs. It was a good three minutes before he appeared again. We could go up. The first door on the right. We went up. Matthews rapped at the door and a voice called "Come in".

We were in a largish room that was bedroom and living-room and office combined. I had eyes for the moment only for the man in front of us, a man whose pale, drawn face looked even paler against the black of his hair. The eyes were sunken and dark. At one time he must have been a fine figure of a man, but now he was in a wheel chair. A man stood behind it, hands resting lightly on the back. His face seemed familiar. He was wearing an oldish tweed suit and he was watching us as a dog might watch us.

"Mr. Cavallo?"

"Yes."

It was a quiet voice, but somehow intense. Matthews proffered the card. Cavallo waved it away with just a movement of his hand.

Matthews looked at the other man. "Aren't you Cray? Shorty Cray?"

I remembered. Cray had been a light heavy-weight. I'd seen him box.

"Yes, sir."

"Well, we shan't want you for a minute," Matthews told him. "All right if he goes out, Mr. Cavallo?"

"Cray stays," Cavallo said. "Anything that I can hear, he can hear."

"Suit yourself," Matthews told him. "You know who I am. This is a colleague, and we've only one question to ask you. You read the papers, so why didn't you get in touch with us and tell us you knew Martin Charles?"

Cavallo's hands tightened on the arms of the chair. He didn't speak for a moment or two but his eyes never left Matthews' face. "Why should I?"

Matthews let out a breath.

"Let's not go round in circles. You know your duty to the law. Just tell us all you know about Charles and we'll go. And we'll be much obliged to you."

"And suppose I've nothing to tell you?"

"We know you have. So don't make it hard for yourself. Anything that has to be confidential will be kept so. It won't be that if we consider it necessary for you to give evidence at Charles's inquest."

"I don't like threats." The voice was harsh and bitter. "Not that you haven't a point. What do you want me to tell you?"

"Just what you know about him. The more you can tell, the better."

Cavallo grunted. It was uncanny, somehow, the way he was watching Matthews. He never glanced my way. He couldn't even have noticed the start I gave when he spoke.

"Martin Charles, he called himself. That wasn't his name. He was my brother."

It shook Matthews a bit, too.

"Your brother, eh?" He grunted. "Older or younger?"

"Me, I'm forty-three." He smiled, if you could call that loosening of the lips a smile. "That surprises you. You think I'm an old man? Mario was older, but you don't believe that?"

"Why not?" Matthews told him. "I wouldn't go saying things you might resent, such as being sorry to see you in that chair. No one told me you were like this."

It was the first time Cavallo had looked away. Cray's hand moved quickly from the chair and rested lightly on his shoulder. Cavallo moved. A quick movement as if he were pulling himself together. Then he began talking. The tone was queerly impersonal: still dry and almost monotonous—and bitter. "You say you know a lot so I won't tell you about my old man. Me and Mario were here till after Mamma died and Mario went to the States. He was hard to get along with, my old man, and Mario was pretty tough. I went out a couple of years later. Mario wrote he had a job for me: a good job, under-chef at a Manhattan hotel, and so he had, only he was taking a cut for himself and I found it out and we had a fight. He was always a twister."

He felt beneath the rug that covered his legs. Cray produced a handkerchief from nowhere and he wiped away the spittle from the corner of his mouth.

"That the kind of thing you want to know?"

"Anything you'd like to tell us, Mr. Cavallo."

He sneered. "Mr. Cavallo. You hear that, Cray? Lead a good life and they call you Mr. Cavallo. The first time I ever have the police here and they call me Mr. Cavallo. Maybe they used to call Mario Mr. Cavallo, the cops in the States. I don't know. I moved on to New Jersey and then to St. Paul. Got me a job and did pretty well. Never saw Mario again till he walked in on me just over a year ago. Said his name was Martin Charles. I told you he was always a twister. I didn't like him no better and I told him so. Said I didn't want him around."

He was panting slightly. He wiped his mouth again.

"But about St. Paul. I got married there. No kids and the wife died about ten years after. Cancer. That's how things work out. Then the old man wrote that he wasn't going to last long himself so I come over. Then I flew back and sold up and came here for good. I got married again. Always fond of kids. Thought I'd raise me a family. You seen my wife?"

"Not to speak to. It was you we wanted to see."

"A fine woman." His lip curled and I wondered why. "Must have been my lucky day when I married her. Ain't that so, Cray?"

Cray patted his shoulder. "Take it easy, boss."

Cavallo let out a slow breath. For a good minute he said nothing. His eyes had narrowed and he was looking beyond us—at nothing at all.

"Well, that's all," he said. "Mario came in a few times but I wouldn't see him. I'd told him so."

"And now he's dead."

"That's right." I thought he smiled. "Now he's dead."

"You knew he'd bought himself a haulage business?"

"He told me so. That time he came here. Said he'd had a haulage business in the States. He was always a liar. You'd like a word with my wife?"

"The missus will be busy, boss."

Cray had cut in quickly. Cavallo mightn't have heard him. "Tell her to come up here, Cray."

Cray gave a slow shake of the head and went across to the inter-com.

"That you, Frank? . . . The boss says he'd like the madame to come up here. Some gents would like a word with her."

He came back to his old position behind the chair. No one said a word. We just waited. Then the door opened and Mrs. Cavallo came in.

She was rather above medium height. The dark dress gave her a slimness and its tightness accentuated the fullness of the breasts. She carried herself well. She halted just inside the door and looked quietly round. "You wanted me, Harry?"

You could feel a curious tension in the room. Cray was watching her and he nervously moistened his lips.

"My wife," Cavallo said. "I keep nothing from my wife and she keeps nothing from me. Isn't that so?"

"If you say so, Harry."

She spoke quietly. Her voice had just the faintest accent. I couldn't place her, but perhaps there was some Mexican about her, too.

"Tell these gentlemen about Mario. My fine brother Mario who's just got himself killed."

She gave a quick shake of the head.

"There's nothing to tell them, Harry. Three or four times he came here and I didn't want him to pay but he insisted. He kept trying to talk to me but—" She turned to us.

"Harry didn't want him here, so how could I talk as if we were friends?"

"You see?" Cavallo said. "Didn't I say she was a good wife?" Matthews cut in.

"And that's all, Mrs. Cavallo?"

She shrugged her shoulders.

"What else is there? When he spoke to me I had to listen. He said he had a business. And he had a flat. He asked me once to come to his flat. I didn't trust him. I think he was trying to turn me against my husband." Her lip suddenly quivered. "Perhaps I am even glad when I know he is dead."

That was all. Matthews thanked her. She looked towards Cavallo but she mightn't have been there.

The door closed on her. Matthews turned to Cavallo.

"Thank you for what you've told us. We much appreciate it." He smiled. "And thank you, Shorty. You're Mr. Cavallo's factotum?"

Shorty grinned. There seemed to be a smile about the whole lean six foot of him.

"I wouldn't say that, sir. I just do what I can. The boss was always a good friend of mine. He came back just in time to see my last fight. Hadn't been for him I might've had a rough time."

"You talk too much," Cavallo told him curtly. "Show the inspector out."

Matthews turned to me. "Nothing else you'd like to ask?"

I shook my head. Cray already had the door open but Matthews took his time. He even turned to thank Cavallo again. I could almost feel Cavallo's eyes on us as Shorty closed the door.

The restaurant was pretty full. Mrs. Cavallo was back at the desk. No one else was there but she didn't even turn her head when we passed within three feet of her. A middle-aged waiter held the outer door for us.

It was cold out there on the pavement. Matthews looked each way and then turned towards Wedlow Street.

"What about a meal? Ought to be something along here."

We walked a couple of hundred yards and then at the Palace end we found a place that looked pretty good. It was apparently full, but a waiter did find us a table.

"You order," Matthews told me. "I want to use the telephone."

I was glad enough to sit down. As Matthews was to say, it'd been the very hell of a half-hour. I suppose I've got a far too impressionable mind, but there was something about that inter-view with Harry Cavallo that made me shake my head and wrinkle up my eyes. I was glad when the waiter brought me a beer. I ordered my own meal but I didn't order for Matthews in spite of what he'd said. I was glad I didn't. It was over ten minutes before he came back.

6

BLIND LUCK

WE COULDN'T do much talking in that restaurant till the meal was over and there was room to sit at ease. You can't do much more than eat when a place is chock-a-block with tables and your chair is hard against the chair of whoever it is behind. It was after two o'clock by the time we'd finished, and by then the room had thinned out. We could actually push back our chairs and get leg-room while we had coffee.

Matthews had tried to get information about Cavallo's acci-dent when he had telephoned just after we'd come in, but no one at Division seemed to know anything. After all, as Matthews said, you don't go poking your nose into the affairs of well-conducted citizens. He'd thought at first that Cavallo was suffering from the after effects of polio, then he remembered that the head waiter had mentioned an accident.

"Whatever it was, it seems to've made him a pretty trying fellow to live with," he said.

You see how that short time we'd spent with Cavallo had made a queer, disturbing impression? We weren't talking about the dramatic unearthing of Charles's history, which, after all, had or ought to have had an enormous deal to do with the case.

"I wouldn't like to judge," I said. "He must have been a fine figure of a man before that accident crippled him. God knows what I'd be like under the same circumstances."

"Not like that," he said. "What I'd do myself I'm not telling anyone. But Cavallo! A damn misery to everyone who comes into contact with him."

"Even Cray."

"Yes," he said. "But Cray's an even-tempered chap himself. Always was too good-hearted. That's why he ended up without a penny. I often wondered what happened to him after we saw him take that hammering that night."

"But Mrs. Cavallo. What's behind the way he spoke about her to us? That double talk and the sneers. And did you notice how Cray was trying in his way to keep the peace? Then there was what Cavallo said. Not *ask* my wife to come up here, but *tell* her."

"Yes," Matthews said. "Even though he was in that chair I felt like smacking him across the mouth. Not that he got a lot of change out of her. I thought she behaved damn decently."

"What was that informer like? The one who tipped you off about Cavallo?"

"I didn't get the actual call," he said. "I'm told it was a man with a rather superior accent. A man of fifty or so. Far as I remember, he asked for the one in charge of the Charles case, and when he was asked for his name he just said, 'Why doesn't he go to the Café Mexique and ask Harry Cavallo what he knows about him,' and then he hung up."

"I was just wondering something," I said. "You remember a middle-aged waiter who nipped ahead of us and opened the door when we were coining out? He gave me a most peculiar look. I thought at the time he'd got some tic or other. Now I'm not so sure. I'm wondering if it'd pay to find out."

"Can't do any harm. Why not drop in for a meal?"

I said I might. Perhaps that same night.

"I'll have a word with Shorty Cray," he told me. "I won't call him in or anything. Try to pick him up somewhere, just by chance. He must get some free time. Cavallo has to sleep."

I remembered another question I'd wanted to ask: the one about Charles's asking to be driven to Charing Cross Station. And how Farrell's wife had last been seen at the same place.

"Yes," he said, and snapped his fingers for the waiter to bring the bill. "We've been thinking a lot about that. It's a coincidence: it has to be. The obvious answer, the way we see it, about Charles wanting to go to Charing Cross, was because he knew the one who'd shot him had made for Charing Cross. I mean that whoever it was would be taking a train from Charing Cross. Don't know if you can get anything else out of it."

I couldn't. Then he was paying the bill and we got up to go. I hadn't known it but he had a car parked about a hundred yards away and he gave me a lift round to Broad Street. We promised to keep in touch.

"Almost like old times," he told me, as I got out of the car. "You picking my brains and everything."

I just caught his grin as he shot the car on. He was out of sight before I'd thought of anything resembling a retort.

I pottered about at the agency till the late afternoon and then I got Bertha to book a table for me at the Café Mexique. Then I went home to change. A black tie seemed too formal so I just wore a dark suit. After that I had a look at the evening papers with nothing new on the Charles case. At a quarter to seven I was hailing a taxi.

When I walked into the restaurant that evening I could see at once that things were different. The lighting was good and the whole place had an air of gaiety. The far curtains were drawn back and I could see through to the other room. It looked larger than the main restaurant, with tables at the side and quite a good space for dancing. A grand piano was on the slightly raised dais at the far end. It was only just after seven but at least two-thirds of the restaurant tables were occupied and a couple, too, in the far room.

A smart-looking girl took my hat and coat, and when I came back that head waiter was waiting for me and you couldn't have told from his expression that he'd seen me only a few hours before.

"You've booked a table, sir?"

I said I had: for seven o'clock.

"And the name, sir?"

"Travers."

"Oh yes, sir. For one, sir?"

He lifted the red cord and replaced it when I'd gone through.

I suppose it was luck that the waiter I wanted should have happened momentarily to be free. At any rate he met us. Lemon waved a hand and the other took over. My table was almost at the end of the room with my back to the room beyond.

"You're dancing later, sir?"

"No," I said. "Just the dinner."

He gave me the menu and the wine list, and left me to myself while he saw to another table. The dinner wasn't out of the way at a guinea and I was pleased when I found a Tavel Rosé on the wine list. A half-bottle stood me back fifteen shillings.

"What's your name?" I asked the waiter, when he came back.

"Walter, sir."

I gave him my order. Five minutes and the wine had arrived and the hors d'oeuvres trolley was alongside. It was a good meal: not the best I've ever eaten by a long chalk, but good enough. The wine was excellent, though just a bit too cold. I'd thought of lingering out that meal but that's the sort of thing it's hard to do when the service is good, and Walter was superlative. He certainly knew his job: courtesy without obtrusiveness and absolute competence that wasn't spoilt by showmanship. Good-looking in his mature way and very well spoken.

While he was clearing the table for my coffee and kümmel he asked me quietly if he hadn't seen me earlier that day. I said he had. We might have spoken a bit louder and not been overheard, for in the room behind me the band had just struck up a rumba. But that was all, and there'd been something in the way he'd said it that told me I was on the right track. I made the advances when he came back.

"What time do you people get away at night?"

"It depends, sir. Sometimes not till we close and sometimes just after ten. This happens to be my early night."

I didn't push things. I'd been optimistic enough to make sure I had paper on me, so I wrote a brief note. No use spoiling the ship for a ha'porth of tar, so I changed my mind about wrapping it round a pound note and found a fiver instead. At half-past eight with everything now in full swing in the room behind me, I signalled for my bill. I managed to find the exact amount and then I slipped that note into his hand. He didn't turn a hair.

"Thank you, sir. Hope you've enjoyed your dinner, sir." I drifted to the cloak-room and got my hat and coat, and as I went towards the door, there he was moving ahead of me. "Thank you, sir. Hope to see you again, sir."

If that old formula had the twist I thought it had, then I'd really be seeing him again. It was a clear, frosty night, so I walked through to Tottenham Court Road and took a train to Leicester Square and walked home from there. I switched on the electric fire, changed my jacket for an old tweed one, and settled down to wait.

It was a quarter to eleven when the night porter brought him up.

"Glad you could make it," I told him as I let him in. "Let me take your coat. And what about a drink? Afraid I have only whisky and beer."

"Whatever you're having, sir."

"I'm a bit of a vulgarian. I prefer beer. A bit cold for it, perhaps?"

"Never too cold for beer, sir."

"A man after my own heart," I said, and fetched a couple of bottles and glasses. As I was pouring it I asked what his other name was.

"Garrow, sir. Not a name you meet often, or so I'm told."

He was absolutely self-possessed. I knew why when we began chatting informally. He'd begun life in the household of a certain peer where his father had been butler. Later the estate had been broken up and he'd drifted into the restaurant business.

"Some people might think it a come-down, sir, but there's no comparison in the financial way. On the whole, tips are very good."

"You've been there long?"

"The only place I *have* been, sir. Started about ten years ago with old Mr. Cavallo. A bit crude, sir, but excellent to work under."

"I suppose you get all sorts there?"

"Well, perhaps yes. On the whole a very good clientele. Now you, sir, if you'll pardon me, I placed you as soon as I saw you this morning."

"Placed me?"

His smile was deprecating. "Sorry, sir. I should have expressed myself more clearly. What I should have said was that I knew you were a gentleman."

It took me aback for a moment. I smiled too. "I must get you to tell that to my creditors."

"Ah, no, sir. I don't think there's anything wrong with your credit. You have some excellent pieces here, sir, and I imagine your pictures are pretty good."

I told him I'd been lucky enough to collect at the right time.

"My name's Travers, by the way. I've been in the detection game most of my life: occasionally working for Scotland Yard and chiefly running my own agency. That's why I want to assure you that everything that's said here will be strictly confidential. I may have to divulge the information itself but on no account the source of it. So set your mind at rest about that. If that's agreeable to you, let me put a blunt question. It was you who gave the police that tip about the Café Mexique?"

He didn't answer for a moment. Then he put his own question.

"Everyone knew as soon as you'd gone this morning that you were the police, but what's your exact part in it, sir?"

I told him frankly that the man in whose flat Charles had been shot was my client, which was why it was good policy for me to work with the police.

"I see, sir." He paused for a moment. "Well, I *was* the one who gave that tip to the police. We all knew that man Charles was the boss's brother as soon as someone saw his picture in the papers, and then word went round that nobody was to do anything about it. The general idea seemed to be that it might bring discredit on the place. I didn't see it that way."

"You don't like Harry Cavallo?"

"I wouldn't say that, sir. He was like his father, a bit brash, as they say, but he certainly improved the place. And he was quite good to work for. That was before his accident, of course. My grievance came later when Fredericks, the head-waiter, died. Everyone'd expected me to get the job but instead it was given to George Lemon, and he wasn't even on the staff. I think Mrs. Cavallo had a lot to do with that. Harry was in hospital at the time, recovering from that accident."

"Yes," I said. "The accident. You know all about it?"

"As much as any of us, sir. It was about two years ago, and the boss and her had a day at Kempton Park races. In those days they had a flat at Hampstead and he used to drive a big American car. At any rate, rumour had it that he ran across some pals at the races and was too far gone to drive back. She hadn't had as much but all the same he wanted to drive, but she wouldn't let him and drove the car herself. Then they had that smash. She only got a broken wrist but he got a spine injury. He had all sorts of specialists but no one could do anything."

"And he changed from then on?"

"Everything changed. He had that room upstairs fitted up and left the flat. She has another room on the same floor. Then he got that man Cray to look after him. A very good man for the job, if I may say so. He does everything."

"I'm getting the picture, so let me put something up to you. You probably know it but my idea is that he's turned against his wife. I think he hates her because he holds her responsible for that accident and what it did to him. Am I right?"

"Quite right," he said. "Everything gets round sooner or later to the hotel staff. I think it's called a grapevine. I suppose Cray talks and there's the staff who see to upstairs meals."

"And I should be right in saying she runs the place now?"

"Well, not exactly, sir. Orders, I suppose, actually come from him and he does the accounts. All the same she's as good as in charge downstairs."

"Easy to work with?"

He smiled. "That's a bit out of my line, sir. I get my orders from Lemon. I don't think it'd do to take any liberties with her. Always very decent to everybody, as far as I know." I gave him an edited account of what had been said that morning in Cavallo's room about Martin Charles, and asked if he had any comments. He thought that what Mrs. Cavallo had told her husband was perfectly right.

"The way I'd put it, sir, was that he used to talk to her when he came in and not the other way round. In fact, I only remember her going to his table once, and that was one night when he had a lady with him."

"A lady?" It looked as if we were going to have a break. "Remember what she was like?"

"I can't, sir. I know she was smart-looking and, well, about thirty. But don't rely on that, sir. It must have been about three months ago and naturally I wouldn't have noticed her at all unless she'd been making herself conspicuous. What drew my attention to her was seeing the madame at the table."

"You remember what waiter was in charge of that table?"

He shook his head. "No, sir. I wouldn't deceive you. Three months is a long while to remember all that. But the madame, sir. I expect she'd tell you anything you wanted to know."

I said he was right. What would be the best time to see her? He thought about half-past ten or eleven. Mrs. Cavallo usually went out for a short walk after breakfast but was always back by then. Cavallo never went out, he said. It was usually two or three in the morning before he went to bed and he never got up till about midday.

Time was getting on. Garrow had to get home, which meant the Underground to Belsize Park. When I pulled out my wallet to pay him for his trouble, he waved a quick hand.

"If you don't mind, sir, no! You've treated me like a gentleman, sir, and I've been very pleased to tell you what I know."

I tried to insist but he'd made up his mind. I saw him downstairs and thanked him again as we said good-night. I watched him move off, and when I moved in out of the cold air, I was thinking what little unseen wheels and cogs worked the machine of life. But for a man who still was nursing a grievance I'd never have learned, perhaps, all I'd learned that night.

It was that chance mention of Charles's lady friend that had been the real gift. I wondered if I ought to ring Matthews, but when I glanced at my watch again it was after midnight. I told myself I'd ring him in the morning. Or would I?

I was frowning away to myself as I took the empty bottles and glasses to the small kitchen. Mightn't it be good policy for me to see Mrs. Cavallo myself? Wouldn't it be better for me to have something to hand out instead of being always on the receiving end? I thought it would. I was still of the same mind when I woke in the morning.

A thaw had set in during the night and it looked as if there might be rain. It wasn't more than six minutes' walk from the flat to Medway Street, and I split the difference in the times that Garrow had given me and reached the café at a quarter to eleven. It wasn't officially open, even if the door wasn't shut, and as soon as I stepped inside, Lemon caught sight of me and made straight for me as if to shoo me out. Maybe that hadn't been on his mind after all, but I spiked his guns all the same.

"Good-morning, Mr. Lemon. I know you're not actually open but I'd like a word if possible with Mrs. Cavallo."

He frowned. "I don't know, sir. I'll see."

He disappeared through the service door. I watched waiters putting the last touches to tables. I didn't see Garrow, and I thought he might be in the other room. It was only a couple of minutes, in any case, before Lemon was back.

"This way, sir, please. And the madame wishes to know, sir, if you'd like coffee."

"Very good of her. I certainly would."

We went along a wide corridor, past the kitchens and round into a smallish room that was some kind of office. I'd hardly got seated when Mrs. Cavallo came in. She was wearing a black dress, highish at the neck, with a slim gold chain on which perhaps was a cross. If so, it was worn inside the bodice. I got quickly to my feet.

"Do not get up," she told me quietly. "You are one of the gentlemen who came yesterday?"

I said I was, and I gave her my name. Then coffee came in. "You'd like it here, madame?"

"Thank you, Pierre."

She didn't smile. There was a queer aloofness about her even while she was pouring the coffee. As I took my cup I told her why I'd come. We'd information, I said, that one night when her brother-in-law had dined at the restaurant he'd been accompanied by a lady. Perhaps she remembered the occasion.

She said she did. Her brother-in-law had sent a message by a waiter that he'd like to see her and she went to the table. She didn't trust him, she said, and knowing her husband's views she'd rather not have gone.

"It was to avoid unpleasantness. If I did not go I did not know what he would do."

"I understand," I said. "But could you describe the woman who was with him? How old was she, do you think?"

She frowned. "I think about thirty. But you never know."

"Her hair?"

"It was blonde."

"Long?"

"But no. Short and in curls. As we say, *en boule*."

"And her name?"

"Her name?" A moment and she remembered. "Laura. That was her name."

"And her surname?"

She shook her head.

"I do not remember." She frowned. "Perhaps it will come back."

"It wasn't by any chance Mann? Laura Mann?"

"Mann," she said. "Mann."

Then she did remember. It was the first time I'd seen her smile.

"Not Mann—Manette. He said, 'This is Miss Manette. Call her Laura.'"

"That's fine," I said. "Anything else you remember about her?"

What little there was came out bit by bit. Mrs. Cavallo wanted to get away from that table as soon as she could and she wasn't there more than a couple of minutes. She'd thought the woman was a bit common. As she said, a chorus girl or something like that.

"Then I happened to see my friend Carlo Manrico and I asked him if he knew this Laura Manette."

"Who's Carlo Manrico?"

She smiled again.

"He is a friend who I know all my life. When he sees me again in Havana he insist that I sing in his band. That was four years ago, and then we have an engagement here and that was when I first see my husband. It was six months after that that we were married."

"And did Manrico find out anything about her?"

"No. He rings me and says she is someone who is not known."

That was all. I didn't question her further and I'd finished my coffee in any case. She didn't smile when I thanked her. For some reason or other she'd gone back into her shell again.

But when I got outside I was walking on air. Not only was there the first contact with Laura Farrell since a cab had deposited her at Charing Cross Station; there was also a contact established between her and Charles. I couldn't get quickly enough to the Yard to unload what I'd discovered. Matthews, when I rang, happened to be in. He suggested a half-way rendezvous at a little coffee-shop we sometimes frequented in the Strand.

7

HITHER AND YON

I THOUGHT Matthews might have been a bit sore, but he wasn't. He laughed.

"Bravo the old maestro! I knew you were going to be up to something when I left you yesterday morning."

He'd finished his coffee and looked as if he was going to make a move.

"No hurry for a minute," I said. "What about something by way of a *quid pro quo*?"

I passed him my case and held the lighter for the cigarette. I wondered what it was that was still amusing him.

"Funny," he said. "They say all roads lead to Rome. You took one road; we took another road."

"You'd known about that woman who was with Charles that night?"

"Oh that," he said, playing it down. "No, we didn't actually know that."

"But it's the only real thing we've run across!"

"I know," he said. "It's just the opening we wanted. But we did find out all about that accident. Shorty went out for a breather yesterday afternoon. Went to see a sister of his at Lewisham, and I picked him up. Didn't learn anything much that you didn't get from Garrow. Shorty was virtually down to his uppers doing occasional jobs at Tom French's gym when Cavallo sent for him just before he left a private nursing home and offered him that job. Ten quid a week and his keep. You'd think Cavallo was God Almighty the way Shorty speaks of him. From what he told me about the hours he had to keep, I reckon that ten quid is slave labour."

"Always something just a bit simple-minded about Shorty," I said. "Anything else did you get?"

He seemed to be hesitating for a moment, and then he felt in an inside pocket. As soon as he began undoing the tissue paper I knew what he was going to show me—that brooch I'd found in Farrell's flat. He held it on the palm of his left hand. You'd have thought it was a miniature pet monkey or something the way he smiled at it.

"Know what this turned out to be?"

"You tell me," I said. "I've got the kind of heart that can't stand suspense."

"Right. I'll try and ease the strain. We passed this on to be checked against the lists of stolen jewellery. Know where it came from? That Kensington job last September."

"Don't remember it. Probably read about it, but I've forgotten it."

"Doesn't matter about names," he said. "A high-class flat occupied by a widow. Has her own maid and it was the maid's night off. The old trick worked. Fake call from a hospital. Accident to the maid, so off the lady goes and in walks someone else, bold as brass. Helps himself to fifteen thousand pounds' worth of stuff. Not much of it, but high-class—all except this. This was probably a family relic."

He began wrapping it up again. "What you've told me seems to tie the whole thing up. You see how?"

"You tell me. My brain's a bit dull these days."

"The hell it is," he told me. "You just haven't had time to figure it out. But what's wrong with this? Charles did that Kensington job, and this piece was a kind of odd man out. So what'd he do with it? Passed it on to his fancy lady, the one who was calling herself Laura Manette."

"Could be," I said. "And she was wearing it that evening in Farrell's flat."

"Got it in one. They tell me the pin's a bit slack. It wouldn't have taken a lot of movement to've come undone."

"As when she was hitting him on the head with that candlestick."

"Well, there we are," he said, and tucked that brooch away in his wallet. "You know what we've done already? Got into touch with America to see if Charles has a record. They ought to have his prints by now. A day or two and we ought to know the devil of a lot. We've overlapped a bit and Interpol's handling it, too."

He made as if to move again and then he was giving me a look. "What're you looking so glum about?"

I said I wasn't. I'd been thinking.

"Suppose," I said, "you do get Charles's record, how's it really going to help?"

"You're losing your grip," he told me. "We're not sure he actually did that Kensington job. The kind of record he has will help to confirm that."

"And if it *is* confirmed? How much nearer will that get you to what happened in Farrell's flat?"

"Listen," he said. "Do we have to dot the i's and cross the t's? This Laura Manette may have been working with him over there. It may give us a lead. And something else we're probably going to do. Send out a call for Laura. You know the kind of thing. 'In connection with the death of Martin Charles, and so on, the police are anxious to get in touch with a Laura Mann or Manette or Farrell or what have you, because they think she can furnish information.'"

"A good move," I said. "She must have been living somewhere. Probably Charles had her parked. If I were you I'd also describe her as possibly known as Mrs. Charles."

He was grinning as he got up to go. "You see? The old grey matter's still working."

I got ahead and paid the small bill. When we got outside a taxi was cruising towards us and he grabbed it. There was only time for a wave of the hand before the taxi moved off.

I suppose I oughtn't to have felt disappointed, and yet somehow I did, and then when I'd had time to stretch myself out, so to speak, on my own couch and do a bit of self-analysis, I knew my only quarrel was with myself. In the old days I'd often remarked ponderously to a witness that the Yard might work slowly but it worked uncommonly sure. And now I stood somewhat outside things. That was my grouch. I wanted to get on. I wanted flashes of inspiration followed by short cuts. What I'd been saying to myself was, "Let's have some action." And things didn't always work out like that. You remembered the times you'd had and used them as a kind of rosy-hued spectacles to tint the times you hadn't.

I put in an appearance at the agency. Nothing much was doing, and I was only cluttering up the place so I went to lunch at a pub near by where you get an honest-to-God lunch with as good a pint of bitter as any in town. I'd bought a newspaper and did some reading while I ate. There wasn't much in it that I hadn't seen in the morning papers. Racing everywhere was off, so there weren't the usual programmes, not that racing ever interested me, and I was just giving a last glance through over my coffee when I caught sight of a name in the half-column headed RESTAURANTS. Dinner and dancing from 7.0 till 2.0. Carlo Manrico's Cuban Band. At the Bellini.

I sat back. Manrico had made enquiries about Laura Manette. Maybe there was something he'd picked up. Something he didn't think mattered but which might have a meaning for me. And what did it matter in any case? Even if Manrico knew nothing, it'd be something to do. Then I had to smile to myself. Ludovic Travers, a man-about-town. A new and dazzling figure bursting on the night life of a great city. Two successive nights of gay living. A pretty high-class place, the Bellini, and I wondered what Farrell would say when he saw his expense account.

When Bertha brought me a cup of tea that afternoon and I asked her to book me a table for seven o'clock at the Bellini, she gave me a queer look. We took Bertha over, so to speak, with the agency. She mayn't be a Mona Lisa but what would happen if she ever left us, I never dare think.

"Well?" I said.

"Just wondering," she said. "Didn't you say Mrs. Travers was away?"

"She is," I said. "Which reminds me. When you book the table, find out what time Manrico's band comes on. And not a word to Mr. Norris."

Her click of the tongue was not too serious. A couple of minutes and she was telling me the table was booked and the band didn't come on till half-past eight.

You remember the final irony of that superb film, *Un Carnet du Bal*? The still youthful widow has always remembered her first ball and her mind has come to see it as a thing of incredible beauty: haunting music, the voluptuous swirl of satin skirts as if it were swans, not women, who danced under the light of the crystal chandeliers. So, twenty years later she goes back to that provincial town, and a dance is once more on in the Hotel de Ville. She looks in. No haunting music: no rhythmic swirl of swan-like white: only a dowdiness and a drab gaiety to the sound of the same violin and accordion in that bare and almost dingy hall.

That was how I felt when I entered the Bellini. I suppose it was a good twenty years since I'd been there, and I'd remembered its glass and chandeliers and how we'd laughed at the endless reflections of ourselves and even the waiter had smiled at us. We'd danced till well after midnight, and altogether it had been a night to look back on. I had almost an affection for the old Bellini, and once when I was on leave and I knew that area had been bombed, I actually took a walk that way and felt a queer relief to see it unharmed.

I don't say it was shabby. What it did have was a dullness, and an emptiness. The Café Mexique, a third full, would still look friendly, the Bellini, into which it could have been unobtrusively tucked, was hardly a third occupied. The mirrors had gone and the walls had murals, and on two or three the paint had begun to peel. The whole place had the look of failure. It's like that, they tell me, in town. For years a place can be popular, and then all at once and arbitrarily as can be, tastes change and whims of fashion ease it on the skids and, before you know it, it's on the downhill way. It changes management and puts up a fight, but it rarely ever gets back.

A youngish waiter took my order. Compared with Garrow, he was practically a mountebank. The wine list was long and the prices high. There was a quick lift of the waiter's eyebrows when, after his gushing recommendations, I ordered iced lager. I looked round at my fellow diners. I'm no snob, but there'd been a change since the old days. And that was when I realised something. I ought to have known that the Bellini was no longer a Monico or a Café Royal, even in miniature. Manrico's band had played at the Café Mexique. The Bellini of my younger days would have been far above his class.

When the waiter brought the consommé I told him what I wanted, and his fingers closed over the ten-shilling note.

"Certainly, sir. A Mr. Travers from Mrs. Cavallo. Soon as he's in, sir, I'll let him know. It should be just before eight."

The main course had that warmed-up taste. I didn't like the list of sweets and took the safer course of cheese, and even then the Stilton was far too raw. But that big room had begun to fill up, younger people mostly, and noisy rather than quietly gay. Then just before eight o'clock my waiter told me Manrico had arrived. He said I could leave by the side door to Dalton Street, so I settled my bill, fetched my hat and coat from the cloak-room and followed the waiter through. A few tables round the dance floor were occupied. We turned left at the end into what looked like a small changing room.

Manrico had one arm out of his overcoat and was fingering some band parts on a centre table. He looked round as the waiter showed me in. "Be with you in a minute, sir."

He was much younger than I'd anticipated: thirty-five, perhaps, or a little more. He was tallish, slim and his face was tanned. The sideburns and pencil moustache gave the Latin look. He hung up his overcoat, looked at himself in the mirror and dusted his lapels with his handkerchief.

"Can't spare you more than a minute or two but you might as well sit down," he told me. "A Mr. Travers, is it?"

I did some brief explaining. He didn't ask to look at my warrant.

"I thought you'd said Carmelita sent you."

"Carmelita?"

His smile was just a bit patronising.

"You know her as Mrs. Cavallo. Her professional name was Carmelita Valle."

"You're not actually Cuban yourself?"

He chuckled. He threw at me the names of half-a-dozen dance band leaders.

"Were they Cuban or Spanish or what-not?"

"No," he said. "I was born within a couple of miles of where we are now. Parents killed in the blitz. I was only a kid at the time and they shipped me out to an uncle in Trinidad. That's where I got the dance band fever. Carmelita got it, too. We were practically kids together. Then I lost sight of her and then, about four years ago, I ran into her in Havana. She'd done pretty well for herself, but I brought her over here."

His tone changed from the expansive to the confidential. "Tell me, was she still looking pretty ill? Last time I saw her I couldn't believe my eyes."

I said I hadn't known her before Cavallo's accident, but strictly between ourselves, I'd judged he was giving her a hard time.

"She ought to leave him." He smiled. "Don't get ideas, mister. I'm married."

A couple of men came in.

"Shan't be a minute," he told them. They went through to what I guessed was a cloak-room. One of them had had his overcoat open and I could see he was wearing some sort of costume: a bolero thing and a bright undervest.

Manrico's tone changed to the brisk. "Now then, sir. What was it exactly you wanted to know?"

I told him. He frowned.

"Laura Manette. Yes." He shook his head. "I just rang up one or two of the agencies. Never heard of her. Between you and me she was just Charles's fancy woman."

Another man came in and this time he wasn't waved through. Manrico moved towards the door.

"If you should ever hear anything you'll let us know?" I said.

"Only to glad to. A thousand to one, though, if you ask me."

He stayed just inside the door and held out his hand. "Sorry I couldn't be of any use to you. Like dancing, do you?"

"I used to."

"Married?"

"Oh, yes."

"Come along some night and bring your wife," he told me. "We're strictly dance tempo these days. Making quite a name at it. We'll be here for the rest of the week."

Two more men were coming in. He waved a hand to me and turned. I called him back.

"Do me a favour," I said. "Strictly between ourselves, what's your real name?"

He laughed.

"Good God! I thought Scotland Yard knew everything. Keep it to yourself, but the name's Charlie Morse."

I'd walked along Dalton Street a good hundred yards before I knew I wasn't likely to pick up a taxi there. I turned back towards Hallam Street. The depression that had seized on me as soon as I'd entered the Bellini wasn't the lighter when I knew it was still short of half-past eight and a good part of the night still ahead of me. A wasted evening: still, that was how it sometimes went. Farrell's expense account had swollen by a couple of pounds and I wished I weren't too honest to add a percentage by way of personal compensation.

And then I didn't go straight back after all. I walked on to Piccadilly Circus and into a cinema, and when I got home it was time for bed.

The newspaper was propped up as usual in front of the coffee-pot as I ate my toast and marmalade, but I wasn't really looking at it. Most of the time I was thinking about the previous night. I've claimed I'm not snobbish, but as I looked back I couldn't help thinking there was something just a bit—well, sordid, about Manrico and his Cuban band. It's not the right adjective but perhaps you guess what I mean. I suppose it arose out of disillusionment. And, when I looked back again, a slight irritation.

Manrico—I couldn't somehow think of him as Charlie Morse—had changed quite a lot in his attitude during the few minutes I'd been with him. He'd gone through the semi-respectful to the confidential and had ended with the patronising. His world and mine, to flog a cliche, were poles apart, and it hadn't taken him a couple of minutes to spot it. Not that he'd regarded his own as inferior. Still, in fairness I had to admit I must have seemed something of a simpleton: the boy at the circus who takes the spangles for diamonds.

The telephone bell shrilled almost at my ear. Matthews was on the line.

"What's the matter? Guilty conscience? Didn't expect to find you up."

I just wasn't in the mind for quips. "It's the best part of nine. You've got some news?"

"Yup." He was always a great one for Westerns. "The first sketch of Charles's record came in last night, and boy! is it some record! He got himself up to manager of a hotel at Columbus, Ohio, and then he skipped. Been milking the takings for years. That was in 1951. Picked up in Butte, Montana, for a hold-up and got away with two years at Deer Lodge. In 1955 he defrauded a widow in Seattle and skipped across the border with a few thousand dollars. Wanted by the Canadian police for a bank hold-up at Nipponik, Ontario, and suspected of being concerned in another near Montreal. That was in 1957. Looks as if he managed to get over here not long after."

"Aliases?"

"A string of 'em. Long as your arm. Charles Martin was used at Butte. That helped to tie him up with Martin Charles."

"What about his passport?"

"Asking for something, aren't you? Lord knows what name he used and how he got it. Which reminds me. There wasn't any passport at that flat of his. Not a single incriminatory thing."

"He was running that haulage business straight?"

"His manager was. Bringing in a nice steady income, too."

He rang off then. He did add that he might be dropping in for a coffee at a certain place near Westminster Bridge round about eleven. Something else might have come in by then.

I dropped in myself and found him there. He'd nothing else for me except an interview with the manager of Charles's bank. Charles had opened the account with just over five hundred pounds in notes. Fivers, mostly no dollars. The Alder from whom he'd bought that haulage business had also been paid in cash, plus a cheque for three hundred on the bank. The total was £6,500, of which £3,000 was left on mortgage, repayable within twelve months. It was duly repaid. Various sums in cash, presumably from the haulage business, had been paid in till the balance was the best part of £4,000 and Alder was paid off by cheque. The balance at Charles's death was three thousand approximately, plus another two thousand on deposit account. Matthews wanted to know if I was beginning to see a pattern.

"Can't say I do."

"Look at it this way," he said. "He must have had money when he came over, probably the proceeds of the Montreal job. Then when Alder was almost due for repayment, he did that Kensington job. That jewellery was high-class stuff. It might have netted him seven or eight thousand."

I still thought that tie-in with the Kensington job was pretty tenuous.

"I was waiting for you to say that," he told me, and grinned. "But listen to this. The widow concerned was a friend of old Alder's, and when Charles was at young Alder's Knightsbridge flat, he happened to meet her there. When he left he gave her a lift in that Buick and she asked him to come in for a drink. She professes not to remember what they talked about but my guess is he got what he wanted. Also she still refuses to believe he had anything to do with the robbery. You know the sort of thing: 'Such a charming man.'"

That was about all I learned. I didn't tell him a thing about that visit to the Bellini. I have enough private misgivings about making a fool of myself without having the facts broadcast.

I did ask him if that appeal for Laura Farrell had been agreed on and apparently it would appear in the morning papers. I think we were just about to exchange the usual banalities about keeping in touch when I asked him what he was doing next. He sat down again.

"Glad you mentioned it. As a matter of fact we've got the net out for a chap called Forester."

He was giving me a quizzical sort of look.

"Forester? I seem to remember the name."

"Come off it," he told me. "That young doctor, Hipman, told me you'd had a word with him."

"Oh, that," I said lamely. "No point in telling you that. Hipman hadn't been there long enough and Forester'd been struck off and disappeared."

"I know. But what were you doing? Trying to follow up that pregnancy business?"

"That's it. If it hadn't been a dead end I'd have passed it on."

"Well, we think there may be something in it," he said. "We think it's a good theory and that's why we're trying to find Forester. We had a tip he was working on one of those ships flying the Panama flag so we're working the docks."

"You've seen the other doctor?"

"Caver?" he grunted. "Not yet. But that Mrs. Back hasn't a great idea of him. Seems he was doing surgery when Hipman was away, so she consulted him about her varicose veins. Wanted to know who her own doctor was and virtually sent her off with a flea in her ear. According to her he's what you and I'd call a scruffy old basket."

The evening and morning, as Scripture hath it, was the fourth day. It was on a Wednesday evening when I'd first gone to Mayes Road, and when I woke up the morning after I'd left Matthews at Westminster, it was Sunday. From somewhere or other I could actually hear the tolling of a bell. My wife was coming back the following day, and after I'd had a quick look at the papers, I did a bit of tidying up. I made a note that in the morning I ought to buy some flowers. The hyacinths in the bowls were pretty well over but I thought I'd better leave them alone.

When I came back to the papers again I remembered what Matthews had said about that appeal. It was at the end of a brief resume of the Charles case in the first paper I looked through; the wording much as forecast.

In connection with the above, the police are anxious to get in touch with a Laura Farrell, nee Mann, and known at various times as Laura Manette and Laura Charles: height about five feet six, blonde haired, thin featured and age now about thirty years. Telephone Scotland Yard, Whitehall 1212.

8

BOMBSHELL

NOTHING happened on that Sunday, except perhaps that the weather changed with the change of month. I was almost tempted in the afternoon to take a stroll in the park. The sun was shining, the wind had shifted south-east and altogether it was the sort of day that makes the optimistic think about spring. The only cloud, so to speak, was the weather announcement: fog or mist at night, dispersing slowly. When I looked out just before going to bed, there was only a slight haze.

When I looked out in the morning, the haze was still there but the sun was breaking through. At just after midday I was meeting my wife at Euston. That made it a sort of broken morning. I didn't feel like going to the agency, so I got an all clear from Bertha and thought I'd call on Farrell. The temperature was in the high fifties and, instead of taking a bus, I walked right through to Sutton Court.

I might have known that Farrell wouldn't be there. Kewton said they were doing a documentary about London's mists and fogs. He caught my slight lift of the eyebrows.

"The average foreigner thinks we've nothing else here in the winter: you know, real old pea-soupers all the time. As a matter of fact there're at least twenty different kinds of fog and mist. You can get the most marvellous effects."

I said I'd like to see that film when it was ready and he said I certainly should.

"As for Paul," he said, "I think you'd do just as well to let me handle things. I wouldn't like him disturbed, if you know what I mean."

I told him just enough to show I hadn't been sitting on my haunches. He was very impressed.

"What I'd like personally," he told me, "is for something to have happened so that he'll never be bothered by that woman any more. I wouldn't call her a nightmare, but what's happened has got her on his mind. He'd practically forgotten all about her till last week and that's how I'd like it to be again. And don't worry about money. Two or three hundred pounds'll neither make him nor break him."

I didn't say so, but there was a client after the agency's own heart. I did suggest he have a coffee with me if he could spare the time, and he looked round as if something might suddenly pop up out of nowhere, and said he'd be glad to. It was nearly half-past eleven when we parted. The morning was finer than ever, so I walked through Chancery Lane. I won't say girls were in summer frocks and men in shirt sleeves, but you could see that morning on people's faces. I actually walked all the way to Euston and had a little time to spare when I got there.

Bernice's train was only a few minutes late. We took a taxi to the flat and had a service lunch. I'd lighted my pipe and was just about to hear the rest of her news when the telephone went. It was Matthews.

"Glad you're in," he told me. "Your Bertha said you'd been meeting your wife. You can get away?"

"Why not?"

"Right," he said. "Be here, if you can, in a quarter of an hour."

He didn't give me the chance to ask him what for. As soon as the car turned west along the Embankment, I guessed we were going to Mayes Road. I'd guessed, too, from the look on his face that we weren't going there to look at the view.

"What's happened exactly?"

"Happened?" he said, and grunted. "Something that's blown the whole thing sky high. Looks as if we've got to start again from scratch. Know what I learned just before I rang you? Farrell's wife is dead."

"Dead!" I stared. "You mean *just* dead?"

"No," he said. "That'd have been a stroke of luck. She died about two years ago."

"But that's impossible. It just doesn't make sense."

"I know," he said. "Or do I? You tell me."

"Tell you?" I said. "It stands out a mile. How could she be dead when she was with Martin Charles in the Café Mexique only a few weeks ago!"

"That was a woman who, we're told, was calling herself Laura Manette."

"But—good lord!—what extra proof do we want? There can't be two Laura Manettes. Laura Mann. Laura Manette. They couldn't be two different women. That'd be stretching things too far."

The traffic lights were with us and we took the right-hand turn into Morley Street.

"We're going to Farrell's flat?"

"Not this time," he told me. "Seeing Hipman's partner, Caver. He's the one who gave us the news."

Morley Street's a shopping centre, typically suburban. Nothing big or high-class in the way of shops. Branches of multiple stores mostly. Sandwich fillings, so to speak, of little millinery shops, furniture stores, a photographer's, tobacconists and a pub or two. We went about half-way down, then turned into a red-bricked street of Edwardian houses. Just inside it, the driver signalled a right-turn and drew across in front of the very first house. It looked the only detached one in the street—Barlow Street. Caver's plate was outside.

Three steps led up to the front door. A side path led left with SURGERY painted on the wall, and an arrow pointing. Matthews pushed the bell of the front door and it was Caver who opened it.

I put him as pretty close to seventy, a broad-shouldered but slightly stooping man of medium height. He looked queerly out of place: almost the spit of an old country doctor I'd known years before: old-fashioned, straggly moustache—white, with a touch of sandy in it—and grey, untidy hair with the same faint touches of colour. His face was heavily veined and the beak of a nose was as mottled as his cheeks. The blue-veined hand he held out had a distinct tremble.

"Inspector Matthews. I was the one you spoke to, sir. My colleague, Mr. Travers."

The hand I took was limp. Somehow it wasn't a hand: just something warm over which my own hand closed.

"Come in, come in."

It was a blurting sort of voice. He led the way down a corridor and into his consulting room. It looked as if it hadn't changed since he first set up his plate. The leather of the flat-topped desk was badly worn. The chairs and couch were horse-hair stuffed, and the books in the heavy Victorian bookcase were askew. A couple of ancient pipes and a half-filled ash-tray were on a side table with a pile of medical journals, and from them protruded the rubber of an old stethoscope. On another table were what looked like piles of forms. The smell of the room I couldn't place. It reminded me vaguely of the medicine I'd sometimes had to take as a boy. But nothing could have been more incongruous, somehow, than the two green metal filing cabinets.

He seated himself in the heavy, round-backed chair behind the desk and waved at us.

"Sit down, sit down." He had that trick of repeating himself. "Don't know what else I can tell you."

Matthews took out his notebook. The old doctor took out a spectacle case and hooked the spectacles on.

"You want me to go over it again?"

"If you don't mind, sir. We'll have to get you to make an official statement later."

"I know. I know. A lot of damned official flummery. Not your fault though. Not your fault."

"Just a minute, sir, before you begin. This Laura Mann. We have reason to think she once lived in Mayes Road, the flat above your surgery there. Is there any record of her ever having consulted you or your then partner, Doctor Forester?"

"None," he said. "None at all. Never clapped eyes on the woman before. Can't vouch for Forester though. My own fault. I ought to've got rid of him long before. No record though."

His speech was a kind of bombardment from under that heavy moustache. We might have been a couple of school-boys in a headmaster's study.

"Records can come later," Matthews told him. "Just tell us what you know about her personally, doctor."

He picked up a card, looked at it for a moment and laid it down again. The woman had consulted him on the morning of April the 12th, 1957. Surgery was actually over when she came in, and as a private patient. Name, Laura Mann, age twenty-seven, of 7 Windfield Road, Westminster. He confirmed that from the card.

"Pardon the interruption, doctor, but why should she come here to you? Wasn't it rather off the track?"

He peered over his spectacle tops.

"I'm a doctor. Here, or Timbuctoo, what's it matter? The woman was a private patient." He waved a hand. "I suppose I asked her if she'd seen a doctor before and she told me she hadn't. Must have told me so, or I'd have noted it."

Matthews didn't interrupt again. The woman, old Caver said, was in a highly nervous state. Suffering from acute constipation. Also she was pregnant. Two months gone, he thought, which probably accounted for the nervousness and general state of health. He'd been tactful about the pregnancy. It'd been for her to mention it. She said she was a private secretary and hadn't any relatives whatever, and, to be frank, hers wasn't a case he was too anxious to handle. He tried to put her off by saying that if she could afford it she ought to have a thorough rest and treatment. Preferably in a nursing home. A month might make all the difference. To his surprise she said she did have the money. Even the mention of eighteen guineas a week didn't frighten her. The upshot was that she went to the nursing home he mentioned: that of an old friend, a Doctor Renfield who ran a nursing home—St. Mark's—at Vigar Road, Hornsey.

He'd had in mind the rest he'd mentioned and probably colonic irrigation. And then, the very next morning after she'd arrived, Renfield rang him that she'd had a miscarriage and was in a bad way. By the time he himself had got to Hornsey, she was dead. He, as the last doctor actually attending her, had had no hesitation in signing the certificate. But there were problems: problems, he said, that he hadn't run across before.

For instance, he'd gone personally to the Westminster address and discovered to his amazement that it didn't exist. He and Renfield had then consulted the registrar about the action to be taken and it was agreed that notice should be placed in *The Times* and the *Daily Telegraph* asking for relatives or friends. No one came forward and Laura Mann was duly buried at Warnham Cemetery, North London. A further extraordinary thing was that she'd brought with her to the nursing home a considerable sum of money in notes: about a hundred pounds, in fact. Quite a bit was left over after paying for all expenses, plus the erection of a stone. That balance was still held by the registrar.

"Naturally we wouldn't have been interested, even if we'd seen the notices," Matthews said. "But about this Laura Mann. Do you remember enough about her for a description?"

What he told us made her Laura Mann: long blonde hair, rather peaked face, height, everything.

"You didn't see our notice yourself?" Matthews asked him.

"Never look at anything but the headlines nowadays," Caver told him. "Sometimes not that. Who the hell wants to know when we're going to be blown up by a bomb! The whole world's gone mad. Clean mad."

"I know. Enough to drive you to drink."

The old doctor shot him a quick look. Matthews kept a straight face. A moment later he got to his feet.

"Well, thank you very much, doctor. We'll have to trouble you again when we've got the whole general picture. Meanwhile, will you do one thing for us? Get on the phone straight away to Doctor Renfield and tell him we're coming. When we've seen him and the registrar, we'll have everything cleared up."

Caver got up much more briskly than when he'd sat down.

"I'd forgotten the whole thing," he told us. "Hardly remembered it when my partner told me about it this morning. Life and death, you know. Life and death. That's all it is. Day in and day out."

He saw us out. He said we could go straight on and take two right-hand turns, and that'd bring us out to the Mayes Road end of Morley Street. Matthews thanked him again.

"A queer sort of old fish," he told me as the car moved off. "Bet he drinks like a fish, too."

He chuckled, probably remembering that hint he'd had the nerve to throw out. "What d'you think of it, so far?"

I didn't know what to think. There were things, I said, I couldn't even begin to understand.

"Such as what?"

"Well, let's leave that business about Laura Mann being dead and then being seen two years later very much alive. Let's take the pregnancy. I mean the one about three years ago. Mrs. Back must have made a mistake. Laura Mann could hardly have been pregnant then."

"I know," he said. "That struck me, too. But let's sort of look at it on the assumption that Mrs. Back was right. My guess is yours. Laura would have had an abortion. She had enough money to pay for it immediately after she left Farrell. But wouldn't she have been a damn sight more careful afterwards?"

I said that was how I'd seen it. She must have had bad luck to get herself pregnant again, and inside a year.

"And if she had, why not go to the same abortionist?"

"Don't know. Plenty of reasons, though. She mightn't have liked the way he did the job. Or he might have disappeared."

It was a longish ride, and we twice had to ask the way to Vigar Road. It was four o'clock by the time we found that nursing home, and we'd already gone by it once and failed to spot the board on which was the name. And we'd both expected a much bigger place. St. Mark's Nursing Home was just a fairly large detached Edwardian house. It probably had five or six bedrooms, and staff quarters, and there was the usual conservatory on the south-west end. It seemed to have quite a big garden, and as we came in we could see a range of outbuildings: probably the stables when the prosperous owner had kept his carriage.

The gravelled drive led round to an ornate porch. A fairly old Daimler stood just beyond it and we drew up behind. The plate by the main door had been well polished: I could hardly read the words.

ST. MARK'S NURSING HOME
H. RENFIELD, M.D.. M.A.

Matthews pushed the bell. You'd have thought from the speed with which the door was opened that that uniformed nurse had been listening within reach for the sound of our car. She was a good-looking woman, probably in the late thirties, who must have been quite a beauty only a few years ago. Now her figure was just too full. What the uniform was I couldn't spot. The grey and blue was something I'd never seen. Matthews was uncommonly polite.

"Good-afternoon, sister. Or is it matron?"

She smiled. Maybe that was meant to answer the question.

She also had a quick look at me. "You're the gentlemen Doctor Caver rang about?"

The voice came as a shock. It had a nasal quality. American or Canadian. I didn't know which: a voice that was far from unpleasant. It was just that I hadn't expected it.

We were in what had once been an entrance hall but was now a reception room. It had a faint smell of antiseptics. A wheel-chair and an up-ended stretcher stood by the far wall. A modern, automatic lift had been installed and it came down while we stood there. A thinnish, middle-aged woman in housemaid's black came out with a small tea-trolley. She went through one of the far doors and I caught a glimpse of a bed.

The first floor, we were told, and the door facing the lift. Maybe Renfield had heard us downstairs. He stood there, at the open door of his office, and his hand was out as soon as we emerged. He was a younger man than I'd anticipated: in the early forties. His accent was noticeable but no more. He was talking from the moment his hand went out till the seconds later when he had us seated.

"You're the inspector from Scotland Yard and this'll be your colleague. Caver rang me and said you were coming. That Mann case apparently. How'd you get on with Caver?" He smiled. "A queer old chap in a way. One of those whose bark is worse than his bite."

"You've known him a good while?" Matthews cut in. "Personally only five years. That's how long I've been back here. Spent most of my life in Canada. I knew Caver's son out there. A great friend of my wife and me."

"You run a practice as well as this nursing home?"

"A private practice. Not far from here. In Westwood Road. But the home is my principal concern nowadays." The smile was deprecating. "I happen to be one of those fortunate people who isn't actually forced to work. Still, once a doctor, always a doctor. Like dear old Caver. I've told him he ought to retire. But will he? Not he."

"Yes," Matthews said. "And now about this Laura Mann business. I'll tell you just what we learned from Doctor Caver and perhaps you'll do any filling in."

Renfield was the very opposite of Caver: of medium height but spare in build and almost dapper. His linen was spotless and his dark hair beautifully parted. His voice had a curious jocular quality: a sort of exaggerated carry-over from a bed-side manner. A mercurial kind of character: all that ebullience and now almost a solemnity as he listened to Matthews.

"Yes," he said. "I don't know that there's much to add. She came straight here after she'd seen Caver, and her manner was much more quiet than he'd led me to believe. However, she said she'd like to come here at once, so we arranged for her to come early that evening. I don't know why but she was much more nervous. Very highly strung indeed: so much so that I postponed any serious diagnosis."

"But you formed an opinion?"

"Oh, yes. Caver was undoubtedly right. Almost certainly an excess of purgatives, and that and the pregnancy were leading to quite a dangerous hysteria. I'm putting it simply but perhaps you gather what I mean."

"Absolutely clear. You assumed, of course, that she was an unmarried mother?"

Renfield smiled dryly.

"Let us say that I was deferring everything till the morning. In my judgment she was in no condition to undergo much questioning. She had a very light meal, and after that my wife—you saw her downstairs; a highly qualified woman, by the way—my wife gave her a sedative. We have two nurses here, night nurse and day nurse, and when the night nurse looked in shortly after midnight she was sleeping. When she looked in again at about five in the morning, the patient was lying on the floor and a miscarriage had occurred. I got here as quickly as I could. The rest you know."

"Yes," Matthews said. "I think I've got the general picture. But what about the clothes she came here in? Mightn't she have been identified from laundry marks?" Renfield smiled.

"I'm glad you asked that. There weren't any laundry marks. All her underclothing, night-dresses and so on, were new. Not unusual, believe me. Also, as soon as Caver discovered the false address, I had a word with the local police. There was just nothing they could do. In fact they approved everything the registrar had suggested, including the notices in the press. We kept her belongings for over a year and then they were given to the Salvation Army."

"Well, that seems about all," Matthews told him. "And thank you for a very clear statement, doctor. We may have to get an official one from you later. It depends on how things turn out. And now if you'll tell me where to find the registrar's office, I'll have a word with him and clear the whole thing up."

"Afraid you're too late. The office'll be closed by now. Ten o'clock in the morning he should be available." Matthews treated him to one of his grins. "You and I ought to be civil servants, doctor."

"I know, I know," Renfield told us genially. "The only consolation is they all come to us doctors in the long run." He got to his feet. I put in my only question. "You have several patients here, doctor?"

"At the moment, only four. One an old lady who's been with us some months and the rest the usual run."

"And that means?"

The smile had a touch of the roguish.

"Oh, dieting. Colonic irrigation. Usually we have a maternity case or two but not at the immediate moment. We have rather fine grounds here, by the way." He drew back the window curtains for us to look out. "Nothing much to see now, of course, but in the summer it's very charming."

They were certainly extensive grounds. I could see a large summer-house behind what looked like a croquet lawn. There were plenty of shrubs and flower-beds and at least one fine tree.

"Quite a nice place," Matthews told him. "If ever my wife gets over-weight, doctor, I'll see what I can do."

Renfield was chuckling as he saw us out to the lift. He gave us a wave and a smile as the doors closed. His wife wasn't there when we got down, and I just caught another glimpse of that elderly housemaid as we went out.

There was a slight haze in that late afternoon air as we moved off, but it didn't look as if it would thicken into fog. The street lights were on before we got back to the Yard. We hadn't done a lot of talking. Matthews had asked me what I'd thought of Renfield, and I'd found it difficult to sum him up. I thought there'd been something a bit plausible about him.

"As a matter of fact," I'd said, "if I had to choose between him and Caver as my doctor, I wouldn't be happy about either."

"Well, I'll get that registrar's version in the morning," he'd said, "and give the whole thing a good going over."

We'd wondered about Renfield's medical degree. There'd been no English university bracketed after it so it looked as if it were Canadian. Not that that was necessarily any kind of slur. But what was noteworthy about the little talking we did was what we didn't mention at all: the growing certainty that Laura Mann had died at that nursing home and had been alive two years later. Perhaps we didn't refer to it again because it was more than incredible. I did do a little thinking about it, and all I could arrive at was that Laura might have had a twin sister. That could explain the bodily resemblances, but it couldn't explain the similarity of name.

I told myself that the age of miracles was long since over, and, if one could only hit on it, there'd be an explanation that would make us wonder why we hadn't thought of it at once. But I did think that twin-sister business was something along the right lines. About the Laura Mann who became Laura Farrell we knew nothing but what Farrell himself had been able to tell us. My guess was that every word she had told him about herself was a calculated lie. Even that step-brother whom she had not seen for years and who she said was a doctor, was almost certainly a sheer invention.

Matthews had said he could do with a cup of tea, so I went up with him. No sooner did we enter his room than Hassack came in.

"This message came through for Mr. Travers. From Mrs. Cavallo."

Matthews and I looked at each other. Then I had a look at the official sheet. Message received at 3.30 p.m. Knowing Mrs. Cavallo's English I guessed from the first words that it had been edited. And it was now in the third person.

"Reference the enquiries made by Mr. Travers about a lady who accompanied Martin Charles one night at the Café Mexique, Mrs. Cavallo thought afterwards she would confirm the information given and spoke to the waiter. He says the name of the lady was not Laura but Lola and this was later confirmed by the head waiter. Mrs. Cavallo is very sorry and asks for her apologies to be accepted."

"Well I'm damned," Matthews said, and gave a little chuckle. "Here've we been worrying ourselves silly about nothing at all. Lola Manette, eh? Sounds like a tart to me."

I ought to have been pleased. Somehow I was—with reservations.

"There's still the coincidence of the initials. L.M. and L.M. And Manette is still pretty near to Mann."

"Easy enough to mistake Laura and Lola. They don't sound all that different." Then he stopped. "What about sisters?"

I told him I'd thought of that. And wasn't the real question the identity of the woman who'd accompanied Charles to Farrell's flat? If it *had* been a woman.

"I like the Lola as a sister," he said. "Might be an explanation of why she was at the flat at all. Might have been looking for something that'd been Laura's."

We argued it all through tea and got no further. We'd probably have gone on for another hour if I hadn't remembered a lonely wife.

9

STRANGE ENCOUNTER

WHEN I woke in the morning I still had that problem on my mind. A new twist was incongruously suggested when I brought Bernice her early cup of tea. She had arrived at Euston in a new hat, and I was telling myself that I'd been rather like a woman in a hat shop, trying on a score or so and ending up by buying none. The thing to do, so to speak, was to buy a hat and give it a fair run. You could always buy another later.

In other words—I've said it was incongruous—I ought to work on that theory of sisters, probably twins. I ought to try it on for size and only reject it when I was dead sure it wouldn't suit. Far better, in any case, than flitting airily from theory to theory. And in that context there was one thing I definitely wouldn't do, and that was to raise false hopes in Farrell. Once Matthews was implicitly satisfied about the death two years ago of a Laura Mann who'd once been Laura Farrell, that'd be different. It might mean the end of Farrell as a client. I didn't know. Maybe he, or Brian Kewton, would still want an explanation of those queer happenings at Farrell's flat that Wednesday night.

I mention the weather again because it has a bearing on what was to follow. It was better even than the previous day. When I looked out at half-past seven, the mist had gone and the sun was through. I thought regretfully of my golf clubs, now stored in a cupboard, and wished I'd never given the game up. Bernice was lunching with two old friends and was hinting at a trip to Kew Gardens. All I could do was walk to Broad Street instead of taking a bus.

There was nothing at the agency that Norris couldn't more than handle, and at ten o'clock I was walking towards St. Paul's. I suppose that sister theory was still at the back of my mind and I was wondering too how Matthews would fare with that registrar. I looked up to see I was close to St. Paul's Station and suddenly, out of all that hotchpotch of ideas, I made up my mind to do an extraordinary thing. I'd get out for a bit to the comparative country. Not to a golf course: to a cemetery. I'd have a look at Laura Mann's grave.

At the moment when I made the decision I admit I was thinking very little about the case as a case. I suppose, in fact, it was a momentary revolt against work. There'd been a month of cold and discomfort, and now the touch of sun was too much for me, and that idea of visiting a cemetery was only a justification. But

I did take a train to the end of the line and then a double-deck bus that went to the cemetery and beyond. It was after eleven by then, and the sun was so warm that I wished I hadn't been wearing an overcoat.

The office was just to the right of the main gate: a squat building hidden among trees and tall shrubs. I asked for the grave I wanted and was given a kind of chart. All I had to do when I got back to the main entrance was orientate myself, and now and again consult one of the unobtrusive markers. I must have been walking best part of a quarter of a mile before I neared the number I wanted. A marker showed I was right on it so I took the little side path. And then I stopped.

I must have been given the wrong number. I checked with my eye and there was the grave: a slight mound, a plain surround and a low head-stone. But it couldn't be Laura Mann's grave. A woman was working at the soil: weeding it by the look of her. She had her back to me and to her left was a bucket basket. She took something from it and I saw she was planting something.

I stepped off the hard path and took to the grass and went slowly by. My shadow fell across her as I neared. She glanced round for the merest second and went on with her planting, and I could see now that what she was planting was bulbs. And I saw something else. That white headstone was clean and its lettering sharp. There was so little of it that I could read it as I passed.

SACRED TO THE MEMORY

OF

LAURA MANN

Born March 14, 1930
Died April 13, 1957
Aged 27 years

R.I.P.

I took the path again. Twenty yards on I moved to the grass again and halted at a grave. I took off my hat as I guessed a sorrowing relative would do. A minute or two of that and I began an inspection, and all the time I was watching that woman at that other grave. The whole thing had so startled me that it had been at least a good minute before I could really think. Laura Mann had claimed to be alone in the world. No relative or friend had answered those press appeals or those sent out by the police. Who, then, was the woman at the grave?

I wondered if I should speak to her. Conversation should be easy enough to make: the weather, the condition of the graves, even what she was doing. And then I remembered something. The balance of Laura Mann's money was in the registrar's hands, and maybe he was spending small sums from time to time to keep that grave in order. The woman at the grave was an employee or a friend.

And then, before I could make up my mind what to do, she got to her feet and I could see her more clearly. Her hair was greyer than the felt hat. Her neat costume was grey. She was tall for a woman and slimly, even bonily, built. And she'd come well equipped. She brushed her hands across the skirt of the costume, then put the small trowel and her gardening gloves into the basket. She picked something up and rolled it tightly. It must have been something on which to kneel. I turned quickly away, and when I caught sight of her again, she was walking with long, mannish strides towards the main entrance.

I followed her and held the gap at fifty yards. I needn't have worried for she never once turned round. At the gate I was nearer, but I halted for a minute after she was through. When I looked cautiously out, she was only fifty yards away, and waiting at that bus stop where I'd got off. I waited, too, inside the gates. Now and again I had another look, and all the time I sat listening for the sound of a bus. And then I saw one, coming from the left. As it slowly passed I took a chance. I let the bus mask me as I crossed the road, and as it drew to a halt I saw two women get in, and one was the woman in grey. I quickened my steps, and as I went up the stairs I saw her settling herself half-way along.

I took a seat at the head of the stairs where I'd only to swivel my head at each stop to see where she got off. I was to have a long ride. It didn't come as a surprise.

The conductor came up for my fare.

"That lady in grey downstairs," I said. "I think I know her. Is she going to Corley?"

Corley was the destination of the bus. He said she was going to Little Warberry.

"Oh, of course," I said, and took a tenpenny to Little Warberry too. Maybe he'd have been suspicious if I hadn't been smoking my pipe, which would keep me on top.

We were in the fringes of the outer suburbs and going north-west. That was strange. It didn't fit in with that theory of a conscientious registrar. And she hadn't had the look of anyone's employee. Another few minutes and we were in the more open country with the roads more like lanes. People got off and on and we went through a couple of villages. We went over an old stone bridge that spanned a smallish river. The river circled across meadows, and in the distance there I could see the tower of a church. I asked a man what village it was and he said it was Little Warberry.

The village was only one narrowish street of houses and small shops, and just away to the left I could see the line of willows that marked the river. The bus drew up at a pub—the Red Lion. I sat tight till the woman got off. When I stepped off she was about twenty yards away and engaged in animated talk with a young-ish-looking clergyman. I went past them. Her voice was arch and just a bit shrill.

A few yards on was a post-office store and I went in. I bought some stamps and looked at the display of picture postcards. When I emerged, the woman was just in sight, a good hundred yards ahead of me. The road curved when I came to where she had been, and the houses were petering out. There was another bridge. I didn't want to get too close, so I looked down at the river. It looked pretty deep and I could see the green of weeds that turned to yellow where the sun caught them. I moved on again. On the right, well back from the road, was the church, and beyond it a Georgian house that would be the vicarage.

When I looked ahead again the woman was turning across the wide grass verge to the gate of a small, creeper-covered house. I stooped down and began tying a bootlace, and when I straightened myself she had gone. I waited a minute and went on. Everything about that cottage was neat. The lettering on the green gate stood clear—Willow Cottage. The brass knocker on the green door shone like gold. There were flowering bulbs in the first window, and then as my eyes moved along I was turning them away. A curtain had moved at that second window and I caught a quick glimpse of a face.

I slightly quickened my pace. The road was narrower as it curved back from the river and I stepped on the verge to let a car pass. It would be lovely there in the summer with the shade of the trees and the river and its fringe of willows. And then, out of sight of that cottage, I halted. There was only one thing to do, and I turned back.

I closed the gate carefully behind me and went along the short, bricked path to the door and knocked. A moment and the door slowly opened but no more than an inch or two. I could just see her face. She had the look of a Victorian governess: erect, thin-lipped and with grey, cold eyes.

"Yes?"

I raised my hat. "May I have a word with you?"

"What do you want?" She didn't give me a chance to speak. The words followed on, vehement and shrill. "You're the man I saw at the cemetery. You've been following me. Go away or I'll send for the police."

A last glare and she closed the door and I heard the click of a bolt. I stood there like a fool and then I went slowly back to the gate.

It was almost one o'clock when I went into the tap-room of the Red Lion. There'd been a bus time-table on a board outside and there'd be an hour to wait before I could get back to Warn-ham. It was a pleasant room. There was no real need for a fire but one was burning in the old-fashioned grate. Only a couple of customers were there: in talk with the landlord, a red-faced, middle-aged man who was leaning across the counter. The talk stopped as I went up to the bar. I ordered a pint of bitter. I asked what chance there was of some bread and cheese. The landlord said he'd fetch it.

The younger of the two men left and gave me a country-man's nod as he went by. The other, who had the look of a farmer, told me it was a grand day.

"Unnatural, some'd call it. Have to pay for it, though, if you ask me."

"You're a farmer?"

"Sort of retired. My son's carrying on the farm now. Old Grange Farm. Do you know it?"

It was on the tip of my tongue to say I was a stranger. "Haven't been here for twenty years and more," I said. "Don't seem many changes though."

"A few o' them bungalows as you come in. And them television aerials all over the place."

The landlord came back with my lunch. The farmer's tankard was just emptying and I asked if he'd have a refill. I brought it across to his table. We drank each other's health. "Who's the parson here now?"

"A youngish chap called Smythe," he told me. "It'd be Braid in your time though. Died about four or five year ago. Not a bad old fellow neither. This one they've got now ain't a patch on him."

"You used to live here, sir?" That was the landlord. "Used to go through it a good many years ago. Always thought it was a nice little place. The river and everything."

"There's many wuss," the farmer said. "Fishin' ain't what it was, though. Do you reckon so, Frank?"

The landlord agreed. They discussed it while I got on with my lunch. I cut in at a pause. "Who lives now at that nice little cottage just past the church? Willow Cottage."

The farmer smiled.

"Ah, you mean old Miss Braid. The old reverend's sister. She kept house for him till he died, then moved into where she is now. Saw her get off the bus when it come in."

"A tall woman. Looked like a school-mistress. Talking to your rector."

He chuckled. "That'd be her. One o' his pets. Allus decorate the church and never miss early communion. Your wife never could stand her, Frank, neither can mine."

The landlord just smiled. "Don't do for 'em all to be like you and me, Tom."

Tom chuckled again. "Reckon if I was to go to church the roof'd fall in. Can't stand old Mary Braid though. Give herself too many airs for me. Allus did."

He emptied his tankard and got to his feet.

"Reckon I'd better be slippin' along. Good-day to you, sir. Good day, Frank."

"Wouldn't think he was worth a penny to look at him," the landlord said. "Got no end though. You knew him?"

"I seemed to remember him."

"Farmed here all his life. And his father before him. Reckon the Finchams are one of the oldest families round here."

I asked him to have a drink with me and he drew himself a pint. Then a couple of men came in: a bricklayer and his mate who'd been working on a wall just short of the pub. They ordered pints and I watched a game of darts to see who paid. At ten minutes to two I patronised the premises in the back yard and waited for the bus. It came in on time. Since that farmer had left I'd learned one other thing. I hadn't wanted to mention that woman again and I don't quite remember just how her name managed once more to crop up. What I'd learned was that she'd been pretty ill in the winter and had only just got about again. As I remembered that I suddenly knew the context in which it had occurred. We'd been talking about longevity in the country and the landlord had instanced that recovery as the resiliency of age. The village, he'd said, had known she was going to die, and here she was, spry as ever.

I was thinking about that as the bus went its staid way towards Warnham. Bulbs should be planted in the autumn. That illness of hers had delayed the planting but she'd been tempted out by the sudden, unnatural spring. But that was only something incidental to what was crowding in on my mind. Why she had been at that grave was utterly beyond me. Not that I didn't have theories. I wished, for instance, that I'd asked if any Manns had ever lived in the village. What Farrell's wife had told him about herself was less to be trusted than a gipsy's prophecies. The fact remained that Mary Braid had known her, and known of her death and burial. How I couldn't conceive. Or why it was that she hadn't answered those appeals.

At Warnham I looked up the time of the next bus to the Underground and found they ran at the half-hour. I'd just missed one so I had that much time to spare. I went through the cemetery gates and made for that grave again. There were quite a few people about, some carrying flowers, but it was lonelier up there past the cypresses, and I quickly stooped down and felt among the loose soil with my fingers. I brought up a tulip bulb. I pushed it back in place.

Away to the open land to the left a man was trimming the path edges. I made my way across. I gave him a good-day and remarked on the weather. He was quite ready to pull up for a breather. I asked him if there was any society that looked after neglected graves.

"Well, there aren't any that are what you'd call neglected. We look after them ourselves."

"But you don't plant flowers and things."

He smiled. "Bless your soul, no sir. Cost a young fortune, that would. The relatives'd have to do that. We just keep the weeds down."

"And suppose I told you that I'd seen a woman, who wasn't a relative, planting some bulbs."

He gave another smile. "Probably some crank, sir. You get all sorts of cranks and crack-pots—women mostly. Something to do with religion, if you ask me."

I moved on towards the gates. Another five minutes and I was mounting the bus. It was after four o'clock when I got back to town.

I went straight to the flat. My wife wasn't back. Neither Matthews nor Hassack was at the Yard so I made myself some tea. At five o'clock I rang again and this time Matthews was in. He told me he'd seen that registrar and everything seemed in order.

"What about that balance in hand?"

"Still intact," he said. "Out of his hands now though. He's passed it on with a statement to his head office. He says they're issuing an appeal to relatives at intervals till it's claimed. No skin off his nose if it isn't."

"About it being intact," I said. "He didn't ever spend anything for the upkeep of the grave or anything like that?"

"How could he? It was the same sum that Renfield handed over. But wait a minute. What's the idea? What's so interesting about that money?"

I said if he was free, I'd be along to tell him. Another few minutes and I was in his room. He stared when I told him where I'd been.

"The cemetery! What on earth made you go there?"

I told him I didn't know. A fine day, thinking about Laura Mann, finding myself at an Underground station—all sorts of things I couldn't really explain. He was staring again when I told him about the woman in grey. I didn't let him interrupt till I'd got the whole thing off my chest—Red Lion and all.

"Well," he said, "if that isn't the damndest thing ever! And not as though she lived near the place. And planting tulips."

"And it wasn't a casual impulse either. That bulb I got out was just beginning to shoot. That means she bought them last autumn and then had to store them because of the illness. Then we had that wicked January, and then as soon as we got this fine spell, off she went to the cemetery."

"Yes, but why? The way you described her, she was the last one to come into contact with Laura Mann."

I mentioned what I ought to have done, if it hadn't occurred to me too late—that idea of a Mann family in the village. He pushed the buzzer at once. What he wanted was the local constabulary at Little Warberry.

"We'll soon know," he said. "But this Braid woman. Has she got a telephone?"

I said she had.

"Better hear what the local police say first," he said. "Also if we have to see her it might be as well if she didn't know." The buzzer went. He picked up the receiver. He gave a quick wave at the set on the side table and I slipped across to listen in.

"Your Little Warberry number, sir."

A moment and a woman's voice said "Hallo."

"That Little Warberry police?"

"Yes," she said, "but my husband's out."

"What's his name?"

"Hilton. Wilfred Hilton."

"Right, Mrs. Hilton. This is New Scotland Yard, Inspector Matthews calling. We want some information about any family named Mann—spelt em, a, double en, Mann. You a local woman?"

"Yes, sir. Lived here all my life. There's no one of that name that I know of."

"What about the immediate district?"

"No, sir. Not that I've ever heard of. I can ask my husband when he comes in, but I'm pretty sure I'm right."

"Right, Mrs. Hilton. Don't bother us unless there *is* someone. Or if there was, say within the last three or four years."

"Yes, sir, I'll tell him that."

"Right. Thank you again, Mrs. Hilton."

That was the conversation. A Mann family at Little Warberry looked pretty unlikely.

"We'll have to go to the fountain head," Matthews said. "Best thing we can do is let the Old Man hear what you've told me."

Jewle was in. Matthews had spoken over the inter-com, and Jewle was looking interested.

"What's this about a queer story?"

I went over the whole thing again from beginning to end. Matthews topped it with his call to Little Warberry.

"It *is* a queer story," Jewle said. "I don't know when I heard a queerer. I know it doesn't affect the case but did she have a screw loose, did you think?"

"Don't think so," I said. "I'd have heard about it in the pub. The only hysteria I saw was when she shut that door in my face."

"Yes," he said, "that showed she was afraid of something. It might have been you, of course. Plenty of cases of widows being attacked in their homes. Doesn't affect the main case though."

He went across to the big wall map and ran his finger along. He had a look through a reference book.

"Hungerford's their Chief Constable," he told us. "I'll have a word with him later. The woman's got to be seen. We've got to know what connection there was between her and the Mann woman. From what Mr. Travers has been telling us, she may be a bit difficult to handle. Still . . ."

He left it like that. A few more words in Matthews's room and I went home. After the evening meal, when we'd settled down in front of the fire, I told Bernice all about that case. She's discretion itself: never asks questions but always ready to listen to anything I feel I want to divulge. The whole thing was as puzzling to her as it had been to me. Then, just after nine o'clock, Matthews rang.

"All set for the morning," he told me. "Nine o'clock be all right at your place?"

I'd had so much on my mind that I'd known I was in for a bad night. The knowledge that the morning would bring a whole lot of answers was as good as a sedative, and almost as soon as my head had warmed the pillow, I was asleep.

10
DOUBLY DEAD

It had rained in the night and the morning was cloudy. The forecast had mentioned thunderstorms and the air was certainly a bit oppressive rather than just warm. The landscape that I'd seen beneath the sun the previous morning was now without its colour, and across the grey meadows as we neared Little Warberry the church tower was scarcely discernible.

Hilton's house was just as one entered the village: an almost new red-bricked house with garage. Matthews had rung him and he must have been on the look-out for our car from the way he appeared as soon as it drew up. He was nearing retirement and had been stationed in the village, or near it, all his constabulary life. When he told us there wasn't a Mann in the whole neighbourhood, you took it as read.

We didn't go indoors: just drifted towards his garage and did a bit of talking there. Matthews said there was a Miss Braid living in the village, who, he'd been given the tip, might have some information. It was all very vague and Hilton must have wondered, after we'd gone, what on earth we'd been talking about. He told us where she lived and had an ear cocked, so to speak, for what we were going to divulge in return.

"I suppose you know her?"

"Know her, sir?" He gave a little chuckle. "Known her all my life."

Matthews gave me a look. "Didn't they hint she was getting a bit queer in the head?"

"That's what I gathered," I said. "Would that be right?"

"Right, sir?" He snorted. "Couldn't be more wrong. I don't know where you got the information from, sir, but she's as sharp as anyone in the parish. And more so."

She certainly had a finger in a whole lot of pies: Sunday-school, Women's Institute, Parochial Church Council and what-not, with a special interest in an Orphanage Society for which she made an annual collection. She'd also put up for the Parish Council but hadn't got in. Matthews looked surprised.

"To tell the truth, sir, she isn't all that popular. One of the old style, if you know what I mean. The late rector here was her brother, and she used to think herself a sort of cut above the village. You know how it was in those days, sir, but things have changed. People aren't going to be treated nowadays as if they were something inferior."

"How old is she?"

"Let me see." A furrowed brow showed laborious calculations. Then he nodded. "Exactly seventy, sir. That's how I work it out."

"Active?"

Hilton smiled. "Spry as they make 'em, sir. Nearly dead of pneumonia a month or two ago and now she's hopping about like a flea—if you get me."

"Well, thanks for the information. We may drop in on her on our way past."

We left a puzzled Hilton standing there and went back to the car. I told the driver to slow as we neared Willow Cottage.

"No need to call attention to ourselves," Matthews said. "Drop us here and draw in at that lane there, by the church."

We walked the hundred yards or so, and it was Matthews who spotted something queer.

"Gone ten o'clock and she isn't up yet. From what Hilton was telling us, you'd have thought she'd been about hours ago."

I saw what he meant. A milk bottle stood by the door. A newspaper was held in place by the brass knocker.

We closed the gate behind us and walked down the path. No upstairs windows were open. The newspaper was *The Times*. He lifted the knocker and took it out, then knocked. A few moments and he knocked again. He knocked a third time and there couldn't have been a sleeper who wouldn't have been roused.

"Funny," he said. "Let's have a look round the back."

The brick path went round. It circled a largish lean-to shed and ended up at the back door. Both doors of the shed were padlocked, and from under the further door was a trickle of coal dust. Matthews stepped back along the grass path that led away through the garden, and looked up.

"No fire. A window open though."

He tried the back door. It was locked, like the front. He knocked and we listened.

"A waste of time," he said. "She must have gone out before the milk and paper came. Can't make out, though, why she didn't light a fire."

He drew back again and had a good look at that open window. There was an old-style sawing-horse alongside the shed. He got it set firm by the side of the lean-to and mounted it. He thought the roof would carry him and he pulled himself up. A couple of careful steps and he was looking through the window. He put his arm round and released the bar, and when that half-window was wide open he had a good look inside. Then he came down.

"It's her bedroom all right. That bag she was carrying yesterday is on the chair beside the bed. Bed hasn't been slept in."

He didn't like it and neither did I.

"You go round to the front and keep a look-out," he told me. "I'll take a chance."

It was a quarter of an hour before he joined me.

"Don't like it at all," he said. "You stay here in case she should happen to come back and I'll do some phoning at Hilton's."

It was quiet down there that morning. Now and again a car went past and that was all. I made like a tourist and sat on the end of the bridge parapet and smoked my pipe. It was quite a time before the car came back. It drew into the lane again and I went back slowly to the cottage. Matthews and Hilton joined me there.

"We called up to see the woman who does for her," he told me. "Tuesdays and Fridays. She says Miss Braid is always up and about by seven."

"You're making an entry?"

"Only through that window. You'd better hang around here. Hilton had better come round to the back."

Ten minutes went by before he called me round to the back. The door was open. I went through into a spotless kitchen. You could have eaten a meal off the tiled floor.

"The key was in the lock," Matthews told me. "Come through here."

I stepped into a small dining-room and my eyes popped a bit. It had a nice Pembroke table and the chairs were definitely Chippendale. An eighteenth-century bracket clock with silver dial was on the mantelpiece and a couple of Meissen groups flanked it. A portrait of an eighteenth-century divine looked like a Romney.

"A young fortune here."

"Belonged to the old rector," Hilton told me. "Only the modern stuff, they reckoned, was in the auction."

"Look at the door," Matthews told me. "Damn the antiques."

I didn't see anything wrong with it.

"No key," he said. "She went out last night, locked the door from outside and took the key with her. Wait a minute, though."

He tried the back door key. It didn't fit and he let out a breath of relief. "Now have a look in here."

We went into what I'd call a parlour, so crowded with furniture and knick-knacks you could hardly move around. They weren't cheap knick-knacks either. There was a beautiful Rockingham tea-service in the Regency corner-cupboard. There were Chelsea figures, miniatures, an early French clock, eighteenth-century water-colour drawings, silk pictures, and a pair of exquisite Sheraton side-tables.

"See that?" Matthews said, when I'd had that quick look round.

By the scarcely visible leg of a chintz-covered chair was a little cigarette ash.

"She didn't smoke," he told me.

So there it was. Some time the previous night she'd had a visitor and that visitor had been of sufficient closeness, or importance, to be taken through into that drawing-room parlour. He or she had smoked a cigarette.

"Yes," I said. "Miss Braid, I'd say, was house-proud. You won't find enough dust here to make a flea sneeze. Does that show that she was pretty agitated while that caller was here? If she'd been normal wouldn't she have noticed that flick of the cigarette ash on the carpet? It's a Chinese carpet, too. You'd be lucky to buy it for a hundred pounds."

"Logical enough," he said. "So what now? You any ideas, Hilton?"

He hadn't. Nor had I. Except that it was just possible that she'd gone off somewhere and had spent the night with that caller.

"Right," Matthews said. "We'll go out by the back door and I'll take a chance with the key. Getting on for lunch-time so we'll get something at the pub. Best thing you can do, Hilton, is make a few enquiries whether anyone saw her last night or today. Be as discreet as you can, and your wife might find something for my driver. Which reminds me, what was the weather here like last night?"

"Drizzling a bit, sir. And black as black hogs. I know. I had to be out."

"Not much of a help. Still, we'll have a look at the front. Might just be some marks of tyres."

No one had driven on either of the grass verges. Hilton set off on foot. We walked to the car. At closing time we'd see Hilton again at his house.

*

A foursome of darts was going on in the tap-room. The old farmer, Tom Fincham, and another man were looking on. I introduced Matthews. A friend, I said. I'd liked the village so much when I'd seen it again that I'd brought him along. And a pity the sun wasn't shining. The landlord said he could find us bread and cheese and pickles, and wouldn't we two gents like to go into the other room. The electric stove would soon warm it up. Matthews said he always preferred the bar.

As I told him, he was lending a bit of tone to the place. The landlord actually spread a little table-cloth on the far table where we had our meal. Occasionally we took part in a conversation but we put no leading questions. When we'd finished our eating Fincham stood us two more pints. He didn't seem in any hurry to leave, and challenged either or both of us to a game of darts. Matthews took him on and just lost. If he could have scored his double he'd have won. That made it a quarter to two. We sat on for a bit. We'd had too much cold beer and we didn't want to make ourselves conspicuous, so we said good-day. Fincham had already gone. He passed us in his car as we came out and he was heading west. We took a stroll to just beyond Willow Cottage. Nothing seemed to have altered there but we knocked at the door, just in case. It was still earlier than we'd agreed but we walked back to Hilton's house and, just as we neared it, Fincham went by in his car. He drew up at the kerb with a squeal of brakes and not a foot short of where our car was parked. When we got there, the front door of the house was open and he must have gone inside. Then he was coming out, and Hilton with him. We met about half-way along.

"Would you mind telling this gentleman what you've just told me, Tom? He's an inspector from Scotland Yard." Fincham didn't even stare: he was too full of his story. He'd gone about half a mile, he said, when a man signalled him to stop. The river just there ran alongside the road and the man said he'd been driving slowly towards Little Warberry, looking at the river, when he caught sight of a curious sort of bundle caught up near the bank.

He drew up his car and went back. The bundle was a drowned woman. Fincham went with him for a look.

"It was Mary Braid," he told me. "The one we was talking about only yesterday."

"Dead?" Matthews said.

"Dead as mutton. We got her out on the bank and there she is now. The other man's still there. I said I'd come along here, Wilfred, and let you know."

"Right," Matthews told Hilton. "Get hold of your inspector and arrange for an ambulance. You go on ahead, Mr. Fincham, and we'll follow you."

About half a mile beyond Willow Cottage we drew in behind Fincham's car. The bank shelved down a bit and the body lay just clear of the river. A short, plump, middle-aged man introduced himself as Otwell. He said he'd been staying with a married daughter at Corley and had been on his way back to town.

Matthews was having a word with him and I was looking down at the body of Mary Braid. There was something curiously placid about her. The lips were partly opened which took away the grimness of the mouth. The sodden hair lay back and made the face more thin, and she looked older: much older than the woman who'd walked with long, mannish steps away from that grave. If I felt any pity, the mainspring came as much from myself as from her, and it wasn't easy to forget the frightened hostility in her face and the shrill hysteria of her voice when she'd closed and bolted the door. In a way it was a double death: hers and the hopes we'd set out with that morning.

I must have been standing there much longer than I'd thought and the sound of a car made me look round. Old Fincham was on his way and Matthews was having a last word with Otwell. He closed his notebook and held out his hand, and watched for a moment when Otwell drove on.

"A good citizen, that Otwell," he told me. "Most people wouldn't have had his sense either. Still, now we've got a chance to talk."

He stood for a good minute looking down. "Seems strange it's the first time I've actually seen her. Notice the coat? The same costume, isn't it?"

It had been quite a smart coat with a fur collar. Under it I could see the skirt of that same grey costume.

"No hat, though."

He stretched up and peered along the river, hoping perhaps to see it. The river was about twenty yards wide and running fairly swiftly, fed by the melting winter of only a few days before. Here and there along its banks you could see the small debris of boughs, and a larger one within a yard or two of us: the one in which she'd been finally held.

He stooped down and felt in the exposed pocket of the coat. He turned the body gently over.

"Thought I might find that door key. Probably had a hand-bag though. A few abrasions on her face. Probably where she was brushed against things."

His fingers were moving slowly over the head. Something was there. He felt for his pencil and drew the hair back.

"Have a look here."

There was an inch-long cut almost at the crown. Around it was the deep brown of dried blood.

"Don't like it, do you?"

He got to his feet. "Mind you, she might have struck her head against something, but only if she jumped in herself. And she didn't dress herself up to come out here and do that. How deep do you reckon that river is?"

"Don't know," I said. "Ten feet in the middle. Maybe more. But does it matter? Once she was in it with all those clothes on she couldn't have swum a yard."

There was the sound of a car. It drew up. An ambulance drew in behind it. The man in the car waved a hand in half salute and came towards us: a tall, burly man of about forty with copper written all over him.

"Inspector Yandle of Corley. Hilton said you'd be here."

Matthews introduced himself and me. Yandle had a look at the body.

"Never thought she'd end up like this."

"You knew her?"

"Known her for years. Had a run-in with her last autumn over an accident: shooting out of Church Lane into the road on her bicycle."

"You've got the background? What we wanted to see her about and so on?"

We brought him up to date. It was my story mostly.

"Slammed the door in your face, did she? Looked and sounded hysterical. You think that's anything to do with this?"

"If you mean suicide," Matthews said, "I wouldn't like to commit myself. Look at this wound on the skull."

Yandle had a look. He pursed his lips.

"One or two other things," Matthews said. "Back at her cottage if you'd like to have a look. Do you want her kept here?"

No point in it, he said. The body'd been moved, so photographs wouldn't help. And he hadn't brought the doctor. Since she was dead, he could handle her better at Corley.

We watched while the ambulance men took her away. We watched it reverse in a lane near by.

"Any relatives?"

"Almost sure there aren't. Her brother, the rector, was a bachelor."

"No one to notify, then. You never by any chance heard of anyone called Mann being connected with her?"

"Never," he said. "And the only Mann I know about here is the schoolmaster at Cottenford, and that's another six miles the other side of Corley."

We went back to the cottage. Matthews opened the front door and the three of us went in. Yandle was told about the key.

"This is your pigeon," Matthews said, "but one or two things you might like to see. Some cigarette ash, for instance. Miss Braid, by the way, didn't smoke."

"Been in here before, when I saw her about that bicycle business."

He had a look at the ash. "Looks as if the one who was smoking it was flicking off the ash all the time. Anything else?"

A door in the near corner opened up to show the narrow cottage stairs. On the small landing there was a choice of three doors: to a small bathroom, a small bedroom and the much larger room which Matthews had entered through the window. There was a four-foot bed with an interior-spring mattress, and a handsome Paisley shawl as an overspread. There was a heavy mahogany wardrobe that must have been brought up in sections; an easy chair, and in the far corner, parallel to the window, a beautiful miniature walnut desk. Well to the back of it a small electric stove was plugged into a power-point, the switch off. A Chippendale round-backed chair was just to the side.

"The way I see it, she used this as an office," Matthews said. "A nice view of the church through those elms, as you see, and got all the afternoon sun. The flap of that desk, there, is locked, and I didn't touch it. I did open the drawers though. Don't know what you'll think but I'm pretty sure they've been gone through. As Mr. Travers here pointed out when we saw that ash in the drawing-room, she'd a mania for cleanliness and tidiness, and my bet is that she had everything in those drawers as neat as ninepence."

Yandle opened a drawer. "Yes," he said. "Looks as though you're right."

He stood looking down for an indecisive moment before he turned away.

"That all?"

"All that stood out. My little visit wasn't all that official and we didn't know at the time if she mightn't be popping in on us."

We went down to the dining-room. The light was getting bad. Yandle drew the curtains and switched on the electric.

"Looks as if this is going to be a pretty tricky job. And in conjunction with your story, Mr. Travers, you'd like to give me an idea of how you're beginning to work things out?"

"The way I see it is this, just as a preliminary," Matthews told him. "She had a visitor last night. Any time after dark. She was induced to go out with that visitor who then cracked her on the skull and dumped her in the river. That's the bare bones of it."

He treated Yandle to one of his best grins.

"If you'd like an expanded version, Mr. Travers can probably supply it. If I know him, he's got things far more worked out."

That was a pretty cunning move. It was Matthews himself who wanted to hear my version.

"As I see it, the available evidence points to this," I said. "When she saw me at the door, there, she was badly frightened, and because of something to do with that visit of hers to the grave. I think that when she recovered from the shock, she rang somebody and told him—we'll say it was a him—what had happened; and that someone also had to be connected with that grave. Then someone came along and heard an agitated story: so agitated that she didn't even notice ash being flicked on to a very valuable carpet. He saw she knew too much: a danger, if you like to put it that way, so he gave her a credible reason for going out. Before he dumped her in the river he took her hand-bag with the door-key and her other keys in it, and then he came back here and searched for any incriminating evidence. Then he locked that door behind him and went. May have dumped the hand-bag in the river on his way."

"Yes," Yandle said. "It certainly hangs together—from what I know. And those are the lines along which you think we should work?"

"Not for me to say," Matthews told him, "but I'm betting it'll turn out to be a team job, you here and we back in town. The whole thing's wrapped in with that Charles case, and this business we came here for is only one angle of it."

"Yes," he said again. "I reckon you're right. And if that's so, what's my best line down here? I mean to get on with it at once."

"Stick to those Laura Mann enquiries, that's the chief thing. See Miss Braid's lawyer and her bank manager. Might be a clue in her will or any payments she made. All the obvious things as well. You know them as well as I. That woman who worked for her, for instance. Any friends she might have dropped a hint to. Even the bus company to see if she paid regular visits to that cemetery." He smiled at Yandle's wry shake of the head. "It's going to mean some hard graft."

"You're telling me!"

"There's one consolation," I told him. "You won't be the only grafter."

"Guess not," he said, and moved towards the door. We went out and Matthews gave him the key.

"You keep us informed," Matthews told him, "and we'll do the same. Needn't wait till the Heads have made up their minds. If you feel like coming up to us, do so, or we'll slip down here to you. Anything for promotion."

It was the first time Yandle had smiled. "Something in that." He waved a hand as lie got in his car. "Be seeing you, then."

We halted while Matthews had a word with Hilton, and it was almost dark when we left Little Warberry. The rush-hour traffic wasn't a help, and it was six o'clock when we drew in at the Yard. We had a brief rehearsal in Matthews's room. I telephoned to my wife and then we saw Jewle. It was another hour before I got away.

Things were panning out much as we'd hinted to Yandle, even if there'd have to be quite a lot of tact. If we were officially called in, that would be different, but Yandle's chief, so Jewle hinted, was a pretty ambitious man who'd probe away at his end till the very last minute. After all that I went home. It was drizzling again when the police car dropped me. Maybe, I thought, it'd be drizzling in Little Warberry, too. A kind of requiem for a sodden body in a country morgue.

11
EVENING OUT

THE next day was a thing of shreds and patches. The best thing about it was that Matthews was almost going out of his way to let me tag along. When that case had opened, he'd been feeling his feet. I hadn't any official status and he wasn't sure just how we stood: then Jewle's implied acceptance had turned me into at least a tagger-along. Also I had the sneaking feeling that Matthews saw virtue in the old saw, that two heads are better than one. And, of course, Matthews still might have a private suspicion that I hadn't yet divulged quite all I knew. After all, I did owe some duty to a client.

Another excellent thing, of course, was that that client was now in the clear. The events of the previous day had been proof of that, and Matthews was never again to resuscitate that old, flamboyant theory about Farrell murdering his wife. I didn't raise it either, even in a moment of reproach. It had always looked mighty thin and what had happened since had sunk it without trace. But there was just the faintest echo when I went into his room that morning. He opened a drawer and handed me a couple of photographs.

"Where'd you get 'em?"

"That one you told me Bill Fraser had. Got some copies made. Just sent some off to Yandle. Thought it might help."

It gave me a funny sort of feeling to look at that photograph again. It was a beautiful bit of work.

"Natural enough," I said, "for you to expect her to open her mouth and talk."

"Wish to God she would," he said. "A couple of minutes and this case'd be over. The same with that Mary Braid. Two women and both of them dead." He gave a slow shake of the head. "That grave business is a snorter. It just can't be as complicated as it looks. There must be an answer somewhere at Warberry."

"Should be," I said. "If Yandle's the man to dig it out. Where's Hassack, by the way?"

"Ah!" he said. "Some more bad news. Forester's dead. Died about three months ago in Rio. Been on a dope jag again and they shoved him into hospital. Hassack's down at the docks getting a full statement."

Another small cloud across the mind.

"That theory of mine," I said, "about Laura Farrell getting herself an abortion."

He got up from the chair. "Matter of fact, we're going out to Mayes Road now. Got to get there before surgery's over."

As soon as the car moved off, I went back to that theory.

"You bet your life," I said, "that Laura had seen Forester and summed him up. So let's suppose it was him she fixed the abortion with. We can find out where he lived and if the job might have been done there. It could even have been done in that surgery after hours. Forester would have his own rounds and who was to know where he was at any particular time."

"It'd have to have been after she left Farrell," he said. "It wasn't till then that she had the money. And she wouldn't have risked going to that surgery."

We had to hang about for some minutes till the surgery had definitely closed. We caught Hipman as he was about to lock up. He didn't look all that surprised when Matthews asked if he could spare a minute. He just unlocked the door again and we went in.

"This is something strictly between you and me. It's not even to be mentioned to Doctor Caver. You can promise us that?" Hipman thought for a brief moment. Maybe he was pondering the Hippocratic oath.

"Don't see why not, Inspector."

"Right. So long as it's perfectly clear. Some news for you by the way. Your predecessor, Forester, is dead. We got the news last night. Died in Rio."

If Hipman responded at all, it was with a slight shrug of the shoulders. "Well," he said. "I never actually met him. He'd gone before I came. I did use to hear about him occasionally from my landlady, though."

"You mean you took the same rooms?"

"That's right." He looked a bit surprised. "Number 126, Barlow Street. Doctor Caver's at one end and I'm at the other."

"And very handy, too. And now to the really confidential question. I mentioned that Mrs. Farrell to you: the one who left her husband about three years ago. We happen to know she was pregnant. We're also pretty sure the child was never born. So tell us, from what you've gathered here and there, about Forester. Was he the kind of man who for quite a nice packet of notes would have been likely to have performed an illegal operation?"

Hipman moistened his lips.

"He's dead now," Matthews reminded him. "If he did, the law can't do anything about it. There couldn't be any scandal."

"Frankly, I don't know," Hipman said. "It's just possible. He was a pretty heavy spender and the money might have attracted him. And towards the end he was definitely unbalanced. But I don't know."

"A fair answer," Matthews told him. "And, still keeping it strictly confidential, a personal question. Have you ever been surreptitiously approached here about such an operation?"

Hipman actually smiled. "About three times since I've been here. Just hints and all that: nothing definite."

"What'd you actually do?"

He stared. "Oh! I see what you mean. Just pretended I didn't hear. There was one girl, though, whom I had to talk to pretty seriously. Had to try to scare the life out of her."

"You reported these cases to your partner?"

"Naturally I did. He had to be protected as well as me. You can't trust women like that. Once he had their particulars, he was prepared. I mean supposing they approached him as well."

"I get you." He held out his hand. "Much obliged to you, doctor. And don't forget what I said about secrecy. There might be pretty serious consequences if anything got out." Hipman locked the surgery door again.

"Shan't be troubling you again," Matthews told him. "Just off to those diggings of yours, by the way, to try to clear up that business of Forester. You're not the only ones who are cluttered up with red tape."

Hipman smiled. "No, I guess we're not. She's a nice sort of woman, by the way. Name of Nash."

We went straight on, took the left turn and left again into the far end of Barlow Street. The house was the last but one. The woman who answered our ring looked a cut above the usual type.

"Mrs. Nash?"

"Yes?" she said.

"You used to have a Doctor Forester living here. Doctor Hipman was just telling us he took over his rooms."

"Won't you come in?" She drew back to let us pass.

"Afraid I must take you upstairs. Has something happened to Doctor Forester?"

She showed us into a room at the head of the landing. It was all her floor, she said. The rest of the house was let off.

"You'll be sorry to hear Doctor Forester's dead," Matthews told her, and gave her his warrant card. It was the first time she'd looked the least perturbed.

"Nothing for you to be alarmed about, Mrs. Nash. He actually died in Rio de Janeiro. We're just trying to clear up some loose ends. He was with you a long time?"

About ten years, she said. And did we know about the trouble he'd been in? For the purposes of the visit, we didn't. It didn't do us much good. All we learned was that Forester developed the drug habit only in the last three years of his stay. Mrs. Nash was the widow of a doctor, and her rooms had always been let to medical students and young doctors, which gave what she told us a certain authority. Forester, she said, had suffered from severe arthritis and had taken to the drugs to relieve the pain.

"Didn't he drink a lot, too?"

"Yes," she said, "but he was never anything of a nuisance. I'd call him a private drinker. I liked him. I always did. Towards the end of his time I was sorry for him. He went badly to pieces but I'd never have asked him to leave. My daughter liked him, too. She's a nurse at St. Thomas's."

"Now an indiscreet question. Did you ever know, or suspect, that he had women in his rooms?"

"Never," she said, and flushed slightly. "I don't think he was what you'd call a lady's man at all."

Matthews smiled. "I wasn't thinking of certain kinds of women: just friends, perhaps, or even a patient." He took a photograph from his wallet. "Like this particular woman, for instance. You've never seen her here?"

She gave it a quick look and shook her head. She looked again and frowned.

"Yes, Mrs. Nash?"

"I wouldn't be sure," she said. "I only saw her for a minute. It mightn't even have been her."

It took some time to establish the date before she made it just about three years ago. She'd been in that same living-room and it was about six o'clock. Forester had just got back from evening surgery. Someone was speaking angrily and loudly and she just drew back the curtain in time to see Forester practically hustling a woman down the path to a car, or taxi, drawn up at the gate. It was when the woman had turned in a kind of protest that she'd seen her full-faced. When he and the woman had got into the taxi, she drew the curtain back.

We looked through the window. The path was well lighted, she said. A street lamp, as we could see, and always a light above the door.

"And did Doctor Forester say anything to you about it?"

"Nothing at all. Naturally I didn't ask him."

"But you had private thoughts?"

"It's a long while ago," she said. "Very occasionally a patient would come here instead of to the surgery or to Doctor Caver. Doctor Forester was always strict about that. He never even saw a patient here."

"And what exactly made you think you recognised the woman from this photograph?"

"I couldn't say. Perhaps the hair. It looked practically white in that light."

"And naturally you never clapped eyes on her again?"

"Never. If it was her—I only saw her just that once. You knew her yourself? Or am I wrong to ask that?"

"Not at all," he told her. "He's dead, as I told you, so it's part of our job to look for relatives. Did he have any that you know of?"

She thought he'd once mentioned some relatives—an uncle was it—in Ireland.

"And you never heard of anyone called Laura Mann?" She hadn't. A minute or two and we were thanking her and going back to the car. The driver was told to make for Camden Town.

"Having another word with Charles's manager," Matthews told me. "What'd you make of what that Mrs. Nash told us?"

I didn't see why I should always be the Aunt Sally. "You tell me."

"Well, I think we're on the right lines. If her daughter can make the date more exact and it happens to be, say January, then my guess is this. Laura Farrell did approach Forester and he arranged to do the job. I think he was borrowing a friend's surgery and that's where they were off to that night. He'd told her to be outside with a taxi soon after six and to wait, but she didn't wait. She had to go and ring the bell, and that's what made him riled."

"Just what I think," I said. "She wouldn't dare pick him up at Mayes Road for fear of running across her husband."

If all that were true, it didn't get us much farther. I think we both knew that. Assuming that that operation was successful, what had happened to Laura Mann from then till the day she walked into Caver's surgery, fifteen months later?

"That second pregnancy. That's what beats me," he said. "Still, I suppose it could have happened. She got herself let in once and she might have done it again. Somehow I don't like it, though. It isn't in keeping. Everything we've heard about her makes her as crafty as they come."

I couldn't add anything—unless it was a damper. Crafty or not, there were the facts. She *had* been pregnant again and she had died of an internal haemorrhage in Renfield's nursing home.

We gave it a rest. It was the same driver who'd gone to Hertford Road before, and just after eleven we were turning into that entry and round to the garage. Cantrill, the manager, had been rung and we went into his office. It was all very free and easy, the little time it lasted.

"Still not found any will, sir?" he was asking, almost as soon as we'd shaken hands.

"No, and we shan't do now," Matthews told him. "That doesn't mean you can start cooking the books."

That was a great joke.

"You don't mean you'd give me away?"

"All depends. Cost you a bit to square both of us. But why don't you start going along to that smart little place his brother has in Soho? He's the only relative. Get yourself in well with him and Bob's your uncle. Which reminds me. Your late-lamented boss. Did he ever turn up here with any ladies in his car?"

"Didn't you mention that once before?"

"May have," Matthews said. "You know how it is: the older, the dottier. Present company excepted."

"Nothing dotty about you, sir," Cantrill told him admiringly. "But about women. Never saw him with a woman at all. Strictly business, sir. That was Mr. Charles."

"Fine. Let that be a lesson to you. You read the Sunday papers, so you know what they said happened? The first time he goes out with a woman, she gives him a bullet in the stomach."

Another great joke. Cantrill was still chuckling as he went with us to the car. Matthews shook hands.

"Well, keep your nose clean."

"I'll try, sir."

Cantrill held out a hand to me. I thought there was something just a bit pitying in the way he looked. Still, we can't all be the life and soul of a party.

Matthews dropped me at the flat. There seemed to be nothing else doing and it was near lunch-time, so we left it, as usual, that if anything turned up he'd give me a ring. It was while Bernice and I were having our meal that I showed her one of those photographs of Laura Mann. I reminded her it was three years old.

"I had the impression she was a common sort of person," she said. "She doesn't look it from this. The hair's too showy, of course, but otherwise—"

"Funny you should say that," I got so far and broke off. For a moment the thoughts were just a bit confused. What exactly *did* I know about Laura Farrell as a person? Deductions from Farrell's own statements? The gossip of Mrs. Back, almost certainly biased? Vague impressions front Caver and later from Renfield?

"The fact is I know very little about her," I said as she gave me the photograph back. "Mind you, this was a kind of etherealised job. Farrell's a first-class man and he'd have the lighting and pose and everything just as *he* wanted."

"But wasn't she a dreadful liar?"

I said she was. All the same she'd been capable of putting up a good enough front for Farrell to have swallowed everything she'd said. I didn't put it exactly so to Bernice, but lying and general astuteness weren't necessarily the hall-marks of a gutter-snipe.

There'd been a threat of rain that morning and now it was really coming down. It was colder, too, and I drew my chair up to the fire. I'd intended to tackle a crossword, but before I hardly knew it I was doing some thinking instead. I was wondering about that Lola Manette, the woman who'd been with Charles at the Café Mexique. On the way back from Camden Town, Matthews had told me, the net had been out for her with no results. The superintendent at those flats had discovered nothing—maybe he hadn't even tried. The word had been put out generally but nothing had come in.

That got me to thinking, not for the first time, how lucky Matthews was compared with myself: a children's roundabout on any odd bit of ground, compared with the Ringling Brothers' Circus. I was the roundabout. Or, put it another way. Travers, the lone wolf. If we'd put every man we had on the job they'd hardly have covered that Lola Manette angle. Then, thinking of Matthews, I went back to that hilarious ten minutes with Cantrill. There'd been that joke about an ingratiation at the Café Mexique. A moment or two and I was calling to Bernice. She was pottering about in the bedroom.

"Why shouldn't we have dinner out tonight?"

And that was why, at seven o'clock that night, we were entering the Café Mexique. I was looking for George, the head waiter, but he didn't seem to be there. It was Garrow who caught sight of us and came forward. From the pad in his hand it looked as if George was elsewhere and he was temporarily taking his place. He gave only the faintest sign of recognition.

"Madame. Sir. You have a table?"

"Yes," I said. "Travers is the name."

He consulted the pad. "Ah, yes, sir. Would madame be going to the cloak-room?"

We both were. Garrow seemed to have been waiting for us. Our table was the one I'd occupied before. He motioned to a waiter to attend to us. He held the chair for Bernice. "Haven't I seen you here before, sir?"

He seemed to be playing a game for the benefit of a chance listener. After that he didn't come back to us till half-way through the meal. The waiter took our order and Bernice was taking everything in. My back was towards the main door but she was facing it. She wanted to know why Café Mexique. I told her. I think she'd expected waiters in some sort of costume.

"That woman at the desk. Did you notice her? She looks like one of those young Italian actresses."

I told her she was the wife of the owner, and later on I mentioned that accident. I didn't say that Cavallo was the brother of Martin Charles. That might have looked as if I'd brought her there on false pretences. She did look at one moment just a bit surprised at my knowing so much about the place, but that was just as Garrow came to our table again. I told him everything was fine.

"You acting temporarily?" I asked him, "or has George left?"

"I think he's indisposed, sir." He was speaking very quietly. "This is almost the first time he hasn't arrived. We didn't see him this morning, and all the time we've been expecting him to be here."

"And everything else here about the same?"

"About the same, sir."

We went on with our meal. The place had been filling up and Bernice was definitely enjoying things. We took quite a time over coffee, and then the band could be heard in the room behind me. Bernice said we might dance for an hour. It wasn't all that often nowadays that we went out.

I'm no great shakes as a dancer. I never was. Those long legs of mine have always been hard to manipulate, though I hadn't minded the old pre-war days when you could get away with just gliding over the floor. Bernice is an expert: a classical dancer before we married, and she hasn't let herself run to seed. I don't say I enjoyed myself, well though she managed me. We sat half one cha-cha out before I'd venture on the floor. At any rate we danced till half-past ten. The floor was getting a bit crowded by then, so we fetched our things from the cloak-room. Garrow was lying handy and went with us to the door.

"Hope you've had a nice evening, sir. And you, madame."

His hand touched mine as he went by me to open the door. My fingers closed over a piece of paper. I slipped it into my coat pocket.

The awning was down but the rain had ceased. We were lucky about a taxi, though at a push we might have walked. Bernice said it'd been a lovely evening and we ought to go back there some time. The dinner had been excellent and the wine superb. That head-waiter, too, had been quite a superior sort of man. It just showed, she said, that there were still plenty of small places just as good as the showier ones if you only knew where to find them. There'd been a kind of half-question, so I said I'd known the Café Mexique because of a case.

It was not till she'd gone to the bedroom that I could look at that note. Garrow had written it quickly on what looked like a sheet torn from a pad:

A violent row upstairs last Sunday afternoon. Told she threatened to leave him and he only laughed. Nothing else here.

It told me nothing, so maybe he'd thought he still owed me something for that fiver and was throwing the information in as a sort of extra. If it had been information about the elusive Lola Manette I wouldn't have minded parting with a fiver or two more. As it was, it put me in a rather awkward position. Ought I to tip him if I ever went back? I didn't know. After all, it was really Farrell's money, and I didn't like the idea of throwing it around for virtually nothing at all. I wasn't even interested now in the fact that Cavallo and Charles were brothers. The only reason, for me, why that restaurant, so to speak, was still alive, was that visit there of Lola Manette.

I had another look at that note before dropping it into the w.p.b. It still told me nothing, even that mention of a Sunday afternoon. I knew already that the restaurant didn't open on Sundays.

12

INTO THE PAST

THE next morning brought what I thought was good news. Matthews gave me a ring just before eight o'clock. Yandle's Chief

Constable had been at the Yard the previous evening and there'd been a conference about the Braid case. The Braid murder was the name for it now. That wound on the skull had been from something heavy and sharp-edged, like a spanner or tyre lever. If she'd committed suicide by jumping from one of the two bridges, there was no projection on which she could possibly have struck her head and there'd been nothing along the banks like the heavy branch of a tree. Also that grey felt hat had been found caught up in a tangle of debris only a few hundred yards past where the body had been found, with a trace of blood inside the crown and an abrasion that must have been caused by the same weapon. The assumption was that she'd been killed just up-stream from where she'd been found and the hat thrown in after her. That stream ran parallel to the road and never more than a few feet from it for at least a couple of hundred yards each way.

If she'd had her tea at her usual time of four o'clock, then she'd died at about half-past six.

The upshot of that conference had been that the Yard was as good as taking over the case. There were far too many ramifications for it to be regarded as something largely for local enquiry. For one thing, there seemed a definite connection between Mary Braid and Laura Mann, and still a possibility that something in the career of Laura Mann held a clue to the Charles murder, and there was still the mystery as to why Charles had been shot in her husband's flat. The whole thing was a piece of string tied in knots and you couldn't get that string unravelled by tackling just one of the knots.

Matthews was leaving for Little Warberry just before ten. It was a fine morning but cold, and when I'd looked out just after dawn, the roofs had been white. Hassack went with us and we were meeting Yandle at Willow Cottage. Our cars arrived practically together. We had a short talk in the dining-room with the electric fire on, and we learned two things.

Mary Braid had once made a will. Her solicitors had asked her to let them scrutinise it but she never had. The actual date of drawing up hadn't been determined. That didn't matter much since it must have later been destroyed. She actually made another will at the end of April, 1957. It was witnessed by the postman—he happened to be going by and was called in—and the daily woman, a Mrs. Allen, and again it had not been deposited with the solicitors, or the bank. And it hadn't been found anywhere in the cottage. Once more there was a good reason—that it too had been destroyed. About the end of last April, Mary Braid told Mrs. Allen she was going to make another will, and Mrs. Allen was to remind her. No one knew anything about any such will, and it, too, hadn't been found.

"Think I could see this Mrs. Allen?" Matthews wanted to know. "Something else might turn up that we want to ask her about."

Hassack went off to fetch her. Yandle told us the other thing he'd discovered, this time from the bank. Mary Braid was a well-to-do woman and always had three or four hundred pounds on a current account, a balance above that being invested at the end of each financial year. Her expenses weren't great—income tax was easily the biggest item—and about once a month she cashed a cheque for thirty pounds. It was such a regular drawing that the Corley cashiers not only guessed the amount but how she'd ask for it—twenty ones and twenty tens. But on the 13th of April, 1957, she did what was for her a most unusual thing: cashed a cheque for a hundred pounds and asked for it in five-pound notes.

"Those dates," I said. "Both happenings in that April. You know what also happened then?"

"Yes," Matthews said. "Looks as if there might be something in it. Laura Mann died on that 13th of April."

"And Laura Mann had a wad of notes when she entered that nursing home."

"But the dates are wrong. Laura's hundred pounds couldn't have been the same. She had hers on the 12th. The Braid cheque wasn't till the 13th. But that will business. It could be that she'd made a will with Laura Mann one of the beneficiaries, and then when Laura died, she talked of making a new will."

Yandle said the coincidences had struck him, too. He himself had gone through every possible place in the house to try to find a will.

"Any secret drawers in that bureau in her room?"

"Good Lord!" he said. "Never thought of that."

We went up at once. The suggestion had been mine so I had to do the examining. I tried all the usual places and even made rough measurements, but as far as I could judge there wasn't a cubic inch of unused space.

"Ah, well," Yandle said. "No one can say we didn't try." It was just then, as we still stood there, that my eye caught something. It was just a momentary trick of the light, but on the wall-paper above that bureau was a small, almost square patch of a slightly different colour.

"Been a small picture hanging here. And look. Here's the tiny hole where there's been one of those pin fasteners." They had a look.

"More like the size of a photograph," Matthews said. "Wonder what it was."

There was the sound of voices from downstairs.

"Sounds like Mrs. Allen. She might know about it. No harm in asking."

He called down for Hassack to ask her to come up. She turned out to be younger than I'd expected. Yandle told us later she was twenty-six. Her husband was an agricultural worker who didn't get home at mid-day, which was why she'd had time to work at Willow Cottage. She was a nice-looking woman: shy and just a bit inarticulate. It took us quite a time to get the history of what had been hanging there. Matthews had been right. It was a photograph, taken, she thought, a good few years before: Miss Braid and Dora sitting and the rector standing just behind them.

"Dora? Who's Dora?"

What she told us brought back memories. I'd got my calling-up notice on the Wednesday before the outbreak of war, and on the Thursday, on my way to Southampton, I'd seen on the platform of quite a few stations the lines of children awaiting evacuation. Dora Clabbon had been evacuated, to Little Warberry, and was one of two girls who'd been billeted at the rectory. Later her parents had been killed in the blitz and later still the other girl had gone back to London. Dora apparently had had no other relations, and as the rector and his sister had grown fond of her, they adopted her. Mary Braid had often spoken of her as a niece. Mrs. Allen said she was spoilt: badly spoilt.

She was sent to the Girls' Grammar School at Corley and left at sixteen. She then had two years at the rectory and there was much talk about her and various village boys. Next she had a job in town. No one actually knew what it was but Miss Braid said she was studying art. For the next three or four years she used to come home at most week-ends, but after the rector died she hardly came at all. Then, two years ago. Miss Braid announced that she'd suddenly got married and gone with her husband to America. Miss Braid had letters from her at varying intervals.

"How'd you know?" Matthews asked her.

"Well, I used to ask after her sometimes and that's when she used to tell me she'd heard from her. She told me where she was living and all about her husband and everything."

Matthews looked at Yandle. Yandle shook his head.

"No letters that I could find. Maybe she didn't keep them."

"What was this Dora Clabbon like?" I said.

"Oh, very good-looking. Had the loveliest hair. Red, it was: well, not red. What they call auburn, if you know what I mean. Sort of a light red. Not ginger or anything like that."

"And a very pretty colour, too," Matthews told her. "But about this photograph. When did you see it last?"

She looked surprised. She was sure it'd been hanging there the very last time she'd been in that room. Not that it'd always been there. About two years ago it hadn't been there and Mrs. Allen had enquired about it. Miss Braid said she'd put it away. Dora had been behaving badly in America, she said, and she wasn't at all pleased with her. And then a few months ago it had suddenly been in its place again. The following brief conversation had taken place.

> *"I see you've got Miss Dora's photograph up again, Miss."*
>
> *"Yes, Carrie, I have. In this life you've got to learn to forget and forgive. Never forget that, Carrie."*
>
> *"No, Miss, I won't."*

"Any likelihood of there being another copy of that photograph in the village?" Yandle wanted to know.

She was almost sure there was: Mrs. Fraser had one, she thought, in her parlour. The rectory had had a house-parlour-maid and a cook. The former had gone away, but Mrs. Fraser still lived in the village: half of the big thatched cottage almost opposite the Red Lion.

"Just one other question while we're at it," Matthews said. "How old would Dora be when she first came here?"

"About nine or ten: somewhere about that. But Mrs. Fraser would know." And that was about all. We went down to the dining-room and did some confirming of that will business, and then Carrie Allen left. There was a short silence when the door had closed on her and Hassack. It was Matthews who broke it.

"I don't know about you two, but I'm beginning to have ideas. Correct me if I'm wrong, but what about this Dora Clabbon having become Laura Mann?"

"Went through my mind, too," Yandle said. "She might have had that hair of hers dyed."

"And Dora Clabbon isn't the most attractive of names. Laura Mann's much more stylish."

Matthews turned it all over for a moment. Too many things to digest in a hurry, he said. So what about getting that Mrs. Fraser to fill in a few gaps.

There was no trouble in finding the cottage, and Ellen Fraser was at home. She looked well on the way to seventy: shortish, ample-bosomed and her tightly drawn-back white hair making her face more plump than it need have been. Yandle did the talking and we had quite a lachrymose five minutes while she told us about the rectory and poor Miss Braid. Then she fetched that photograph.

"I was there, of course, when they had it took," she told us, "and I said how I'd like to have one, so Miss Mary give me this one, and I had it framed, like you see. Very good it was, just like life."

Yandle passed it to Matthews. He asked how old Dora was at the time. She had to do quite a bit of thinking.

"Just before she left school. I remember now. She didn't like her school uniform and Miss Mary wanted her to wear it but she wouldn't. Rare headstrong, she was."

"And about ten, was she, when she first came here?"

"That's right, sir. Her birthday was the following year."

"That'd be in March?"

"Oh, no, sir. Just after Christmas, far as I remember."

"You're sure? You're not confusing her with the other evacuee?"

She did some more thinking.

"I don't know, sir. Perhaps I am. Doris—that's the other one—and her was much of an age. It's a long while ago." Then she looked up. "No, sir. I'm sure I'm right. It *was* in January. There always used to be presents and things and I had to make a special cake."

"Glad you remembered it," Matthews said. "We can borrow this photograph for just a couple of days? We'll see it comes to no harm."

"Have it and welcome, sir. Better let me dust it first, though."

"Those evacuees all came from Bethnal Green, didn't they?" Yandle asked her.

"That's right, sir. I once went through it in the train and I wouldn't have lived there, not if you'd paid me."

"You liked this girl, Dora?"

She smiled. "Couldn't help liking her, sir. Very pretty she was. Got a bit wild, though. Too fond of the boys, as they say. Used to worry Miss Mary no end."

"You knew she'd married and gone to America?"

"Oh, yes, sir. I always saw Miss Mary quite a lot. She sometimes used to tell me about her. A pity, I told her, the rector wasn't alive and then we could have had the wedding at the church, 'stead of one o' them registry offices."

We said good-bye. She'd still be there if Yandle should think of any more questions. We'd drawn Yandle's car up a little way on, and we stood there talking for a minute or two.

"I think our place is back in town," Matthews finally said. "There's more than a chance of picking up the trail of Dora Clabbon if it was true about her studying art. What about you? Think you ought to fill her dossier in a bit more from down here?"

Yandle thought it a good idea. We said good-bye and walked on to the police station. The car was there and I sat in it while Matthews did some telephoning. It must have been a good quarter of an hour before he came back. He thought we ought to push on to Warnham and get some lunch there.

That's what we did. We found a promising pub and did our talking over the meal. I'd been a bit worried about that birthday date. Laura Mann had been born on the 14th of March. I had to admit that otherwise the ages seemed to fit in.

"Doesn't worry me," Matthews said. "When she changed her name she changed the whole bag of tricks, birthday and all. Everything fits in, doesn't it?"

There was still a snag. "How did Mary Braid know Laura—let's call her that—was dead?"

"Easy," he said. "There was the money, so that registrar had notices of death in the columns of *The Times* and the *Daily Telegraph*. Mary Braid took *The Times*."

"And that hundred pounds? Mary Braid didn't pay anything towards the funeral expenses."

"Might have bought herself some black clothes for all we know. And she didn't come forward because she'd washed her hands of her. That yarn about an American husband was just to save face. Later on she got a fit of repentance and put that photograph up again. And planted those bulbs."

"That's how I saw it," I said. "Still another snag, though. Just why was she killed?"

"There you go," he said, and not too seriously. "Never satisfied. Here we get all this clean out of the blue and you expect it to solve the whole thing. So what about taking it nice and steady? Get the tie-up between this Dora Clabbon and Laura Mann, and if I know anything, we'll pick up a whole lot of other things on the way."

"You're the boss," I said. "I never thought it'd come to it but there we are. And what're you actually doing?"

"It's being done," he said. "By the time we get back there might be some answers from one of those schools of art." But there weren't. It was after three o'clock when we got back, and the only information that had come in was from Somerset House. Dora

Clabbon had been born on January the 3rd, 1930, at Instow Road, Bethnal Green. If she and Laura Mann were the same person, then she'd been twenty-seven at the time of death, as had the Laura Mann of the death certificate. There was no birth certificate for a Laura Mann at any comparable time.

I asked about the marriage certificate. Matthews said he'd got that from Paris a few days ago. Laura Mann, spinster, aged twenty-six years, was given as the daughter of an Alfred Mann, artist, since deceased, of Brick Street, Chelsea.

"And that's a lie," Matthews told me. "There isn't a Brick Street, Chelsea, or anywhere near." He clicked his tongue in annoyance. "Why that moon-struck Farrell never found out more about her, I'll never know."

"He was just a receiver," I said, "and she the transmitter. She just fed him this and that. And, far as he was concerned, the whole thing was an extraordinary emotional experience. He didn't know if he was on his head or his heels."

"Well, God save us from geniuses," he told me. And that was about all that was said. He was reporting to Jewle, so I made my way home. Or that's what I'd intended, and then it suddenly struck me that there was quite a bit of daylight yet, so I looked for a taxi. It was an elderly driver who picked me up. I told him to take me to Instow Road, Bethnal Green.

We went by the Embankment and turned up past Liverpool Street. Then came an area I didn't know so well. There were still open spaces left by the bombing, and on others there were new blocks of flats. The taxi came to a halt.

"Here you are, sir. Instow Road. Want me to wait?"

I got out and had a look round. Instow Road now ran north of one of those new flat areas. There must have been a lot of bomb-ing: those flats had plenty of space.

"Not much use to me," I said. "You didn't happen to know it before the war?"

He'd known it well. He'd been born less than a mile away and had had a sister living in Nethercott Road.

"That one there, sir, on the far side. She was evacuated, and when she come back there wasn't nothing there. Lived with us for a time till she got herself a place."

There was no point in staying there. I could hunt for a month and never find a soul who'd known the Clabbon family. I did mention it, just in case.

"Clabbon," he said. "Clabbon. I think there was a Clabbon kept a newsagent's and tobacconist's shop in Instow Road. I was in it once or twice when I was down this way just before the war."

"This Clabbon was killed during the bombing. He and his wife."

"Not the only ones," he told me. "All round here they copped it pretty bad."

I let him take me right back to the flat. I gave him a good tip when I paid him off.

"You didn't happen to know anyone called Mann round those parts?"

I gave him a private card. It'd be worth a quid to him if he should happen to pick anything up.

I made myself some tea and later on rang Matthews. I said I'd been a bit at a loose end after I'd left him and had mooched along to Instow Road. The whole area had completely changed since the Clabbons' time.

"Just got the death certificates," he told me. "Both killed in almost the first big raid. What was your idea, though, in going there?"

"Local colour," I said. "Just something to do."

"Right," he said. "Give you a ring if anything else turns up."

Bernice came in and later we had dinner and then I moved my chair to the fire and sat thinking about the day that had almost gone, and somehow I was always coming back to what still seemed to me a snag—that difference in birthdays. I didn't like that off-hand theory of Matthews's, that Dora Clabbon had had a complete change of personality which had included a change of birthday. What point had there been in changing a birthday? What earthly difference could it make?

It wasn't as if she had changed the year only as a means, say, of making herself out to be younger than she was. All that was needed was just to tell the lie. How old are you? So-and-so, just like that. And the change of date hadn't meant a change of year: just on from January to the March of the same year. Matthews might be right but I didn't see it. People did queer things—I did myself—but behind the doing was usually some reason or justification. In the case of Dora Clabbon I couldn't see either.

Then I was wondering about that photograph and what use Matthews expected to make of it. There's all the difference in the world between a girl of fifteen or sixteen and the woman of twenty-seven. Traces maybe of the same person but surely not enough to make really possible an identification of the woman. I was pondering all that, or maybe I'd shifted on to something else when the telephone went. I wondered what Matthews had for me.

"Is that you, Mr. Travers?"

I knew the voice and yet I didn't. "Yes. Who's speaking?"

"Garrow, sir. Of the Café Mexique. Just slipped out for a second, sir. You've heard about Lemon?"

"Lemon?" I said. "Oh, yes: the head waiter. Anything happened to him?"

"Dead, sir. You remember he was away yesterday and when he didn't arrive this evening, Mrs. Cavallo sent someone round to his flat to find out. The police have just been here, sir. I rather gather it's suicide."

"Haven't heard a thing," I said. "Where's he live?"

"Mayworth Street. About three minutes from here. Don't know the number but it's on the left-hand side going down. Above a little restaurant. Chez Victor. Anything else you want to know, sir? I ought to be getting back."

I thanked him and rang off. As soon as the receiver was back I wondered if I should have congratulated him. That ill wind would almost certainly blow him into Lemon's job. My hand went out to pick up the receiver again: to call Matthews, not Garrow.

But I didn't pick it up after all. Matthews wouldn't be in charge of a suicide. His plate was full. And though liaison at the Yard is superlatively good, I doubted if anyone as yet was linking the suicide of Lemon with the Charles case.

If it *were* linked up. At the moment I didn't see how it could be and I went back to my chair. In the morning I'd mention it to Matthews. If he didn't ring me first.

13
THE LONG, LONG TRAIL

I DID the telephoning, around nine o'clock the next morning. Matthews hadn't heard about the death of George Lemon. In fact it took him a moment or two to recall who Lemon was.

"You think there's some sort of tie-in?"

"Don't see how there can be," I said. "I got the news from that waiter pal of mine."

"Can't see how Cavallo and Charles being brothers could affect a head-waiter," he said. "Tell you what: I'll ring you again in a minute or two."

I had to wait nearer half an hour. Might as well have a look at things, he said, so what about meeting him there. It wasn't far to walk and the place wasn't hard to find. Mayworth Street is an architect's nightmare: a jumble of everything and most of it less than a hundred years old. Chez Victor had once been a private house with its yellowish brick now a greenish grey. The ground floor had a pair of windows that looked nearly new, and the usual twin tubs with clipped shrubs were nicely balanced each side of the door. It looked a cross between the second class and the fly-specked. The other floor was entered by a side door. The general lay-out was rather like that of Farrell's flat in Mayes Road.

I was crossing the street to wait on the other side, when the police car drove up. Matthews and another man got out. He was an Inspector Brimbell, the one in charge of the case.

"So you people think there might be a tie-in," he told me. "Won't do any harm, though, if there ain't."

He led the way up the flight of stairs and unlocked the door.

We went straight into a small living-room. Lemon hadn't wasted a lot of money on furnishings, nor was the room particularly clean. For twenty pounds a dealer could have bought the lot: worn carpet, pair of easy chairs, fumed oak table and sideboard to match. There was a cupboard, once white, with a door open, and Brimbell was making for it.

"Did himself well in the drink line." He waved a hand. "Whisky, sherry, liqueurs—the lot. Especially this."

This was the usual green bottle, a Martini e Rossi Vermouth Vino Secco.

"This one's empty. The half-full one's at the Yard. And this is the stuff he took the sleeping pills in. Cenophine. Don't know yet how many he took but the box was empty. They hold twenty."

Matthews had a look at the bottle. "Not so hot on Italian myself but looks like dry vermouth. The stuff they make cocktails of."

"It wasn't a cocktail glass. It was a tumbler. Only just a little in the bottom."

"Might have been a big Martini," I said. "A Bronx would be better. Orange juice and three parts gin and the rest Italian. A Martini's made with French if I remember right."

"Plenty of gin as you see," Brimbell said. "In here is where he was found."

The bedroom was about ten by ten: just room for the medium-sized bed, a small wardrobe, a chair and a rather battered chest of drawers. There was a bedside table with a lamp.

"That's where the glass stood, and the empty box," he told us. "That's where he was curled up. Must have gone off like a baby."

The rest of the flat comprised a small bathroom and a still smaller kitchen, with a gas-ring, a cupboard and a tiny sink with draining-board and plate-rack.

"And that's the lot?"

"That's the lot," Brimbell told him. "What'd you expect? The Chamber of Horrors?"

"Always hopeful," Matthews said, and gave me a wink. "Didn't do a lot of cooking here, did he?"

"No need to. He had all his meals where he worked except breakfast. Only had to walk downstairs or across the road for that."

Matthews had another question in the sitting-room. "Anybody any ideas on why he took sleeping tablets at all?"

"Nobody knew he did. There was another full packet in that bathroom though."

"Anybody think he had anything on his mind?"

"No," he said. "We were up to all hours questioning the staff at that restaurant. Saw everybody including Cavallo himself. And he looks a pretty mess, too. Saw his wife who's running the place. Gave this Lemon the best of characters and reckoned his references had been first-class. No chance of embezzling anything or cooking accounts. Wasn't too popular with the staff, but a man doesn't do himself in for that, not when he was making the sort of living he was."

"Might have got in deep with the bookies."

Brimbell shrugged his shoulders. "Haven't been over the place yet. Haven't had time. A lot depends on what the lab. boys turn up."

"That Cenophine," I said to Matthews. "You remember that Marstead case and that chap Tweed?"

"Yes," he said. "Remember it well. He did himself in with Cenophine."

"And wasn't it soluble in water?"

"That's right. He took a dose in the kitchen before he opened the door."

"What's it all about?" Brimbell said.

"Just keep quiet for a minute," Matthews told him. "Mr. Travers is working up to a theory."

"Not at all. It isn't my job and it isn't my place." Brimbell wasn't satisfied. "You must have had some reason, sir, or you wouldn't have mentioned it."

"If you put it like that, maybe I did. Only that since Cenophine is soluble, you could drop it in somebody's drink. It has a slightly bitter taste but, on the other hand, what's more bitter than dry vermouth?"

Matthews grinned. "You see? Always looking on the bright side. And leaving you with a fresh headache. Did he fall or was he pushed?"

Brimbell didn't even smile. "Against what we've learned so far," he said. "And just a bit far-fetched. No offence meant to you, sir."

I was wondering if I should tell him about Garrow, and somehow there seemed a kind of treachery in it. Garrow had hated Lemon.

"You said the staff didn't like him," was what I said, "so I was wondering if any of them was ostensibly friendly enough to come here at all. Not that the whole thing isn't, as you say, very far-fetched."

Matthews was looking at his watch. "Well, I've got to be getting along. You staying on, Jack?"

Brimbell said he was. He saw us off from the top of the stairs. As soon as we'd turned back into Medway Street, Matthews was asking if I'd really believed what I'd suggested—that Lemon's death wasn't all it seemed. I said frankly that I didn't know. I knew nothing about Lemon's private life, but that talk of Cenophine had happened to recall that Marstead affair. I washed the whole thing out by wanting to know if we were going anywhere special. Then we were doing a bit of a sprint to catch a Victoria bus and it wasn't till we were on top that he told me.

"We've got a clue or two to that Dora Clabbon. She hadn't been to either of the big art schools and then they struck lucky at one of the smaller ones. The New—" He got out his note-book. "The New Barbizon. Always thought a barbizon was something like a trumpet."

I didn't disillusion him.

"A smaller place in Bayswater. She was there three years off and on, principally off. Practically gave up day classes and finally only turned up occasionally in the evenings. We got the address of the last rooms she was in, but she'd left. Just before I saw Brimbell this morning, we got a message from the Barbizon place to say one of their students thought she'd gone to a dramatic school, the Mendel School at Notting Hill. That's where we're off to now."

I wondered what she'd been up to if she'd practically abandoned day classes.

"Don't know," he said. "The old lady must have been paying up for everything, and she wouldn't have taken a lot of hood-winking. The great thing is this. Know how old Dora was when she left that art school? Twenty-one. The way I see it is that she was then on her own with a fixed allowance. Yandle's seeing the bank about that."

We got off the bus at the foot of Whitehall. Inside ten minutes we were on the way to Notting Hill and we'd the usual driver. Matthews had told me he knew the suburbs like the back of his hand. All I know is we went through streets I'd never seen. I might have been anywhere northwest till we turned into a main road. A couple of minutes and we turned off it into Charter Street. The school was just on the left-hand side: a Georgian survival with a little semicircular drive.

"They should have been rung," Matthews told me, "so we shouldn't be long. Either they know something, or they don't."

The fine Georgian door was wide open, and we went through to a spacious hall. A period staircase led up from the back and what looked like an office was on the left. From somewhere at the back came the sound of music.

Quite a pretty girl emerged from a door behind the office. Matthews showed her his card and said we were expected. She didn't look surprised. Mr. Julius would see us.

We went through that door and just along a corridor to another door on the left. She looked in, announced us, gave us a smile and showed us in.

Julius Mendel was about seventy: bald but for a fringe of white. He wore a grey moustache and imperial, and if he hadn't been a bit too full-faced he'd have looked like an ageing Napoleon the Third. His gestures were a bit theatrical and his manners charming. To my surprise he spoke without a trace of accent. He gave a quick look at Matthews's warrant card and shook hands with both of us. If I'd been asked to place him, I'd have said he was what my wife would have called a dear.

"I'm afraid no *Dora* Clabbon," he told us. "A Dorothy Clabbon. The name's so uncommon we think it must be the same person."

"If she came here in 'fifty-one, she'd be just twenty-one," Matthews said. "Height about five-foot-six, good figure and light-ish auburn hair."

"Yes," he said. "If you will pardon me a minute, I'll have a word with my sister."

The sister came back with him: a tall, Wagnerian woman of about sixty. I didn't quite catch her name but it sounded like Lydia Lodovski. She, too, had the most charming manners.

"She must be the one you want," she told us. "I remember her well. Dora, of course, isn't the most fashionable of names."

"She re-christened herself."

"Exactly. If it's any help, she had an aunt who came here shortly after she enrolled. We're always very happy to see relatives."

"The aunt was a Miss Braid?"

"Of course," she said, and smiled. "I remember the name. The country gentlewoman type."

"Describes her exactly," Matthews said. "And what course was Miss Clabbon taking here?"

It turned out to be the Barbizon over again. She actually enrolled for a general course in drama. Then she dropped the day courses and came only in the evenings. The only things in which she showed any interest were elocution and deportment.

"I was making some enquiries just before you arrived," Madame Lodovski said, "and Helen Franks, who's still in charge of that department, seems to remember that Dorothy was doing some kind of day work. She thinks it was modelling."

"You have a whole series of courses here?" I asked her.

"Quite a few," she said. "The house is quite large and we were able to make an extension at the back. In addition to the usual dramatic course, we have a ballet class and another in voice production. Guenevere Lane is in charge of that. Daughter of Frederick Lane, you know: the composer."

"And how long was Miss Clabbon actually here?"

She smiled. "Off and on, for two years."

"And you have her address—her then address?"

"I think so," she said. "It should be in the files."

Julius seemed to be the business manager. It took him quite a time to find what he wanted. Dora Clabbon had lived at 17 Oldbury Street. He said it was only about five minutes' walk. You just went straight on and took the first to the right.

They were nice people. It was a pleasure, somehow, to have spent those few minutes there. We thanked them and moved on to Oldbury Street: an old-fashioned backwater that hadn't gone too badly down. Number 17 was a three-storied house in late Victorian Queen Anne. An elderly maid answered the bell.

She had a look at Matthews's card. I don't know if she was scared but she just looked at him as she handed it back. "You've been here a long time?"

"Yes."

"You remember a Dora or Dorothy Clabbon who had rooms here about four years ago?" He smiled. "Nothing to be frightened about. We're just trying to find her, that's all."

"Wait here and I'll speak to Miss Tait."

We waited. She'd left the door just ajar and Matthews pushed it open with a foot. We could see an entrance with stairs leading up. There was a warmish smell as of long-eaten meals.

The maid came back. "Will you come up, please. Miss Tait has had influenza and she's in the sitting-room."

We followed her up the carpeted stairs to a wide landing. A door was open. She showed us through and closed it behind us. Miss Tait, a thinnish woman of about sixty, was in an easy chair and a dullish coal fire was in the grate. She swivelled round to look at us. Matthews gave her the card, and the patter. He added an extra about the influenza. As she handed back the card he introduced me.

"I'm practically well again," she told us. "Just taking things easy for a day or two. Ethel tells me you're making enquiries about Dorothy Clabbon. She left us about two years ago, you know. I hope it's nothing serious?"

Just wanted as a possible witness, Matthews said. He gave a description, just to make sure. Everything tallied.

"Sorry to keep bothering you, but do you happen to know where she went?"

"I think I may do. Of course I don't know if she's still there." She was making for a mahogany bureau-bookcase. "She left some of her things behind and came back for them later."

Her back was towards us and we could see her going through this drawer and that.

"I'm sure it's here somewhere. I always write down the addresses of my girls."

Another minute and there was a triumphant, "Ah!" Matthews took the address down, saying it aloud for my benefit.

"Twenty-one Westgate Street, Knightsbridge. Thank you, Miss Tait. We're very much obliged. And you haven't seen her or heard of her since she fetched these things?"

She hadn't. A minute or two and we were back in the car. It was getting on for one o'clock but I wasn't hungry. We'd had so much luck that I wanted to get on. Matthews was praying, too, that the vein wouldn't peter out.

No use worrying about extras, he said. We could always go back.

"Two years with that Miss Tait." He took out his notebook and began making entries. "I work it out that she was then twenty-five. Wonder where she was modelling."

Westgate Street was another backwater, tucked away a few hundred yards from the Park. Number 21 was a maisonette wedged between a little millinery shop and a Georgian house. Matthews pushed the bell. It was quite a time before it was answered, and this time by a slightly bent, elderly woman. Her black dress was high at the collar and there was something of the Victorian governess about her. Matthews introduced himself and me and followed up with the spiel.

"Dorothy Clabbon," she said slowly. "I'm sorry but I don't know the name."

"About twenty-five. Five-foot six, and well built. Had what I'm told was very nice auburn hair."

Something was ringing a bell. "Dorothy Delaine! It sounds exactly like her." I heard Matthews's sigh of relief.

"May we come in for a minute?"

"Of course," she said. "I have the downstairs rooms now. This was Dorothy's little room. It's a small flat, really."

It was a pleasant room with the one large window overlooking the street. The one other door led doubtless to bedroom, bath and miniature kitchen.

"She isn't with you now?"

"Oh, no," she said. "She left—when would it be?—just over two years ago. In the January. I believe she was joining a friend in a bigger flat. I think she mentioned Streatham. Won't you gentlemen sit down?"

Matthews and I shared a small chesterfield.

"And do smoke if you wish. I think I'll have one myself."

I offered my case and held the lighter.

"This is rather exciting," she told us. "I never thought I'd be talking to two officers from Scotland Yard. And I'm glad nothing's happened to Dorothy. She was a nice girl, really."

"So I believe. Dorothy Delaine, of course, was a sort of stage name. What was she actually doing?"

"She was a model. Wait a moment. I think I can find something."

She began looking through the drawers of a reproduction bureau.

"I must have put them somewhere else. There's only this. I had several once."

What she showed us was a travel brochure. A strikingly beautiful girl in a bikini was smiling and waving. Her back was to a palm tree, the blue sea and a stretch of beach just beyond.

"A fine-looking girl," I said. "She looks pretty tanned."

"It suited her. She always had one of those sun-ray lamps in her bedroom. She took it with her when she left."

"You have her address?"

"No," she said slowly. "I felt a bit hurt about her never writing. She'd promised she would."

Something was dawning on me. It was dawning on Matthews, too.

"What is your name, by the way?"

"Francis. Margaret Francis."

"Mrs. or Miss?"

"Mrs. My husband was a solicitor in Bedford. He died about two years ago."

"Then tell us, Mrs. Francis, if you know anything about a holiday Miss Delaine took about three years ago. Our information is that she was in France just before the Christmas and came back in the January. You remember that?"

"It's wrong. She never took a holiday. She was what you call a free-lance and she was always working. It must have been somebody else."

He gave her a smile. "Excuse me if I have to be very careful about this. From our point of view it's highly important. So let me put it another way. Cast your mind back to the mid-winter of three years ago. Miss Delaine had then been with you for about a year. She was here all the time?"

"All the time. Very occasionally she was away for a night or a week-end but she was always here. Never away for any longer."

So that was that. The rest was an anti-climax.

"Thank you, Mrs. Francis. Our information was obviously wrong. Can you tell us, by the way, any of the people she worked for?"

She frowned. She'd forgotten the names. There was a big advertising firm if only she could remember it. Then she smiled.

"But of course! Riccardo's. She did quite a lot of work for them."

Riccardo's turned out to be Riccardo, court photographer, of Lerwick Street. From where we were, about a hundred yards past Harrods. Just inside that side street to the left.

Another few moments and we were walking back to the car. From the look of our faces you'd have thought we'd been robbed.

"Well, there we are," Matthews told me. "It's the very devil. Another theory blown sky-high. I thought it was getting too good to last."

We waited for a gap in the traffic and crossed the road to the car.

"Where to now, sir?"

"Nowhere," Matthews said. "Go on reading your paper."

I don't know what he was thinking about. I was thinking about that theory: now, as he'd said, blown sky-high. Dora Clabbon and Laura Mann weren't one and the same person. Laura Mann had been marrying Farrell while Dora was still in Westgate Street. You couldn't get away from it. That Mrs. Francis had been too sure and emphatic.

"Right," Matthews said resignedly. He looked at his watch. "Might as well get a bit of lunch and plan the next move."

We waited for another traffic gap and made a right turn. The driver said he knew of a place but we tried Harrods. We didn't do a lot of talking during the meal. Before it came we'd decided what we'd do, even if we hadn't much heart in it.

"No use getting there much before half-past two." It was Riccardo he was talking about. "Probably closed till then."

It was just about half-past when we came out. We moved on to Lerwick Street and turned left. You couldn't miss the place: a double-fronted establishment with class written all over it. The windows had a backing of dark velvet and on small easels were photographs framed in light wood. There weren't more than a dozen of them, women for the most part. One was definitely of an ex-Prime Minister. Above the door in a long, flowing script, was just the one word—RICCARDO.

14
END OF TRAIL

THAT reception room was handsome in a decorous way. A deep-piled carpet matched the reddish brown of mahogany. The hanging portraits were framed in red maple, and on the reproduction Chippendale table a huge bowl of scarlet and blue anemones went superbly with the old gold of the walls. It was a room in which you wouldn't feel like speaking too loud.

A tall, beautifully coiffeured brunette smiled at us languidly from the reception desk.

"You have appointments?"

The smile went as we came up. Her eyes had been over us and there was something just a bit wrong. Matthews gave her a smile of his own.

"Afraid we haven't. Just making an enquiry."

He held out the warrant card. There was quite a hesitation before she took it.

"From Scotland Yard. Just making a few enquiries. This gentleman is a colleague."

The powdered nose wrinkled as she gave the card back.

"How very interesting. What do you want to enquire about?"

"Well, just this and that. Any of the management available?"

"Not at the moment. Mr. Hammond isn't back from lunch yet. He's the one you should see."

"He's one of the principals?"

"Mr. Hammond *is* the principal," she told him severely.

"Sorry," he said, still smiling. "Any idea when he'll be back?"

"I can't say. He hasn't an appointment till a quarter past three."

"Then perhaps you'll help us, Miss—is it Miss?"

That brought back the smile. Matthews always had a way with him.

"Yes," she said. "Miss Conroy."

"Right. Miss Conroy. We're trying to trace a Miss Delaine. Dorothy Delaine. I believe she occasionally worked here."

Her nose had been wrinkling. The lip definitely drooped. "Oh, yes. Dorothy Delaine. I'm afraid we didn't have very much in common."

"She still comes here?"

"Not now. She hasn't been here for—how long would it be?— well, at least two years."

"I see." He turned on the charm again. "Just between ourselves, she wasn't popular round here?"

"With some people she was."

Her voice suddenly changed. It took on a certain hauteur. "Here is Mr. Hammond."

She'd been facing the door; we hadn't.

"These gentlemen are from Scotland Yard, sir. They wish to make some enquiries."

He, too, was beautifully groomed. He was tall, well built and looked about forty. His hair was just beginning to grey at the temples but the trim beard was a golden brown.

"Enquiries?" He frowned. "Here?"

"About Dorothy Delaine."

We didn't know why, but it shook him. For a moment or two the whole of him was curiously still. He cleared his throat.

"Delaine. . . . Of course. Perhaps you'd better come to my room."

We went through the door by the desk into a beautifully fitted office. The furnishings and colour scheme were the same. A vase of narcissi stood on his desk and their scent made me think of funerals.

"May I see your credentials?"

Matthews handed over the card.

"Thank you, Inspector." His eyes ran over me. "And this gentle-man?"

"A Home Office colleague," Matthews said blandly. "He doesn't carry a card."

"The name's Travers," I told him.

He nodded. He took his time about hanging overcoat and hat on the corner stand. The dark brown worsted suit must have stood him back at least thirty pounds. I couldn't place the tie but it looked rather like an Old Reptonian.

He went down slowly behind the flat-topped desk. He moved the flower-vase a little farther to one side before he looked up.

"Inspector, you were talking to my receptionist. I strongly resent that. I insist on hearing precisely what you were told."

Matthews smiled. "I don't think I'd worry, sir—"

"Worry?"

"Well, make an issue of it. She told us virtually nothing. Simply tacitly agreed that this Dorothy Delaine had worked here."

Hammond's lip curled. "You really expect me to believe that?"

I cut in. "I think it's a matter of indifference to both of us what you believe or disbelieve, Mr. Hammond. You asked a question and you had a true answer."

"You realise that I have influence? Plenty of influence."

"No need for argument," Matthews told him. "All we came here to do, sir, was ask a few simple questions. If you don't wish to answer them, then we might have to ask you to go with us to Scotland Yard."

"I haven't refused."

"Glad to hear it, sir. So about this Dorothy Delaine. What sort of work did she do here?"

"She was a professional model," he said almost curtly. "We enter studies for international exhibitions. And sell them to high-class periodicals and magazines: here and on the Continent and in America."

"I see, sir. And when did she first come here?"

Hammond's expression had changed. Something had suddenly struck him.

"Would you mind telling me what this is all about? I rather resent being kept in the dark."

"We'd have come to it in good time, sir," Matthews said imperturbably. "We think she can help us in a certain case."

"May I ask what case?"

Matthews smiled. "I'm afraid not, sir. These things have to be kept quiet till the right time."

"Nothing's happened to her?"

He was being uncommonly pertinacious. Matthews didn't seem to have noticed. "That again, sir, we don't actually know. But to go back to the question of when she first came here."

"A pity the enquiry wasn't made earlier," he said, and leaned back in the chair. "We never keep an ex-employee's card after a year, but I think I'm right in saying she was first employed in 1955. The last time she was here was—let me see—yes, in the March of 1957. After that we ceased to employ her. Her work had become too casual. Not the quality we wanted."

"You remember her address when she left?"

He looked up at the ceiling.

"Yes, I think so." He smiled. "After all, we don't have that number of employees. The address was Westgate Street. Quite near here, in fact."

"No other address?"

For some reason or other that question worried him. His eyes narrowed.

"I'm afraid I don't understand."

"Well, sir, she had a card and she'd have been supposed to notify you in case of a change of address. Did she ever notify you?"

He looked relieved. When you've questioned as many people as we have, you learn to read faces.

"Never. I'm positive it was her only address."

"Then listen to this, sir. She left that Westgate Street address in the early January of 1957. Yet she was employed here up to the March."

Hammond fingered his neck-tie. "I don't quite see what you're getting at."

"Perfectly simple, sir. Why didn't she notify you of a change of address? How could you get hold of her if you wanted her?"

"I see." He fingered that tie again. "Perhaps I'd better make enquiries." Then his face lit up. "But of course! The arrangements would be verbal. When she left, say, on a Monday, she'd be asked to come on, say, the following Friday." He smiled. "Perfectly simple. I can't think why I didn't remember it."

"Well, that clears that up," Matthews said. "And now, sir, if you'll let me recapitulate the main facts, we won't give you any more trouble. You last saw this Dorothy Delaine in the March of 1957, and you haven't seen her or heard from her since. Correct?"

"Absolutely correct."

"Just one other little thing," I said. "You knew her and you knew her work. Have you seen anything connected with her, shall we say, in any magazine or periodical since that March?"

He frowned. "Now you come to mention it, I believe I did. For a very little while. A year perhaps." He gave me the smile. "Funny you should ask that. I was thinking about it only the other day. Still, these people come and go. Probably got married if we only knew."

Matthews closed his notebook. "Right, sir. Thank you very much. There may have to be an official statement later but I can't say for sure."

Hammond ushered us through the door. I'm sure he was going with us through the reception room but a youngish woman, swathed up to the ears in a mink coat, was sitting by the desk. Hammond shot back.

“Miss Courcy, will you show these two gentlemen out?”

The farewell smile that Matthews had given Miss Courcy had left his face the instant we were through the doors. He hardly troubled to look for traffic as we went across to the car.

“Move along and reverse,” he told the driver. “Then draw in again if you can find a spot to park.”

“Well, what’d you think of that stuffed shirt Hammond?” he threw at me before I’d settled to the seat. “What was biting him? Every now and again he was like a cat on hot bricks.”

“Frankly, I don’t know. At a guess I’d say he and our Dorothy’d been very good friends. Maybe he ditched that brunette for her.”

“Think you’re right,” he said. “All I know is he’s a liar and the hell of a way from being a good-un.” He smiled. “Do you know I’m quite looking forward to taking that official statement. I think he knows where she is.” The smile was a bit more cunning. “Wonder if that receptionist could be induced to do a bit of talking.”

The car reversed at the end of the street. The driver manipulated it back into a gap in the line of cars.

“Wonder if I might make a suggestion,” I said. “We still haven’t established the connection between Laura and Dorothy.”

“Hassack’s in charge of a probe in that Bethnal Green area now,” he told me. “We rushed some prints of that photograph. They aren’t so early as we’d have liked but they might help. The two might just have lived somewhere close and known each other when they were young. Plenty of people living there who could have known them both.”

I said I’d been thinking of something along the same lines. Admitted that the yarn Laura Mann had spun to Farrell had been nothing but a pack of lies, it still might have had just a little convenient bit of truth. That bit about the dancing engagement, for instance, at Nice.

“We got into touch with Nice. They had no knowledge of a Laura Mann.”

“They’ve seen her photograph?”

“No,” he said. “That was before we had it. And what was the point if they didn’t know her?”

"Leave it," I said. "And leave off hunting for Dorothy Delaine. Try to unearth the contact instead and see how far that gets us. Try the long shot, that Laura *was* a dancer."

"Try it how?"

I smiled a bit diffidently.

"That's the long shot. The two just might have known each other at the Mendel School. Dorothy was studying things that would help her to become a high-class model, so why shouldn't Laura've been doing dancing?"

"A long shot? It's a thousand to one."

He told the driver to take us to the nearest post-office and we moved off. We had to cross to the other side of the road to find a new place to park. It was another quarter of an hour before Matthews came back from telephoning. Something had happened.

"Hassack was just back," he told me. "Got that connection. The two families lived within a hundred yards of each other. The two girls must have gone to the same school."

"If so they should both have been evacuated to Warberry."

"Not necessarily. Laura's parents might have been away already."

He told the driver to get back to the Yard.

"Wait a minute," I said. "If you don't mind I'll get out here."

"Going somewhere?"

"Still going to try that long shot," I said. "Those two might have known each other as girls but that doesn't seem a strong enough connection. Not to me."

He clicked his tongue resignedly. "All right. Might as well make a day of it."

We set off back to Notting Hill. It wasn't a long way off dusk when we drew up again before that school. The same pleasant-faced girl was there. A minute or two and we were in Julius Mendel's room again.

"Sorry to trouble you, sir, but something has cropped up since we saw you last. To do with the time when Dorothy Clabbon was here. What we're wondering is if you had a student here at the same time called Laura Mann."

"Laura Mann," he said. "I don't seem to remember the name. Perhaps my sister would know. You haven't any idea what course she was taking?"

Matthews smiled ruefully.

"To tell the truth, sir, we don't even know if she was here at all. It may have been dancing."

"Laura Mann, you said? It should be in the files. Let me see now. We'd better begin at 1952."

A few moments and he was looking round.

"No Mann that I can see. A Laura Manning, though. I suppose that isn't any help?"

"Might be," Matthews told him quickly. "What was she studying here?"

It was singing. Voice production, as they called it.

"Think we could have a word with whoever was in charge of the course?"

"Miss Lane," he said. "I'm almost certain she's still here. She usually doesn't go till five."

Guenevere Lane was a willowy woman in the early forties. She had a beautiful speaking voice. Matthews showed her a photograph.

"That's Laura Mann, Miss Lane, taken three years ago. Do you think she might be your Laura Manning?"

She smiled. "I'm sure of it. I remember her very well."

"Any particular reason?"

"Well,"—she tittered slightly—"she was really so unsuitable."

"For the course, you mean? Put it in simple language for us. We're neither of us what you'd call nightingales."

She laughed.

"Well, the voice had a very small range. Not unpleasant but—well, incapable of much development. We did our best, of course, and I will say she tried to co-operate. It was the evening class, three evenings a week. She left us after a few months and then about a year later she came back again. I think she came for another three months after that."

"Well, we're very grateful. Just what we wanted to know. I suppose you didn't know if she was friendly with a Dorothy Clabbon who was here at the time? She was doing deportment.

A girl of about the same age. Had very nice auburn hair. Came in the evenings, too."

She frowned. "I seem to remember seeing her once or twice with a girl like that. Do you remember, Julius?"

Julius didn't. Matthews said it didn't matter all that much. The great thing was we'd tracked down Laura Mann or Manning. So Miss Lane left us. We thanked Julius and left, too.

"Well, if you're not the luckiest bloke unhung," Matthews told me. "You take a blinder into the blue and come up smothered in diamonds."

I said it wasn't all that much of a blinder. Somewhere there had to be a later connection and the luck was that we hadn't had to dig back earlier still.

He was going straight back to the Yard to report progress. I asked him to drop me at the flat.

"About this connection," he said. "Now we've got it, what use can we make of it?"

"Sounds a tall order, but I think it should be traced right up to the time of Laura Mann's death. Unless we can trace Dorothy Delaine through one of the firms she worked for, we should stick to Laura."

"But how?"

"Well," I said, "what about wangling a holiday? If it's going to be of any help you can quote me, but why not say it's now essential to see the authorities at Marseilles?"

"Marseilles? It was Nice she was supposed to have gone to."

"Marseilles was where Farrell had his first contact with her," I pointed out. "They didn't know her at Nice. That isn't to say we can't pick up a good deal at Marseilles."

"*We,*" he said. "Even if I could wangle it, you can't be wangled in, too."

"I'd go privately, on Farrell's behalf. All you'd have to do is book two seats on the same plane. Do you speak French?"

"Yes," he said. "The way you speak Yiddish."

"Well, I can get by," I said. "That should be a help."

"Be a bigger help if you could use that gift of the gab of yours at tonight's conference. Still, I'll give it a try. Ought to be nice in the South of France. A damn-sight better than it is here."

He was right. The day had been cold and the rain was now coming down. I was glad to get back to the flat and a cup of hot tea, and I made up my mind that nothing short of an earthquake would get me out of doors again that night. And nothing did happen. Nothing, that is, till just before ten o'clock when we were talking of going to bed. That was when Matthews rang.

"It's all fixed," he said. "Two seats booked and you pay later. London airport at eight o'clock sharp. Okay?"

"If a car's taking you, why not me?" I said.

"Give me time," he said. "Be down here at just after seven."

"Right. Any other news? Hassack pick up anything else?"

"Not all that much. The Mannings used to do a double act on the halls. Called themselves Manning and Manning. Never really played the big circuits, and then he died. Tuberculosis. And the mother married again. A widower with a son. Hassack's following the whole thing up."

"Anything else about that head waiter?"

"Not that I've heard of. I'd say Brimbell's taking it as suicide. Lemon had a cold coming on, by the way: that's why he had that drink in bed."

Seven in the morning, he reminded me, and rang off. I was dog-tired that night and went straight to bed. It had been a long, long day and so many things had happened, in so many different places, that a tired mind just couldn't take them all in. There'd been the nice and the unpleasant: the normal and the unusual: familiar streets and strange ones—a kaleidoscope of a day. When the alarm woke me at six the next morning I think I was smiling: on my mind the final incongruous thing with which I'd gone to sleep—the sight of Julius Mendel's bald head as he hunted painstakingly through his files.

15

CLOSING CIRCLE

THEY were expecting us at Marseilles and an Inspector Frigout met us at the airport. Beyond the fact that the Yard was interested in an Englishwoman named Laura Mann or Manning, they'd no definite ideas of what was wanted. To be perfectly frank, we didn't know either. Any information would be gratefully accepted. As Matthews and I had agreed over lunch on the plane, we'd have to extemporise. If we'd been a Prime Ministers' conference we'd have talked about flexibility.

But first let me make something very clear. I can get by in French, and no more. My French was acquired a very long time ago and so, in the matter of vocabulary, I've been left high and dry. What I have to do is use low cunning and try to keep a conversation within the scope of that vocabulary, and you can't do that if the other fellow talks first.

Frigout, I soon realised, had an English of exactly the same quality, and with the same defects as my French, but whereas I've been brought up, like the average Englishman, to a certain restraint, Frigout had no such inhibitions. Where I groped for a word, he'd flick the missing word away with a quick gesture and gallop steadily on. What I'm getting at is that I might perhaps raise an occasional chuckle if I set down our conversations exactly as they took place and if you could bear at least half-a-dozen chapters. So let's suppose that my French was as good as Frigout's and his English as good as mine. Everything in English, then, and cut down to mere facts: not even a *m'sieur* or *eh bien* or *qu'est-ce c'est que ça* for verisimilitude.

By the time we got to police headquarters we'd given him Farrell's story. What Laura Mann had told Farrell didn't seem to him unreasonable. Such things, he said, had happened often at Marseilles but he had doubts about Nice. Nor could he recall any communication from Nice about such a case. Laura's photograph conveyed nothing either. As he said, Marseilles and all its suburbs meant best part of a million people. There were areas, chiefly in the neighbourhood of the docks, where every kind of crime was a commonplace. There were slum areas, middle-class areas and high-class residential areas, and considerable foreign elements or even colonies.

The Yard had nothing to teach them in the matters of filing and cross-reference. We soon learned that. Frigout's assistant brought in various files and almost at once something was found. Another file was fetched and consulted.

"Sorry," Frigout said. "No Englishwoman of the name of Mann."

He ran a finger along the column. "Macklin, Malliston, Manette, Manvers—"

"Just a minute," Matthews said and went across to the table. I went too. "Manette, did you say?"

There it was. Manette (Lola). See File 357 (b).

I explained. We were also interested in this Lola Manette. Frigout shrugged his shoulders. I guessed he thought we might have said so in the first place. The assistant was despatched to fetch the necessary file. Frigout consulted a file already on the table, then pressed the buzzer. He asked if a Brigadier Carosse was available.

While we waited we told him some more about the Charles case. It was possible that Lola Manette might be wanted for murder. File 357 (b) came in. Almost at the same moment Carosse came, too.

Frigout was a man of fifty: very tall and heavily built. With his slightly receding chin and pouched eyes he had about him a look of General de Gaulle. Carosse was younger: slim, dapper and with a permanent look of ironical amusement. There was something about him of David Niven. Frigout made the introductions. Carosse's English, as he confessed, wasn't very adequate.

He was told what our interest was in Lola Manette. He had a look at the photograph.

"Ah, yes," he said, and mentioned that file. Frigout passed it across. Carosse undid the tape. It was a fairly thick file, with several photographs. He passed one across. He smiled dryly as Matthews took it. Matthews put it under his glass, had a long look and passed it and the glass to me. Frigout peered over my shoulder.

The scene was a busy street in what looked like a second-class suburb. To the left in the middle-distance was a café and you could see a small shop or two and those tall, shuttered houses with woodwork a dingy grey. Almost the whole of the photograph was occupied by a woman, leaning negligently against a wall. Below the short coat she was wearing a dark skirt and you could just discern the cigarette at the corner of her mouth. She was hatless and her fair, almost white hair was drawn back into a pony-tail. There wasn't a doubt about who she was: Laura Mann, *alias* Lola Manette.

Carosse had been in charge of the case and it took a fair amount of unravelling, with Frigout wanting apparently to display his English and acting, often unnecessarily, as interpreter. It took a fairish time to tell. Matthews was taking careful notes. Almost at the very beginning there was an interruption.

Carosse began with the background. The brothers Lemonde, he said: two of them—Louis-Philippe and Georges. The father was French and the mother English. When the father died, Louis-Philippe inherited the restaurant: a third-class café-restaurant called the Esperance, situated in a street just off the Avenue de la Rose. On the huge wall map he showed us the exact spot: about five kilometres from where we were sitting.

Georges had been a chef. When the mother died, shortly after the father, he worked for a time in the café. There was some trouble to do with a customer who claimed he'd been robbed. Nothing was proved but Georges disappeared. The events of that winter of 1955 were to prove that he'd gone to England and that when he returned it was with a British passport. The passport was in order. Georges—he spoke excellent English—had applied for and had been granted British nationality. He was then thirty-six.

"Just a minute," Matthews said. "What was that name again?"

"Georges Lemonde."

"Got a photograph of him?"

There were three or four in the file. We didn't need more than a second to know who Georges Lemonde was. Again there had to be explanations. Carosse even then didn't see where our George Lemon fitted in. Neither did we, unless it had been Martin Charles who had managed in some way to get him the job at the Café Mexique. Even then there was only the vaguest of connections.

Carosse went on with the story. At the end of August, 1955, Georges arrived in Marseilles. He was accompanied then by the woman Manette, who'd passed as his wife. Her passport was never traced. It was later assumed that Georges had run into trouble somewhere in England and was staying with his brother till it blew over.

During that absence in England, Louis-Philippe had blossomed out. A property next door had been acquired and the café had now become an hotel. Not exactly a one-star Michelin, Carosse ironically told us, but an hotel for all that, and with five bedrooms. Louis-Philippe had never married and Georges and Lola occupied one of the original bedrooms above the café.

It was not till the December that the police learned that for some weeks the hotel had been used for the badger game. In case you don't know it, it's this. A guest, carefully chosen for his apparent means and circumstances, would be inveigled into getting acquainted with a woman in the café. When the man was sufficiently fuddled, they'd adjourn to his bedroom. As soon as they were in bed, a man would burst in—the woman's husband. Georges filled that role: Louis was, of course, the shocked proprietor. What would follow was blackmail.

One such victim, a well-to-do garage owner from Toulon, paid up to avoid scandal, then did some thinking and approached the police. A trap was laid. That victim—call him Dubois—had paid and was then being blackmailed for more, and it was on the *more* that Carosse worked. The money had to be handed over to a certain person at a certain place. Carosse had a man posted across the street with a film camera. That still from it—the picture of Lola Manette—had been taken before the time fixed for the actual handing over. Evidently she'd been sent to reconnoitre the ground, and, when she left, Georges took her place. The film then showed the actual handing over of the money as the victim slowly passed, and then Georges was seized by two of Carosse's men.

"And Lola?" Matthews said.

Carosse shrugged his shoulders. Maybe she'd been waiting somewhere near by—a woman of her description had been in a café not far along the street. When the police went to collect her, she'd disappeared.

"No trace of her afterwards?"

Carosse said she'd gone into thin air. A description had later been circulated but nothing had ever come in. And after that, as Carosse said, there'd been other crimes. Always other crimes. Crimes beside which that affair would appear comparatively trifling. At any rate, Georges had got two years. Louis-Philippe, who'd claimed an ignorance of the whole racket, had got eighteen months. The café-hotel, Carosse added with that ironical smile of his, was now in other hands.

What we did then was get to work on dates. In less than no time everything was clear. It was on the afternoon of the very day when Georges had been apprehended that Lola Manette had met Farrell, and several kilometres away, in that dock area. The police had probably missed her by seconds and she'd bolted in what she stood up in. Later she'd let down her hair as her only disguise, and she'd chosen the docks in her panic with the hope of telling some convincing tale that would get her aboard an English ship. And then she'd seen Farrell.

As for Georges, the police knew nothing of him since he'd left jail. There'd been no reason to keep track of him unless reports had come in of a renewal of the racket with a man of his description involved.

"And now, you say, he's dead," Carosse said. "If he committed suicide it was not because of what happened here. There'd been no reason for us to make enquiries in London. And you say he had a good job."

"True enough," Matthews said. "Still, you never know. What happened to the brother?"

"He sold the business and went away. To Perpignan." He smiled. "Believe it or not, he also acquired a garage. Maybe he manages to acquire illicit petrol. I don't know. It isn't my affair."

It was after four o'clock. Carosse asked if we'd like to have a look at the various places concerned. Matthews gave me a look.

We'd been hoping to take a plane at six o'clock. It was true we'd each brought a bag, just in case.

We went on that tour and Carosse drove us. We saw the hotel in the rue Henri Marreau, just off the Avenue de la Rose, and the very spot where that photograph of Lola Manette had been taken, near the Boulevard Longchamps. By the time we'd seen some of the dock area it was getting dark. It had been a fine day, but a cold wind was now blowing in from the sea. Carosse found us a hotel a stone's throw from police headquarters and later we had dinner at a restaurant with Frigout. The fact that he was probably on an expense account was a long way from spoiling a wonderful couple of hours. We left him with the promise that he'd look us up if ever he came to London.

We were back at the Yard at three o'clock the next day. Jewle was in his room. He heard all we had to say and he'd spotted what had been troubling us on the planes.

"You couldn't have done a better job," he said. "All the same, something's still badly wrong. Mind if we look into it?"

It *was* badly wrong. Lola Manette was Laura Mann, there wasn't any doubt about that. But a Lola Manette had been in the Café Mexique with Martin Charles only the last October. Mrs. Cavallo and the waiter at their table would swear to that. So would Lemon, if he'd still been alive. And Laura Mann was dead and buried. It didn't make sense.

"Any possibility that someone else could have adopted the name?"

"Where's the reason?" he asked me. "And Martin Charles was definitely not connected in any way with that Marseilles affair. There's overwhelming proof he was in the States at the time."

We tossed it this way and that and it still didn't make sense. Jewle let out a breath and leaned back in his chair.

"Looks as though you'll have to get on the track of that Dorothy Delaine again. She must be tied in somewhere if we could only work out how."

We left it like that. Matthews had his full report to write up so I went home. Bernice didn't happen to be in, so I made myself some tea and had a bath and changed. There was a queer unreality about the flat after that short spell abroad, and even if I'd wanted to do any thinking, I'd never have got very far. What I kept thinking about was that trip, and Frigout and Carosse, and the sights and smells. I was even smoking a cigarette from a packet of Gauloises that I'd brought back. Now and again I saw the docks and Farrell and an imaginary café and then it would merge into that café-hotel in the rue Henri Marreau.

At six o'clock Bernice came back. I was still talking about Marseilles during dinner. Matthews rang soon after nine o'clock.

"Looks like back to the grindstone," he told me. "Going to find a firm or two the Delaine girl worked for. There mayn't be anything to interest you."

I asked him what time he'd be moving off.

"Not before ten," he said. "Need a rest after that Marseilles trip."

I laughed. He'd slept almost an hour on the way to Paris.

"Be all right if I drop in?"

"Don't make it too early," he told me. "It may take some time to get things going."

In the morning I woke at my usual time, and if anything was uppermost in my mind it was still that day in Marseilles. I'd drawn the curtains and peeped out as I always did and it looked about as miserable a February day as we'd had. A cold rain was coming steadily down and I must have been contrasting that weather with the sun we'd had abroad. As I made the toast I was thinking of the *croissants* we'd had the previous morning. Mind you, I don't say that brief obsession with a day just spent out of England was any justification for a general slowness of wits. It must have contributed. As I used to be told in my youth—you can't do two things at once.

We weren't hurrying that morning and breakfast wasn't yet ready when the telephone went. It was Brian Kewton, wanting to know if there was anything to report. I said that with luck we ought to have the whole thing cleared up in a few more days.

"The real reason I rang," he said, "was to let you know Paul's off to Jamaica tonight. A commission for a travel film, so we can have a real good chat any time you like to drop in."

I said I certainly would. It mightn't be that day or the next but definitely in the very near future. I rang off and then I could hear from the bedroom Bernice talking to herself. I made the coffee, and when she came in I asked facetiously whom she'd been having a chat with.

"Talking about grey hairs," she said. "I really ought to do something about it."

"Grey hairs? I didn't think you had a grey hair in your head."

"That's because you don't look at me."

You see what I'd let myself in for? I should have kept my big mouth shut.

"You shouldn't say that," I said. "Of course I look at you."

She bent down to let me see. There *was* a grey hair or two and you could really see them among the black.

"I wouldn't worry," I told her. "If they get really visible you could get them tinted."

"I couldn't do that," she said. "I suppose, really, I'm being stupid. Realising I'm getting old."

I did what you'd have done: denied indignantly that onrush of age. And wasn't I ten years older, and did I consider myself as getting old? Not a bit of it.

"By the way," I went on, "I was reading something last night about some new process for tinting hair. An article in one of the magazines. You might be interested."

I found that article, ran an eye over it to get the facts again and told her about it.

"It says here that they've discovered a way of colouring hair so that the colouring is absolutely permanent. You can do it with either liquid or cream, with a base of some stuff called paraphenyl-enediamene, whatever that is. It works its way right into the core of the hair and then combines with oxygen to make the colouring absolutely fixed."

She laughed.

"Darling, you don't know women. Most women who have their hair dyed would hate to have it permanent." She rushed on in a burst of illogicality. "Besides, grey hairs can be very becoming after you get a certain age. I think it's a stupid invention. Women will just go on doing what they've always done."

I was hunting for something to change the subject when she found a new aspect: "I don't like colouring or bleaching or any of those things. You can always tell."

She quoted a friend of hers. A charming soul, of course, but she never ought to have had her hair tinted.

"But she's only one."

"Heaps of women," she said. "Now take the other night and that woman at the desk. Her hair had definitely been dyed. I saw her quite closely."

"You mean Mrs. Cavallo?"

"Of course," she said. "So you see what I mean. A man mightn't know but a woman always does. The hair's never so bright. There's a sort of dullness."

A lucky thought managed to change the conversation. We didn't say another word about hair till it was time for me to leave. I admit I left a bit early, and it was well before ten when I went into Matthews's room. He was telephoning. He waved a hand at a chair and went on talking. The room was warm and I hung up my hat and coat. I picked up a morning paper and went through the motions of reading it. Matthews was evidently talking to Hammond, *alias* Riccardo, and he was being pretty brusque. I heard him say a name and then he was writing something on the pad. A word of thanks and he was replacing the receiver.

"The Ajax Agency in Fleet Street," he told me. "Not far from Farrell's place. Think I'll just give them a preliminary ring."

It turned out to be a pretty long business. Ajax seemed to be an advertising agency, and he was wanting to speak to any one of their artists for whom Dorothy Delaine had worked. And meanwhile would someone look up her last known address. There were more delays and more spasmodic spasms of conversation and then something.

"Westgate Street? She left that address in the January. Sure you haven't got a later one?"

On it went for another five minutes and then at last there was something happening.

"Mr. Frome? Inspector Matthews here. As you've probably been told we're anxious to get into contact with a Dorothy Delaine who used to do quite a lot of work with you. . . . Not for over two years? . . . I see. But you knew her very well indeed, so have you seen any examples of her work since she left? Work for any other firms? . . . I see. . . . Well, thank you, Mr. Frome. You have saved me a visit. Goodbye."

He sat back in the chair.

"Well, what d'you think of that. She never worked for them after just before that Christmas. They wanted her but couldn't get into touch. And either he or Hammond's a liar. Hammond told us he'd seen work of hers over a year after he'd sacked her, and Frome says he's seen nothing. He says he sees everything and he'd have spotted it."

"Hammond's the liar," I said. "Don't ask me why."

"I *do* ask you why." Then he frowned. "Didn't he suggest she might have got married? Could there be any truth after all in that yarn Mary Braid was telling everyone about Dora marrying an American?"

Before I could speak, he waved that theory away. "No. Can't be that. Not if Hammond was right about seeing some of her work a year later. She couldn't be here and in America at the same time."

He got to his feet. "Think I'll have a word with the Old Man."

He was half-way to the door. He turned back, took a small file from a drawer and gave it me.

"Hassack's full report. Be back in a few minutes—I hope."

It was a beautifully documented account of those enquiries at Bethnal Green. It made me envious of the Yard. Everything was there: the details of every person interviewed and exactly what had been learnt. It wasn't a big file as such files go, but there were over thirty typed pages.

I skimmed through it, got my pipe going and settled back. I read all about the Clabbon family. Dora had been the only child. The report on her ended at the evacuation to Little Warberry, and a cross reference to another file. That would be the one now being compiled on the death of Mary Braid, and I stopped reading for a moment to wonder what Yandle was doing and what he might have unearthed since we'd seen him last. I told myself that when Matthews came back I'd ask him.

I turned over the page to the Manning section. Laura had also been an only child, and she must have had a pretty bad time of it till she was six years old, when her parents were doing minor halls with that variety act. When the tubercular father was in a sanatorium, she went to the local school, attended also by Dora, and it was remembered that the two played together in the same group.

The father died and just over a year later the mother married a widower named Arthur Morse. He had a son two years older than Laura and when the bombing started the family moved to Watford where Morse had a sister. The boy, Charlie Morse . . .

Charlie Morse. For a moment my mind was a blank. I began to remember things. Laura had claimed that she'd had a step-brother. Charlie Morse, for the purpose of impressing Farrell, had become a doctor with whom she'd long since lost touch. Charlie Morse, I said to myself again. And then, I don't quite know why, I remembered the morning's little argument at the breakfast table. And then, as suddenly as that light that had blinded Saul of Tarsus, I knew. *Except*, maybe, for things that could be cleared up later, the case was as good as over.

I stood for a moment irresolute, then put that file back on Matthews's desk. I went as I was along the corridor to Jewle's room, tapped at the door and went in.

16
DECISION

IT HAD taken quite a time to unearth Morse. Even when we knew where he and his band were performing, we had to get his address. Then Matthews went off to fetch him. Jewle had briefed him very carefully on the kind of approach.

What a nice fellow Jewle is! He hadn't uttered a word of reproach or even surprise while Matthews was with us, but as soon as he'd gone, he leaned back in his chair. He gave a slow shake of the head. "What am I to say to you, sir? You go and see this Morse on your own and hear certain facts and you never even mentioned his name to us."

I tried to placate him, and I had a good case. Mrs. Cavallo had told me she'd asked Morse to use his show-business knowledge to find out what he could about a Lola Manette, so I'd seen Morse to ask him if he'd found anything out. He hadn't. So what was there to report?

"You didn't know," he told me, still severely. "There always was something just a bit fishy about the way she discovered that mistake of hers and made the Laura into a Lola. We'd been neglecting that restaurant but if you'd told us about Morse we'd have done a lot more thinking. And we'd have spotted Morse from Hassack's report."

He was right. I said I was sorry. He shrugged his shoulders, but when he reached for his pipe, I guessed the ticking off was over.

"Better late than never," he said. "Better give us a full report now. That'll be something to work on when Morse gets here."

A stenographer came in and I went slowly over the events of that evening. I stressed that I couldn't vouch for every word of the conversation but what I was remembering was pretty near. A few minutes later a couple of typed copies came in. I checked and signed. Jewle had a look at a copy.

"This is going to be awkward," he said. "I doubt if we can trust this chap Morse. We'll have to make an excuse to hold him for twenty-four hours."

I didn't see why.

He told me a couple of things I hadn't anticipated. Once they'd been done, Morse could do what talking he liked. Everything had to be dove-tailed carefully and the trap sprung at the one precise moment. One false step and we'd be back where we'd started from. Given only average luck, the whole thing ought to be settled in those twenty-four hours.

"There's only one thing still worrying me," he went on. "I can't fit in that Charles killing. I can't see how it was necessary. He couldn't possibly have known the facts. And why was he shot in that flat? Still, we'll see. I'd better get this report of yours off by heart. Morse might be here any minute now."

It was only ten minutes later when Morse and Matthews came in. Jewle wasn't affable but he was courteous. Morse had been uneasy from the start and he didn't look any happier after the preliminaries.

"Now, Mr. Morse," Jewle said. "I have here a report of a visit Mr. Travers paid to you at the Bellini Restaurant on a certain evening. You remember it?"

Morse gave me a look then said he did.

"You knew that Mr. Travers was making an official enquiry?"

"No, sir. I never thought anything of the kind."

"I see. Well, it's only fair to you to let you hear Mr. Travers's actual report. Don't interrupt me. You can ask any questions later."

The report was read. Morse squirmed more than once in his chair.

"That isn't my version, sir. I didn't know it was official. It says I never asked to see his warrant card. Don't that prove it?"

"We know for a certainty that you knew it was official," Jewle told him. "I'm not prepared to tell you why—not at the moment—but you can take that for a fact. What follows is that you fed Mr. Travers nothing but a pack of lies."

"No, no, sir!"

"Yes, yes, sir. Nothing but a pack of lies. And why didn't you admit that Mrs. Cavallo was your step-sister?"

The shrug of the shoulders was more of a cringe. Then he looked up. He'd made an admission. Jewle *did* know more.

"I'm not talking," he said. "I want to see my lawyer."

"You've read too many detective novels," Jewle told him. "Let's assume that we've only asked you to help us. You're prepared to do that?"

"I'm not talking."

Jewle beckoned to the stenographer. "You'd like to read what you've said so far?"

Morse shook his head.

"In that case we shall have to hold you."

"You can't do that!"

He got to his feet. For a moment I thought there was going to be some kind of a scrap.

"I can and I will," Jewle said. He nodded to Matthews. "Take him away. When he changes his mind he can come back."

"What about my band? We've got to—"

"We'll see to that," Jewle told him. "You should have thought of it before. Unless you think you'd like to talk after all."

Morse didn't. Matthews took him gently by the arm and he went quietly out. Jewle chuckled.

"Couldn't be better. He played right into our hands. All we've got to pray for now is that he doesn't change his mind."

"Everything's clear as daylight," he told me. "As soon as you left her that day she got on the telephone to him and told him exactly what yarn to pitch in case you saw him. And I bet she was in a bit of a dither. Making out that woman with Charles to be a Laura Manette and realising she'd opened her mouth too wide, and then faking the name to Lola." He chuckled again. "Always the way. Sooner or later they always make a slip. You've just got to be patient, that's all."

Matthews came back, looking pleased.

"I'd offer you some coffee," Jewle told me, "but we've got this conference. About tonight, if it comes off. You'd like to be there?"

I said I would. He said they'd ring me at the flat and he didn't think it'd be much before six.

It was nine o'clock at night and the rain was still coming down. I'd been at only one other exhumation in the whole of my career, and that had been on a summer night. Now, as Hilton had once said, it was black as black hogs, except at the actual grave where the headlights from two cars were blindingly focused. Matthews and I were about twenty yards away in the partial shelter of a cypress. Near us was the faint sound of digging and away to the right the sounds of traffic. The street lights were uncannily clear against the intervening blackness.

I turned the collar of my waterproof still higher. I'd smoked too much and my mouth had the taste of all the staleness there'd ever been.

"Shouldn't be too long now," Matthews said. It was more of a mutter. In a way it was like being in a church. "Going to be a nasty mess, though. Still, mightn't be so bad. The soil's all gravel around here."

Now you could just see the head of the one digger. The three men at the grave-side moved forward. One of them turned. The rain on his waterproof almost flashed in the light and then he was a darkness against the glare as he neared. It was Jewle.

"Shouldn't be too long now," he said. He wrung out the sodden handkerchief he'd had across mouth and nose. "Shouldn't be too unpleasant. Two years is a long time though."

"A hell of a night, sir."

"Yes," he said. "But you can't pick your weather. Better have that light handy for rigging above the grave. The ambulance might draw up, too."

You could see the flicker of Matthews's torch. His feet left the path and the sound of him was lost. All at once it was very quiet. Jewle just stood there, shoulders hunched against the rain.

"Cigarette?"

"Thanks," he said. I held the lighter and cupped it with a hand. I took a draw at my own cigarette and I could have spat it out.

"Like being in some extraordinary outdoor cinema," he said, "and we standing here watching the screen. Makes you think of Burke and Hare, only they had to work in the dark."

Matthews and another man were coming into the light. There was what looked like a heavy gas-container. The grave-digger emerged and a hand was held to help him out.

A spade clattered on a stone. A minute and the light was focused into the hole itself. The headlights of the cars were turned off. Now it was a much smaller screen. One of the men took a look down.

"Sanders, the Home Office pathologist," Jewle said quietly. "I'd better get along there."

I stood there alone. A minute or two and I heard what I guessed was the ambulance, and I wondered how long it would be before it was all over. A long quarter of an hour and Matthews came back.

"Having a job getting out what's left," he said. "Wouldn't be surprised if we don't get away for another hour yet. Like some coffee?"

He had a Thermos and he poured me a cup. It was over-sweetened but it tasted good.

"A drop of rum wouldn't have done it any harm. Like to come over and have a look?"

He saw or felt my shake of the head. He went off somewhere in the dark. There seemed to be less traffic now and everything was uncannily quiet. They might have been mutes who were working in and around that grave. I'd no real official standing, but that wasn't why I kept in the almost useless lee of the cypress. I'm allergic to what I'd call morbidity. I didn't even dare imagine what lay in the exposed bed of that grave.

Another few minutes and there was a movement. Something was being transported to the ambulance, and the head-lights of the cars went on again. More minutes went by and one of the cars was being backed out. The second followed it. The flare was tilted and that gravedigger was standing by. The light flashed now and again on the bright metal of the spade.

Then Jewle came across.

"All over now," he told me. "They've got all they need."

Matthews was in the car already. The driver moved the car slowly on. Where Jewle was I didn't know. I looked at my watch and it was half-past eleven.

It was well after midnight when we got back to the Yard. We had some more hot coffee in Matthews's room and I felt as if I'd never get the damp out of my bones. We didn't do a lot of talking. In this life you can never be really sure, and a lot would depend on what that grave had held.

Matthews was yawning. After the chill of that cemetery, I was sleepy, too, and yet somehow I'd never felt less like sleep. And then at last we heard Jewle's steps in the corridor. He didn't say a word till he'd hung up his hat and coat.

"Everything as it had to be."

He felt in his breast pocket and brought out a small envelope. He shook it and a few longish hairs fell out. With the corner of the envelope he moved them to a tiny heap. Even in that artificial light you could see a colour.

"That's right," he said quietly. "Doesn't matter what else they've found. It was Dora Clabbon who was buried in that grave."

You could feel the heavy silence in the room. Jewle was looking almost bewilderedly at his hat and coat as if he were suddenly realising he'd come to the wrong room.

"Might as well stay here the little time I'll be here."

"What about the morning, sir?"

"Seven o'clock," Jewle said. "Caver and Renfield will be picked up at eight and kept well apart. Details will keep for the morning."

"Any chance of my being here?" I said.

"I want you here. You were at both original interviews. Make it eight o'clock. There might be a thing or two to talk over."

He held out his hand for a good-night.

"You did a pretty good job. Forget all about that Morse business."

I said I'd rather walk home than have a car. The rain was still coming down. Cars still swirled by on the sodden roads and there was something friendly in their company as they broke the still reflections of the lights above.

It was old Caver who came in first that morning. He gave a quick peer round from under his heavy eyebrows but he didn't look in the least perturbed: not till he'd held out a hand to Jewle and found that Jewle's hand wasn't there. I don't know what yarn they'd pitched him to get him to come, but the frigidity of that room couldn't help but tell him that something had gone wrong.

"Doctor Caver, I'm Superintendent Jewle. Your full name is Robert George Prentice Caver?"

"Why, yes."

"Of 2 Barlow Street. Pimlico; a medical practitioner?"

"Yes, yes." He cleared his throat. "I don't know what all this is about but I ought to remind you that I have a surgery in under an hour."

"Your partner will be taking both surgeries," Jewle told him. "It's all arranged. Sit down, doctor. You've no idea why you're here?"

"Not really. They said they wanted my help about something. Thought it was my duty to come."

"Then I'll get to the point. I could charge you. Robert George Prentice Caver, with at least three serious offences: falsifying medical documents, making false statements with an intent to impede justice, and being an accessory to an illegal operation. I may charge you yet. It depends. I think you know what I'm talking about: that woman who consulted you under the name of Laura Mann. If it helps, I can tell you we're already holding Doctor Renfield."

I won't say that Caver collapsed. His hands were shaking as he slumped a bit in his chair.

"Yes," he said. "Yes. I knew there'd be trouble. I told him so."

"Well, tell *us*. Start right at the beginning. Your relations with Renfield."

"Nothing wrong there. Nothing at all. He'd known my boy in Canada and when he came here he had a letter of introduction. I liked the fellow. I think he suggested it but I used to put things in his way. Women who wanted confinements in a nursing home."

"And Laura Mann?"

"Exactly as I told these officers here. I signed the certificate. I had to. No reason to suspect anything wrong. Then, a day or two before these officers came to see me, he rang me up. Wanted me as a special favour to change the woman's description. Spun some cock-and-bull yarn or other. I told him I'd have nothing whatever to do with it. Nothing at all. Then he hinted at an illegal operation and threatened to have me involved. I thought it over and I agreed. I shouldn't have done. I didn't want trouble. The man's a scoundrel, sir, an absolute scoundrel."

"Yes," Jewle said. "But you realise we shall have to check what you've told us and in the meanwhile we must hold you. Later on today you'll have to give a full, official statement. Think very carefully, Doctor. The truth, the whole truth and nothing but the truth. Otherwise—well, you know the consequences. All right, Inspector. Take the doctor out."

"What d'you think?" Jewle asked me. "He was telling the truth?"

I thought he was. A man like Renfield had been able to twist him round a finger. Not that Caver hadn't been guilty of grossly unprofessional conduct. And he'd probably done pretty well from time to time. A case of whisky occasionally, or a cheque.

"Yes," Jewle said. "He'd got to the stage when nothing much really mattered. Everything was perfunctory. Just enough and no more."

I remembered something. "What about Morse? Changed his mind yet?"

Jewle chuckled. "Yes. At six o'clock this morning when he realised he'd be coming into court. Spun the whole yarn. Claimed, of course, he only did it as a favour for her." He looked up at the clock. "Might as well have Renfield in and get it over."

Renfield was a different kettle of fish: no shambling in, no peering around, no blurt in the voice: just his suave and dapper self. He gave me a nod and a smile, and stopped just short of Jewle.

"Good-morning."

"I'm Superintendent Jewle. Your full name is Horace Renfield?"

"Why, yes. These gentlemen—"

"Just answer the questions. Doctor Renfield. You're a medical practitioner of 154 Westwood Road, Hornsey, with a private nursing home known as St. Mark's Nursing Home, at Vigar Road, Hornsey?"

"I am."

"Then, Horace Renfield, you're under arrest. I charge you, Horace Renfield, that on the 12th or the 13th of April in the year 1957 you performed, or caused to be performed, an illegal operation on the body of one Dora Clabbon, known to you as Laura Mann."

"But this is outrageous. You must be mad!"

He looked round for confirmation.

Jewle warned him. Anything he said might be taken down and used in evidence.

"And, for your information. Doctor Caver has already made a statement. Is there anything now that you wish to say?"

There was nothing. I doubted if he could even have said it if anything had come to his mind. Jewle told Matthews to take him away. The stenographer went out on their heels.

"That settles *him*," Jewle said. "I hate that shiny type. Abortionists." He grunted. "Must be hundreds of 'em in the game. And how many do they grab? Not a dozen a year."

"A holding charge?"

"That's right," he said. "We'll keep him just long enough to fix that Braid murder on him. If we can't we can always stick. He'd get a pretty long stretch."

"What about his wife?"

"Plenty of time. We'll turn that nursing home inside out. Once she knows about him, she may even come clean."

Matthew's came back and we had a brief conference. Everything so far had turned out fine, but it wasn't enough. Caver, Renfield, Forester, Lemon, Mary Braid; all were just spokes of a wheel, the hub of which was the killing of Martin Charles.

That was the real mystery—and we knew about it little more than we'd known from the start. It was the old simile of a jig-saw puzzle. We had all the pieces but never a clue, except here and there a matching piece of colour, as to how to make the picture whole.

In the end we arrived at what may seem an extraordinary decision. It was only half-past nine when Renfield left and we had plenty of time, and necessarily we did a lot of harking back. It was Matthews who brought up Cavallo. There was that hatred he had of his wife. That curious scene that had followed when he'd told Shorty Cray to have her come up. It was hard to convey it to Jewle.

"She'd like to leave him but she can't," I said. "I don't think she's hanging on because of any sense of duty. I mean about that accident."

"Maybe she hasn't any money," Matthews said. "Cavallo does all the accounts himself and I don't reckon there's any chance for fiddling."

"All right," Jewle said. "Let's suppose he has some kind of hold over her. He might even have known she was associating with his brother."

"That brooch," I said. "If we saw him alone, couldn't he be questioned about it? And then told the facts? He may have hated his brother, but he might like to see us get the one who did it. Especially when he knows she's played him for a sucker all along."

We threw it around for a few more minutes and then Jewle made up his mind. Cavallo didn't get up till about midday. By two o'clock the restaurant would be practically empty, so that was when we'd see Cavallo alone. We agreed where to meet, and when.

"Just one other thing," I said. "Could I see Morse's statement?"

Jewle and Matthews were due for a brief conference with the Higher-Ups. A minute or two and Hassack brought the statement in, with a couple of cups of coffee.

17
CAVALLO LISTENS

THERE were only half-a-dozen people in that main room when we went in. There was no sign of Mrs. Cavallo. Garrow caught sight of us.

"Mr. Cavallo's expecting us," Jewle told him. "Any reason why we shouldn't go right up?"

We went up. Jewle rapped at the door and was told to come in. Cavallo was alone. He must have had a couple of chairs. This one had a kind of handle that made it self-propelled. When we came in he was across the room by his desk and it looked as if he'd been working at accounts. Jewle said afterwards that the sight of him had been a shock. He looked even older than when I'd seen him before: thinner, and the eyes darker and more deeply sunk.

"Mr. Cavallo? I'm Superintendent Jewle." He held out his hand. "We wouldn't have troubled you if there hadn't been something we knew you ought to hear."

Cavallo's eyes took the three of us in. Matthews went out to the corridor. The last thing we wanted was a listener at the door.

"Sit down, sir. You can talk just as well sitting as standing."

We sat down. Jewle's chair was quite close.

"Something about my brother?"

"Yes. And your wife."

He just swivelled his head and practically focused his eyes on Jewle. He smiled.

"Superintendent, you're just too late. I know all about my wife."

Jewle stared. "You do!"

"She's a bitch," he said. "I had her watched. Knew she was two-timing me with that Lemon. And with my brother."

"And you didn't do anything about it?"

"Why should I? I couldn't give her what she wanted." The half-sneer was there again. "Didn't even sack Lemon. She fixed it for him to come here while I was in hospital. He did his job."

"You didn't even let her know that you knew?"

He was still for a minute.

"Let me ask you something, sir. You're a fine, big, well-built man. What would you do if you were all at once like me?"

Jewle didn't speak.

"You'd think about blowing out your brains, and then you wouldn't. You'd sit here and you'd think. You'd begin to pick up things. Kinda feel as if you were directing things. My wife was two-timing me. So what?"

"I think I get you. It sort of gave you a sense of power."

"Yes," he said. "Maybe you've got it. You didn't say a word. Just let her know that you knew."

"I see. And did you ever suspect that she'd anything to do with your brother's death?"

Cavallo's eyes narrowed. "Did she?"

Jewle took out that brooch and unwrapped it.

"Ever see your wife wearing this?"

Cavallo looked at it. From his face you couldn't tell a thing. "Just a minute."

He swivelled the chair round to the inter-com. He told someone to send up Shorty. There wasn't a word till Shorty came in.

"You want me, boss?"

"Look at this. Ever see my wife wearing it?"

Shorty shot a look at the pair of us as he came over. "Yes, boss. Don't know when but I've seen her."

"Right," Cavallo said. "Get to hell out of here and keep your trap shut. You hear that?"

"Yes, boss."

Shorty went out. Jewle told Cavallo where and when that brooch had been found. Cavallo didn't say a word. "Another shock for you. Think you can stand it?"

"You do the talking, sir, and I'll listen."

"Mrs. Cavallo isn't your wife. She was definitely married once before she met you and she's never been divorced. She may even have married before that."

Cavallo slowly moistened his lips. His hand went to the chair lever. Jewle held the wheel.

"We'll do the talking, not you. You promise us that? You'll just sit there and listen? . . . You will? Right."

He went out for a word with Matthews.

"Something I want," Cavallo told me and swivelled the chair round to his desk. I didn't know what he wanted. Maybe some papers. Some kind of private proof. He opened a drawer and took something out, adjusted the rug across his knees, and swivelled the chair round again as Jewle came back.

Mrs. Cavallo came in and Matthews again went out.

"Take a seat, Mrs. Cavallo," Jewle said, and drew a chair up for her. "Certain important matters we'd like you to hear. Things we've just been discussing with your husband. You know Mr. Travers. He knows more about these particular things than anyone, so you might be interested to listen."

"Thank you."

The voice was just as quiet. Everything about her had the same queer aloofness.

"It's a long story," I said. "It begins with two little girls who lived near each other, played together and went to the same school. One was a Laura Manning, the other a Dora Clabbon."

She was on her feet and making for the door. Matthews pushed the door open as the knob turned.

"Sit down!" Jewle told her. "Or do you want me to handcuff you to the chair?"

"You can't. You can't make me listen to a pack of filthy lies."

They grasped her arms and put the cuffs on her. They got her back to the chair. Matthews had his hands on her shoulders. There wasn't much need.

"Carry on, Mr. Travers."

"Later these two happened to meet each other again," I said. "Laura was then working as a sales assistant in a certain shop. Laura had stage ambitions. She had a stepbrother: a man who ran a small band. He thought he might use her but her voice wasn't good enough, so in her free evenings she began taking lessons. That's when she met Dora Clabbon again.

"Then some time during 1955 Laura met a man named George Lemon. Plenty of details about that have to be filled in, but the facts are these. He'd probably got himself into some kind of trouble, so he slipped across to France to lie low with his brother in Marseilles. George had got himself naturalised over here but his brother was French. He kept a small hotel-restaurant. Laura joined George there, changed her name to Lola Manette and later passed as George's wife.

"Then all three started a profitable badger-game racket. One of the victims squealed and the police laid a trap. The brothers were pulled in but Laura got away. And that very same afternoon she got herself attached to an Englishman who happened to be working in that dock area where she'd gone. She pitched him a very plausible tale and he fell for it, and the upshot was that he took her back to England, after marrying her in Paris. She lived with him for a few days at his flat, then drugged him and bolted with all the money she could lay her hands on and he never clapped eyes on her again.

"There were two complications as far as she was concerned. She had to get a job, and she was pregnant, and almost certainly by Lemon. Underneath the flat was a surgery and she arranged with the doctor there, now dead, for an abortion at a certain nursing home. It was successful but she still had to have a job, so she went to Morse again. The upshot was that she went back to the same place for more lessons and then he arranged for her to be the vocalist in his Cuban band. Her hair was dyed and altogether she was meant to be a regular South American. One of the band, a Venezuelan, used to help her get the words off by heart. That band played here, Mr. Cavallo, and you saw her. Later on you married her.

"Two things happened next. Lemon came out of jail, and while you were in hospital she got him back here and found him his job. The other thing was that she'd been in touch with Dora Clabbon again and Dora was in trouble. She'd become a Dorothy Delaine, a model, and she was pregnant. Laura arranged for her to have an abortion under the name of Laura Mann. You see the point? Dorothy didn't want any scandal and Laura didn't want the name. The original doctor wasn't there so it was worked through his partner and at the same nursing home. Dorothy Delaine died there on the twelfth of April, almost two years ago.

"It was Laura who'd done some confidential fixing with the same doctor who'd done her own operation, and she was notified. Now we go back a bit. Dorothy Delaine had been evacuated during the war to a certain village. Her parents were soon to be killed in the blitz and she was adopted by the well-to-do people with whom she'd originally been billeted. The woman actually came to regard her as a niece, even if the two drifted very much apart when Dorothy came to London. So Laura saw this aunt and told her the truth. I don't know if she blackmailed her, but the aunt wouldn't want any scandal and agreed to let Dorothy be buried under the name of Laura Mann. I think she was even glad to.

"So that was that. Laura Mann was dead and buried. Unfortunately for the live Laura Mann, other things happened. Your brother came back, Mr. Cavallo, and he and Laura got acquainted. I'll be perfectly frank and say we haven't yet got quite to the bottom of everything—we shall do very soon—but your brother was shot in the very same flat where Laura had once lived. Unfortunately for her she left something behind: a brooch which has since been identified as hers. That gave us a clue. We began delving into the history of Laura Mann and naturally our enquiries brought us here.

"At all costs Laura had to throw us off the scent. Luckily there'd been a woman with your brother one night when he'd dined here, and Laura tried to lead us on a false trail by saying that woman was a Laura Manette. Unfortunately she'd also said she'd asked her step-brother, Charlie Morse—Manrico to you, Mr. Cavallo—to use his connections to find out if anything was known in the theatrical world about this Laura Manette, and then, of course, as soon as I'd left her, she had to get hold of Morse and fix up what he was to say if we questioned him. He certainly told a very convincing tale. He was brought in yesterday, by the way, and now we have his true and complete statement. Needless to say, it verifies everything I've said.

"There are just two other things. Something alarmed Dorothy Delaine's aunt the other day and she got at once into touch with that abortionist. The same night she was murdered. There was also Lemon's death. What we know about that, we're not at the moment prepared to say. Still, I think you can put two and two together, just as we've done."

"Yes," Jewle said. "And what's going to happen to this Laura Mann, you can guess. Bigamy's a small crime; murder isn't. She's been responsible, directly or indirectly, for at least four deaths. The only thing that might possibly help her is to talk. Any questions, Mr. Cavallo?"

Cavallo didn't speak. And that was when things began to happen. They happened more quickly than I can relate. Just seconds and it was all over.

Laura was struggling to get to her feet and she was beginning to shriek. Cavallo's hand came out from under the rug and there was a shot. Jewle was wrenching the gun out of his hand. Laura was writhing on the floor. Shorty Cray came bursting in. Jewle had the gun and was pushing Shorty away. And then, so suddenly that it was more of a shock than the din, the room was quiet. Only Shorty spoke.

"What'd you go and do it for, boss?"

Cavallo didn't speak. On the floor the woman was moaning: faint sounds that were somehow more eerie than the shrieks.

"Ring for an ambulance," Jewle told Matthews. Then he turned to Cavallo.

"You shouldn't have done that, Cavallo. You're not the law. You realise we'll have to take you in?"

He didn't speak. He looked at that heavy Webley in Jewle's hand and shook his head. I knew that if Jewle hadn't grabbed him when he did, he'd have turned that gun on himself.

"And you, Cray, keep your mouth shut about this. One word to a soul and I'll have you where you can talk to yourself."

Shorty didn't speak either. He looked like a man whose world had blown to bits.

"You can get this chair down the stairs?"

It was Matthews who answered.

"Easily, sir. Only needs carrying and him in it."

"Right," he said. "Ring the Yard. And you, Cray, start packing a bag. Make it two bags."

Laura Manning had stopped moaning. Jewle knelt down and looked at her. He felt the pulse before he got to his feet. "Through the stomach, Cavallo. You meant it like that?" Cavallo sneered. "You think I'm that kind of a shot?"

"Why d'you have the gun?"

He didn't speak. Shorty, kneeling by the chest of drawers spoke for him.

"Used to be a lot of money up here, sir. Anyone'd come up and he'd been alone, he wouldn't have stood much chance."

"That didn't give him authority to have a gun."

He was going to say more, but he didn't. Maybe he was remembering what Cavallo had told us. Some people would have blown out their brains. Maybe that gun had been there, just in case.

Matthews went out to wait for the ambulance. Ten minutes and a young doctor was helping the stretcher-men to carry her out. Another few minutes and Cavallo was carried down, too. Shorty came behind with a couple of handbags. Matthews was staying on. The restaurant had long since been closed and only Garrow was there. I could feel his eyes on me as I went through, but it wasn't for me to speak.

Jewle and I walked on to the car.

"You won't want me," I said. "Might as well get back home."

"A hell of an afternoon," he said, and looked at his watch. "God knows where it's got us. According to that doctor, she's got a good chance. Another few hours and we might get her to talk."

I waited. He was still standing there. He looked at his watch again.

"Three o'clock," he said. "Five. That gives us a couple of hours to start straightening out this mess. Might have Hammond in. Matthews is staying here so you're the only one who saw him. Say half-past five. Six o'clock if it suits you. Do him good to kick his heels."

At half-past five I was back in Jewle's room. He'd been pretty busy, and he was going to be more so. The stenographer had just taken his own statement and, later, there'd have to be one from me. He'd sent another inspector down to Little Warberry to get things stirring, and turned Cavallo over to the Higher-Ups. I asked him what he was expecting to get out of Hammond.

"Just clearing things up." His smile was a bit tired. "To tell the truth, it's something to do. Still, you never know. What do you say? Let him cool his heels a bit longer or have him in now?"

We had him in. The suavity was there: only a slight uneasiness as he glanced at the stenographer. The same overcoat, hat and suit. Even the same necktie.

Jewle didn't waste a lot of words. Courteous enough, but he made it clear from the outset that he wanted the truth.

"We should have warned you to bring a bag, Mr. Hammond. We might have to keep you here quite a time."

The look was incredulous. "But why?"

"Giving false evidence with the deliberate intention of impeding the course of justice."

"You must be wrong, Superintendent. I don't remember giving any false evidence. You mean to this officer here?"

Jewle smiled. "Mr. Hammond, we've talked to hundreds of people here and half of them with that air of innocence you're trying to put across now."

"I must say I resent that."

"So did they," Jewle said. "But let me just put one question to you. A year after she left you, you saw an example or examples of Dorothy Delaine's work. Where did you see it?"

Hammond smiled sheepishly. "If I may say so, that's not a fair question. It's quite a time ago. I suppose I see scores of magazines. How can I remember which?"

"You're a liar," Jewle told him bluntly. "Dorothy Delaine did no work a year after she left you. You've said you last saw her on March the twelfth or thereabouts. We know that a few weeks after that—on April the thirteenth to be exact—she was dead. What's more, we know that you were well aware of it."

He was beaten, and he knew it. It's like that sometimes. Bluster at one minute, and the next eager to tell what they know. Still, perhaps, with reservations.

"Let's build it up," Jewle said quietly. "She left that little flat of hers to come and live with you. Right?"

Hammond moistened his lips.

"Yes or no?"

"Well, yes."

"Right. Then she found herself pregnant. She said she had a friend who could arrange for an operation. How much money was needed?"

"I don't know. I think it was a hundred pounds."

"Whatever it was, you probably found it. You were told in confidence where she was going. When you learned she was dead, you were scared to death. How much more money were you bled for?"

He didn't know. Maybe about another two hundred pounds. Jewle leaned back.

"You see? If you'd come clean with us, we'd have tried to protect you. Now I don't know. Things have gone too far. What I'll have to do is keep you here till you've made up your mind to tell the whole story. Everything, Mr. Hammond, and heaven help you if you don't."

He pressed the buzzer.

"You realise you were an accessory to that illegal operation? . . . I see you do. Think of that when you're ready to make your official statement."

A uniformed sergeant came in.

"You know what he has to do, Sergeant. See he has a meal and I'll see him again about eight."

"Another smarmy type," he told me. "God, how I hate 'em! Came in here as if you and me were dirt."

I got up to go. I remembered Laura Manning. Was there any news?

"Heard just before you came in," he said. "A successful operation. She's got at least a fifty-fifty chance. A slug from a gun like that makes a hell of a mess."

"Any use dropping in in the morning?"

"Can't say at the moment. Wouldn't do any harm to drop in about ten."

18
FULL ANSWER

MATTHEWS rang me next morning to save a wasted visit. He wouldn't be available till eleven o'clock when the preliminary hearing was over. Shorty had made a statement and had gone. For Cavallo there'd be the usual remand in custody. I felt sorry for Cavallo. The law might have stretched a point and let him loose on bail. That made me wonder what Shorty was going to do now, and whether Garrow was in charge at the Café Mexique.

At any rate I did meet Matthews soon after eleven, and at the hospital. The early morning report on Manning hadn't been so good. I thought there'd have been a man at the bed-side, but there wasn't. Manning wasn't a victim who'd be anxious to help the police. I asked if anything special had been found in her room, but there hadn't.

"No key to Farrell's flat?"

"No," he said. "And no key to Charles's flat either. Nor to Lemon's flat. And no gun. You know what I think about that?"

I didn't.

"I reckon that she and Charles drove to that flat that evening and Charles did the ringing from that call box at the end of Mayes Road while she kept an eye out for Farrell leaving. When she'd shot Charles, she just walked on to the car, got out for a moment at the Embankment to ditch the gun, and went on to Charles's flat with the car. Took a bus home and was ready for opening at half-past six."

As he said, it'd be easy enough now to check times and movements. The trouble before had been that she hadn't even been a suspect.

"All the same," I said, "she's the only one who can tell us why she went to that flat at all. And whether they got what they went for. I'm open to bet she'll never open her mouth, not even a sixteenth of an inch."

"Why all the pessimism?"

I said it wasn't pessimism: it was facing up to facts.

"Even if you were to tell her she hadn't a hope, she wouldn't talk. She isn't the type."

We went up in the lift to get the news at first hand. We saw a sister and then the doctor. He doubted now if she had an even chance.

"Strictly between ourselves, I don't think she wants to live. If she'd only put up a fight, she might pull through."

"She's under constant watch, as suggested?"

"No need at the moment. She's under sedation."

"We can have a look at her?"

He went with us to the small private room that Jewle had asked for. The same sister was there when we went in. Laura Manning had the sheet drawn up to her chin and she was on her right side. Matthews had told me that a sun-ray lamp had been in her room to retain that tan that had originally been necessary for her role with Charlie Morse's band. The tan hadn't gone. A normal face would have been deadly white; hers was now a kind of sickly yellow. The bed-clothes hardly rose and fell as she breathed.

"She came to all right after the operation?"

"At about seven o'clock," the sister said. "Fully conscious. She looked like becoming hysterical and that's why she was put under a sedation."

"She said anything?"

The sister smiled. "Nothing much more than they usually do. It took her a minute or two to realise where she was. And then she wanted something: a sort of locket she'd been wearing. On a thin gold chain and inside her vest. That's what she was getting hysterical about."

"You fetched it for her?"

"Oh, yes. And she's wearing it now."

Matthews grunted. He stood there, looking down. "Wonder why she was so insistent? Superstitious, probably. It was some kind of charm?"

"I can't say. It was about so big"—she indicated the palm of her hand—"and a coloured photograph on the front. A plain back."

"What about our having a look at it, doctor? She wouldn't wake?"

"You couldn't wake her if you tried."

He gently turned back the clothes. There was the thin chain round the neck. It disappeared somewhere beneath the night-gown and between the breasts.

"Don't like that amount of disturbance," the doctor said. "Be easier if we cut the chain. But no. Probably the first thing she'd notice."

"Wait a minute."

That was Matthews. He bent down and fingered the chain. He felt for his pocket-knife and opened a small blade and began a gentle prising at one of the tiny links.

"There you are, sister. Now you can draw the locket up and off."

It was a circular locket about two inches in diameter. The photograph looked as if it had been cut from a magazine. It was a coloured photograph of a man. There was something familiar about it. The sister had a look.

"Why, it's Michael Redgrave!"

It was. The doctor said she must have been a Redgrave fan.

"I doubt it," I said. "It isn't in keeping."

"Better have a closer look," Matthews said. With the same knife blade he began gently prising at the back. It came off. Then he was prising something out, what looked like a tight, thin fold-ing of blue paper. He began unfolding it. His mouth gaped a bit as he looked at me.

"Afraid we must keep this, doctor, for about an hour. She won't be round by then?"

"Oh, no. Not for at least a couple of hours."

Matthews changed his mind. "We'll do it another way. You got something I can fold up in place of this?"

Another five minutes and the locket had been replaced. Matthews closed the open link. There wasn't anything for Laura to notice when she came to and she'd be in no condition, the doctor said, to open that locket and make sure that what had been in it was still there. She'd be aware, perhaps, that the locket was there, and no more. And he didn't think a receipt would be needed for what we'd taken. After all, as he said slyly, he didn't know what it was.

"You will do," Matthews told him and left it at that.

It wasn't till we were back at the car that I knew what had been found. *Two cloak-room tickets at Charing Cross Station. The numbers were very close.

"It's incredible!" I said. "If these are what they were after in Farrell's flat—"

I couldn't go on.

"Must have been," he said. "Simplest way is to go along and see."

Matthews was driving the car himself. We drew up in the station forecourt and we had another look at those tickets.

Each was for a bag: the charge sixpence. Each had been deposited on the morning of Wednesday, January 28th. And that, we remembered, was the date of Charles's death.

"Look," he said. "We won't call in the Old Man, not unless we have to. We'll try and do it the straight way. I'll go first. Got any money? There's threepence a day overcharge."

He left a ticket with me and went off. He was back in three minutes carrying a bag about two feet by one and a half. It didn't look too heavy. He put it in the back of the car.

"Better wait a minute or two or it might look a bit too brown."

He bought a couple of papers and we sat looking at them. A porter came up and told us we couldn't wait there. Matthews showed him his card, the porter shrugged his shoulders and went back.

"Better go now before he spreads the news."

I had no trouble at all. The attendant hardly looked at me, except for a second when he gave me my change. My bag was much like the other. It had seen a deal of service. Once there'd been some sticky labels on it but they'd been scraped off. Only the fainter white against the brown showed where they'd been.

We nosed out to the Strand. The lights were with us and we shot down Northumberland Avenue. We humped the two bags up to Matthews's room. He rang through and Jewle came in. His guess was as good as ours.

A sergeant came in with a selection of keys. The bags had different locks but a couple of minutes saw them both open.

"Blimey!"

That was Matthews. Those bags were full of notes: ten-shilling notes, pound notes, fivers and a few tens. We began stacking them on the table. Even Jewle let out a breath.

"Must be well over ten thousand quid. You stay here, Sergeant. Better divide them up and make a rough count."

We made the rough total about thirteen thousand pounds.

"Can't make it out," Jewle told me. "January the 28th. This looks like the proceeds of that Butter Lane job. So what was Farrell doing, mixed up with a thing like that?"

"Don't know," I said. "The whole thing's incredible. I remember reading about that Butter Lane job. Three men, weren't there? One big, one slim and a shorter one."

"Yes," he said. "But something must be wrong somewhere. We all saw Farrell. The last man in the world to take part in a hold-up. Not that you always know. You can't get away from the fact that Charles and that woman knew he had the cloak-room tickets. Where *is* Farrell?"

"In Jamaica. Brian Kewton, his partner, said he was going there to make a film."

"Sounds a bit too convenient. Wait a minute, though." When he came back he had with him Farrell's statement. "Here's the statement I heard him make. He has a sort of alibi, but only his word for it. He was—"

He stopped. He looked through us across the room. He smiled.

"Well, I'm damned!"

He actually laughed. We were staring.

"Get someone in to sit on these," he told Matthews. "We'll do a proper count later. The bank ought to have the numbers of some of the new notes. And you, Mr. Travers, get hold of that Brian Kewton and see if he can see us. Say in half-an-hour."

He and Matthews went out and I managed to get hold of Kewton. I told him I knew no more about it than he did. All I could guess was that it was something to do with that queer evening in Farrell's flat.

"Heard from him yet?"

"Had a cable," he said. "He likes it there."

"If you're writing, give him some news," I said. "Tell you more about it when I see you, but that woman never *was* his wife. We think she might have been married to a certain man in France, weeks before she met him in Marseilles."

I heard his gasp as I rang off. What I'd told him mightn't be true but the moment had looked right for me to end my part of the contract. Just why I didn't know. Maybe it was just another hunch. And I'd remembered Jewle's laugh.

Jewle had a good look round.

"Nice little place you've got here, Mr. Kewton. Plenty of money in this—I almost said racket."

Kewton smiled a bit nervously. He was still wondering what it was all about.

"We get nicely by," he said. "As a matter of fact it's like I heard someone say the other day. All this television, shorts and documentaries, home and foreign markets, it's like there was a chute and money coming down and you stand underneath holding out your pocket. Got to produce the right stuff, mind you. You can't get by with just anything."

"And you people do produce the right stuff?"

He smiled. "Well, it's hardly for me to say. What I will say is that there isn't a better man at the game than Farrell. Not a quick worker, mind you."

"Perhaps that's all to the good. Any chance, by the way, of seeing any of his work?"

"Of course. Love to show it to you."

"As a matter of fact we'd like something rather special. We know that Farrell was doing some filming on the morning of January the 28th: somewhere in the neighbourhood of the Embankment. The Charing Cross end. Any chance of seeing what he actually did?"

Kewton smiled.

"As a matter of fact, you can, sir. I've got the whole thing here. You know all about it?"

Jewle said he didn't.

"Well, to put it briefly, London under fog and mist. Real smog and ordinary fog and patchy fog and so on. What you'll see is actually a pilot film, taken with a Kodak Special. Colour film, eight millimetre. We cut that kind of thing and put it together and, according to how it turns out, decide whether or not to do a sixteen millimetre on the same lines. You follow that?"

"I think so. A pretty expensive business, though?"

"Mistakes are more so," Kewton told him. "Here's the pilot film. If you gentlemen will sit down here I'll draw the blinds and run it off."

The light was focused on the screen. There was the familiar whirr and then, out of a queer sort of yellow blackness, there was a light. A man was walking slowly forward, the light of a torch thrown back over his head. There was a touch of red that slowly became a bus. Inside you could just see the passengers as it crept forward. The scene merged into a length of railings through which you just caught a glimpse of shrubs. Two women were slowly working their way along in the now whiter fog and one was laughing as if the whole thing were a joke. That scene dissolved into another; somewhere down in the docks. A visibility of only a few yards. Seagulls swooped in it. There was a glimpse of stevedores at work up and down a wide gangway, and every now and again the mist would blur it. That scene dissolved into a suburban shopping street. The visibility was now about fifty yards and there was snow on the ground. A bus drew up and moved off again. People, mostly women, went by with shoulders hunched and somehow you could feel the very cold. The scene dissolved again and the visibility was now slightly greater. You could pick up the Embankment.

"Taken with a telephoto lens," Kewton said quietly. "Probably at about eighty yards."

There was plenty of mist on the river. A launch emerged from it and its wake was white against the dull grey. The camera picked up the line of the parapet and the narrow pavement. A car drew up. A woman looked out of the off-side window. Two men emerged, each carrying a bag, and were lost to the left in the invisible road. The woman emerged. She was coming towards the camera. Suddenly she swerved away and was also lost to sight. I gave a little gasp. *The woman was Laura Manning!*

Half an hour later we were back in Jewle's room. I was still feeling just a bit shaken. The drama of it all was still with me: that sudden startling glimpse of what should have been part of a forgotten past: a part of limbo.

"Well, there it is," Jewle said. "One of those men was definitely Charles and the other was probably Lemon. We'll have to wait till we see some stills. And for checking up on that abandoned car. The Cavallo woman almost certainly drove the car in the gateway from Butter Lane. Probably wore slacks and that's why they took her for a man."

It fitted snugly in. She'd recognised Farrell but he couldn't have recognised her. She'd changed far too much. But what they had to do was get that film. And there again, things had changed. Laura had expected that flat to be what it was when she'd last been there. But it wasn't. Farrell had taken that office, and his stock of negatives and cameras and even the dark-room itself had gone.

"She was going to get rid of Charles in any case," Matthews said. "Otherwise she wouldn't have brought the gun."

That had to be it. The way we saw it was that Charles had taken both cloak-room tickets: his own and the one given to Lemon. He was the boss, and the share-out could come later. Laura knew all that. With Charles out of the way, the loot was all hers. And Lemon's. So later, Lemon went too.

What upset things, as Jewle said, was the very thing that ought to have made everything smooth—the killing of Charles. If he'd been killed outright or elsewhere, things might have gone much better. But there were enquiries. However badly she wanted to get away from her husband, she had to stay put. Once things blew over or we could be diverted to a false trail, that'd be different. Even there, though, there was a bit of luck. It gave her time to get rid of Lemon.

"Mind you, we'll never be able to prove half of this," Jewle said. "Luckily we shan't need to. We've got more than enough as it is. Wish we had as much on that swine Renfield." He pressed the buzzer and asked for the hospital. He was going to ask the latest about Laura Manning. Somehow I didn't want to listen. I'm like that. I hate the grim end of things. I wanted her to live and be hanged and yet I wanted her dead. That's why I muttered something to Matthews and went quietly out of the room.

THE END